1937

A tale of hollywood's nastiest scandals

DAVID WALLACE

ISBN: 1534680799
ISBN 13: 9781534680791
Library of Congress Control Number: 2016909821
CreateSpace Independent Publishing Platform
North Charleston, South Carolina

Also by David Wallace
Lost Hollywood
Hollywoodland
Dream Palaces of Hollywood's Golden Age
Malibu: A Century of Living by the Sea (contributor)
Exiles in Hollywood
A City Comes Out: How Celebrities Made Palm Springs a Gay and Lesbian Paradise
Capital of the World: A Portrait of New York City in the Roaring Twenties

ACKNOWLEDGMENTS:

The late Marilyn Monroe, who once said: "Hollywood is a place where they'll pay you a thousand dollars for a kiss and fifty cents for your soul."

And those still lively ghosts of Hollywood who didn't sell out for a kiss… well, not always.

CHAPTER 1

"Hello, Joe. Wadja know?"

"Benny, could you please lay off the slang this morning? Makes my head hurt, and it's bad enough anyway this a.m. And, damn it, don't call me Joe."

"OK, OK, Oakey. I mean, OK, Mister Oakley Webster, Hollywood's favorite gumshoe. I was only tryin' to make a joke to start the day. Too much 'caddy' last night?" Benny asked, using, as he often did, an outdated slang word; in this case, "Cadillac" was one of the previous decade's terms for an ounce of cocaine. It was a drug still all too common in Hollywood and one that Oakley usually has avoided despite his need to escape the ups and downs of the life of a private investigator in Tinseltown.

"No…no." Oakley sighed as he dug into his trouser pocket to retrieve his nickel pouch of Bull Durham smoking tobacco. He opened it with a yank by his teeth and shook some of its contents into the thin paper cigarette wrapper in his left hand. He licked the edge of the paper and rolled it, one handed, into a slim cylinder; the entire process was accomplished with the dexterity of a person who had already done it too many times in his life.

"Why don't you save yourself all the trouble by getting ready-made cigarettes like Luckys or Fatimas?" Benny asked. "Would save you lotsa time."

"Maybe that's the reason," Oakley replied. "I guess because doing it this way takes my mind off things. Like the next stupid thing you're going to say…"

"Aw, boss, I doan" mean to be a problem—jus' tryin' to brighten the new day."

"I know," Oakley said. He walked over to one of the office's pair of grimy windows and looked at the traffic on Broadway, four stories below, before seating himself at his scarred and scratched wood desk. "But it just doesn't sit well with me this morning. Sorry."

"So, boss, if it wasn't too much Caddy last night, why are you not feelin' up to par this a.m.? Too much partyin' or some cheap hooch?"

"No. No…the main reason is that I didn't get much sleep last night," Oakley explained.

"Some new guy? You get lucky?" Benny interrupted.

"No, unfortunately," Oakley replied. "Wishful thinking."

"Then if a guy ain't the problem, what's goin' on?" Benny asked, reaching into his "hope chest" as he called a crushed pack of Camel cigarettes, retrieved one, tapped it, and lit it. As he took a long drag on it, he asked, "Some new case I don't know about?"

"Not that either, unfortunately," Oakley replied.

That's no surprise, Benny thought. His boss was always worried about where the next dollar was coming from and, more often than not, had to ask him to wait a couple of days for his paycheck. "So what's eatin' ya, then?"

"Well, over the weekend, when I was catching up on the trades, I saw this item in *The Hollywood Reporter* that caught my attention. It seemed very odd."

"An' what was that?" Benny asked, finally seating himself in one of the office's pair of aging leather lounge chairs.

"There was this item about Eva Sanderson," Oakley continued. "Seems she lost her baby after contracting measles. And the item went on to say that because of this, she pulled out of consideration for the lead in Metro's big bucks, sound remake of an old, 1916 silent movie, *The Matrimaniac*."

"*Matrimania*? What was that about?" Benny asked. "I can hardly pernounce it."

"I never saw the original," Oakley explained, "but the trades said it starred Connie Talmadge and Doug Fairbanks and was a sort of early screwball chase movie about a girl and a boy racing to find a minister to marry them before her irate father caught and stopped them," Oakley continued. "Had to be good, 'cause it was written by Anita Loos…you know, the writer who started with Griffith and has written lots of screenplays since…like rewriting *Redheaded Woman* for Jean Harlow a few years back when Fitzgerald tried and couldn't deliver the script. And then she really hit the jackpot when she wrote her first novel in the midtwenties," he added. "A nifty little book called 'Gentlemen Prefer Blondes.'"The point is," Oakley added, "it would have been a great role for Eva. I hear that her husband, Stan Damon, was slated to play the Fairbanks role and that Loos is going to consult on the whole project. It's all such a pity…"

"So she lost her kid and wanted some time to recover," Benny said. "No surprise."

"It may not be surprising to you, but it was to me," Oakley said thoughtfully after taking another drag on his cigarette before stubbing it out in an overfilled, chipped glass ashtray on the desk. "First thing that bothered me: she wasn't merely up for consideration for the lead in *The Matrimaniac*, a part that most actresses in Hollywood would kill for. From what I had heard, she *had* the part…at least Mayer had offered it to her, and she had accepted it, although nothing had been signed yet. And a date to begin filming had actually been picked based on her pregnancy…one month after the baby was due to be born."

"So how d'ya know this?"

"Let's say I have a friend who is a close friend of Ida's who knows everything that happens at the studio, and she told him that it was all set."

"You know someone who actually talks with Ida Koverman? I thought she was harder to get to than her boss Mayer himself!"

"She can be. In this case she was talking with a friend who is a friend of mine…"

"OK, OK. I'm impressed. But I still don't see…"

"Just listen. You and I both know that people drop out of movies for all kinds of reasons, but not often and hardly ever when movies like this one are involved. Here, you have one of the biggest stars in Hollywood cast to star in one of the biggest roles in her life in one of biggest movies to be made in some time by the biggest studio in town. Then, suddenly, she loses her baby and drops out, leaving the field wide open for everyone else—"

"Who would kill for the role," Benny said, echoing Oakley's earlier comment. "But she wasn't killed."

"Yeah, yeah, I know. I know. But it doesn't make sense—to me, anyway. The pregnancy was going along just fine, but then, out of the blue, the country's most famous mommy-to-be gets the measles and loses her baby. The fan mags that splashed the story of her and Stan's oncoming bundle of joy on their covers for months must be going nuts."

"Maybe there was somethin' else," Benny said. "Measles is a kid's disease that don't kill grown-ups…"

"Not true," Oakley interrupted. "I've heard grown-ups can catch them, too, and they can kill you in some parts of the world where our doctors and medicines aren't available. And I've also heard that measles can sometimes cause a pregnant woman to lose her baby or, more often, give birth to a child who's deformed," Oakley continued. "Eva lost her baby. And then she went into an emotional tailspin and decided that she's done with everything: her career, movies, maybe even her marriage to Stan Damon, America's most famous boy next door. So now the way is wide open for all those actresses who wanted the part and…"

"Are you sayin' that you think it was the baby who someone wanted to kill?" Benny asked."

"Could be," Oakley said slowly.

"This is gettin' to be a crazy time anyway, so why should this be any different?" Benny added. "Like that flyer dame—Amelia somethin' or other—disappearin' over the ocean last week when she knew how to fly better than anyone? And how about blowin' dust buryin' half of Oklahoma a month ago, while a million folks were gettin' flooded out in the Middle West? Everthin's goin' crazy lately, so I guess it's natural that you suspect somethin's fishy when a grown-up catches measles.

"Anyway, Oakey, as I see it," Benny continued, " there's a big difference between dyin' and bein' killed. And where'd you get the idea that because of the miscarriage she dumped her career and maybe her hubby?"

4

"Amelia something or other's name is Amelia Earhart, and with all her flying experience, I agree that she's the last person you'd think would simply vanish, even somewhere over the middle of the Pacific Ocean. It's a puzzlement. But the ocean is huge, so I guess it's possible. But, as far as I know, catching measles when you are an adult is even less likely than a veteran flyer like Earhart getting lost. So, because I was curious if others besides me might be wondering about Eva's measles, I called Docky Martin, and he gave me an off-the-cuff update."

"Louella's hubby? You called Parsons's husband, an' he told you what Louella and her friends might be thinkin'? No one does that!" Benny yelled, jumping up from the chair in excitement. "How the hell do you know him?"

"Everybody knows Docky, Benny, even parking-lot attendants," Oakley said of the man married to Hollywood's most powerful gossip columnist. "I've told you over and over again that half the battle for getting ahead in this town is by knowing the right people. So it's not hard getting to know him.

"Docky Martin makes his living as a urologist who some people call Hollywood's clap doctor because he is really good at curing it. But I'm told he makes even more as Hollywood's Happy Docky by keeping actors working even when they shouldn't. One Hollywood doctor said he'll shoot up the stars with anything to make them perform. But he has a little personal problem with gin. The trick, I'm told, is knowing when Docky is sober enough to be reliable."

"Yeah, I heard he has a booze problem. What's that story again about his being so drunk one night at a party he fell asleep under their piano?"

"As I was told it," Oakley related, "when one of the guests told Louella he was asleep on the floor, she said, 'That's OK, let him sleep. He has surgery at seven in the morning.' He seemed fine when I talked with him, though."

Oakley, like most of Hollywood, knew Louella Parsons's personal story by rote, or as much as she allowed anyone to know it. In fact, as her gossip column was said to be read daily by more than twenty million readers of press czar William Randolph Hearst-owned and syndicated newspapers and magazines, the story of her rise to fame and fortune was as familiar and probably more accurate than that of any film star profiles in *Photoplay* or *Motion Picture*, the powerful film fan magazines.

Born Louella Rose Oettinger in Illinois, she had her first newspaper job as a local news columnist for the *Dixon Star*. After divorcing her first husband, she moved to Chicago where, in 1912, she began writing movie scripts (her first sold for $25), and some of the resultant movies actually starred her infant daughter, Harriet, billed as Baby Parsons.

In 1914, she began writing one of America's first gossip columns for the *Chicago Record Herald*. After moving to New York in 1918, Parsons wrote a movie column for the *New York Morning Telegraph*, switching to William Randolph Hearst's flagship newspaper, the *New York American*, a couple years later after attracting the publisher's attention by writing a flattering interview of his mistress, the actress Marion Davies.

After contracting tuberculosis in 1926, she moved to Palm Springs, California, where, after recuperating, she moved on to Los Angeles because of what Hearst considered the "compelling, glamorous, and economic phenomenon of the movie industry. He also sweetened the move by announcing that her column would be syndicated throughout his publishing empire with its then four hundred outlets, and raising her salary from the already-astronomical $200 weekly to $350 (and eventually to $500 in 1929).

From the moment she arrived in what was becoming America's film capital, Lolly, as she soon was called by most people who knew her (usually, though, behind her back), ruled the roost despite some competition. From the start, she laid down a rule that was inviolable: "You tell it to Louella first." Nearly everyone did, and her policy brought her some of the biggest scoops of the era, including, in 1933, when "America's Sweetheart," Mary Pickford, confided to Parsons that she and Douglas Fairbanks, the universally worshipped "king and queen" of Hollywood, were divorcing.

In the 1930s, she also began to host a radio show, *Hollywood Hotel*, during which stars could sneak preview upcoming films by reading excerpts from their scripts.

"OK, OK," Benny exclaimed. "So Docky said Eva told Louella she had given up on life," as he said as Oakley shook his head affirmatively. "But why do you suspect a problem with the ever-lovin' hubby?"

"Louella also told Docky that Eva's blaming him for her catching the measles. She's saying that he was exposed by being around a bunch of kids being used as animation models while he was doing voice recordings for Walt Disney's new *Snow White* movie, and he brought it home."

"So, America's girl next door and America's boy next door are splitsville over a case of measles which had a bad outcome? But what you're thinkin, don't make sense," Benny said. "As I said, far as I know, grown-ups don't get measles."

"I think grown-ups can get them if they didn't have measles when they were children and then were immune afterward," Oakley suggested. "Parsons asked Eva that exact question, and she said she never had them when she was growing up."

"So, Oakey, you think someone gave it to her deliberately? And anyway, how would you go 'bout doin' that? Maybe she just caught them from somethin' floatin' around in the air, like how kids catch it. You think someone knew she wasn't immune, knew how to get the measles germ or whatever it is you catch it from, and somehow managed for her to catch it?"

"Yep, that's exactly what I think," Oakley asserted. "One of the reasons I think I'm right is that no one else around her caught it, not even her husband. I know, I know, maybe he was immune, but not everyone she palled around with was necessarily immune. It was Eva, alone of all the people she knows and the hundreds of actors, extras, and everybody else at her studio, who got the measles. And remember, a studio is a place where everyone works so closely together that if one of them has the sniffles, the whole place is calling in sick the next day."

"So, OK, let's pretend that you're right," Benny said. "But only pretendin', because I still think your idea is all banana oil. But if you're right, and someone figured out how to get the germ or whatever, how do you think they infected her?"

"Well, Benny, I pretended I was Sherlock Holmes and tried to figure that one out by doing exactly what John Barrymore did in the silent I loved when I was a kid: by eliminating the ways it couldn't have been done. And I finally came up with the one place where she probably could have caught it—the MGM studio commissary."

"Why the commissary? Seems to me Eva's reason makes more sense. Maybe Stan did bring it into her home like she told Parsons, and he was immune to it so he didn't catch it himself. How do you know that someone else didn't visit her and bring it into the house?"

"Could be but I doubt it," Oakley said. "Stan didn't catch the disease; neither did her maid nor her cook, nor her secretary, nor anyone who worked at their house. And as far as visitors are concerned, as far as I can tell, none of her friends—Marlene and Greta and the others whom she sees fairly regularly—have gotten sick. I agree that doesn't eliminate this possibility, and I can't be a hundred percent certain. But it seems easier to have done it at the commissary."

"How…"

"Listen to me. There are two reasons that I think this was the way it happened. The studio commissary would be an easy place to infect a person; just get the germs or whatever it is on the rim of a glass of water or cup of coffee that the person you want to infect is using and maybe they could be infected. Anybody working at the waiters' station could easily do that. And you could do it fairly easily since a couple thousand people eat lunch there every day, and everyone is so busy no one would notice someone dressed as a waiter fooling around with a glass or something. Maybe put something in Mama Mayer's famous chicken soup that everyone seems to order in the commissary.

"And point two, I called Eva's secretary this morning and explained that Louella said it was OK for me to call—a little white lie because it was Docky who said to use his name—and she told me that Eva was terrified about losing the baby…seems that her mother had lost a baby or two before Eva was born. So she's been sticking, pretty much, close to home. For the last couple of months, apparently the only public place she has gone out to the studio for a couple meetings with L. B. Mayer and the film's director. And both of those meetings took place at lunch in the commissary.

"The commissary is also the one place where whoever did it could control the situation…well, mostly control it. That wouldn't be the case if the germ or whatever was used was just sent willy-nilly into her home where anyone around her could have been exposed. But if it was done in the commissary, the person who wanted her to catch measles could be sure she and no one else was infected because they could be certain…well, ninety percent certain…that it could have been her glass or plate, and hers alone, that was doctored. Unless of course she shared some of her food, which is why I said ninety percent."

"So boss, you think someone was smart enough to know how to both bring this off as well as knowing that the loss of the baby would destroy her life and career? Seems a pretty roundabout way to do it—infect a person with measles to eliminate a rival or whatever you think the motivation was. Why not just shoot her and have done with it?"

"I don't think whoever did this intended to eliminate her permanently. I think that all that whoever it was wanted to accomplish was to get her out of the way. The obvious reason was so someone else could get the role in *The Matrimaniac*. Which is my point," Oakley said, getting out of his chair and walking over to the window again. "Looks like it's going to be another hot day," he mused, looking down at the traffic once more.

Chapter 2

"Back to my point," Oakley continued. "Like you said, I believe someone who knew that getting measles when you're pregnant could cause the fetus to be aborted or born deformed was close enough to Eva to also know that her whole life was wrapped up in that child. He or she knew that losing the child would be worse than death in her mind. And then they had to figure out a way to make it happen."

"Unless you're being paranoid, and it was just an accident," Benny said, "which any sane person would conclude."

"Which, dear Benny, if it was a deliberate act, is exactly why the plan was so brilliant."

"So, OK. But where's the margin for us…I mean you? No one is paying you to solve the mystery—which you claim is a murder. Sort of a secondhand murder anyway."

"I know. That's just one of the questions that kept me up all night."

"So, boss, not to change the subject, but what do you want me to do today?"

"I'd like you to take a hike over to the main library and look up everything you can on measles," Oakley directed. "And check out the books you find. Here's my library card for you to use."

"OK. Anything else?"

"No. Wait. Yes, there is. Look through the back issues of the trades and see who else was originally in the running for Eva's role in the movie. Once it seemed that every actress in Hollywood was fighting for the part, or at least their flacks were telling the press that they were in the running, so it might be interesting to see who the other candidates were."

"Flack?" Benny looked blank. "What's a 'flack'?"

"A term meaning 'promoter.' *Variety* started using it recently as a sort of compliment to the talent of Gene Flack, a very good freelance movie publicist."

"OK. So, if what you think really happened, don't you mean 'who may be the suspects'?"

"No, no…well, not really. But it would be interesting all the same."

"What else are you up to today, boss?" Benny asked, changing the subject.

"As you might imagine"—Oakley laughed—"it's about time for me to spend serious time getting some bookkeeping done and getting bills sent out so we won't have to eat beans next month."

For as long as he could remember, Oakley had always been curious about the world around him and why people did what they did. "I should have been a journalist," he often jokingly told people who asked him why he chose the profession of private investigator. "But I discovered I was a better snoop than a writer." Actually, it was by accident that he ended up as a professional "snoop," and it all began after he graduated from college at the University of Missouri.

Oakley had chosen Missouri for two reasons. It was fairly close to his family who lived in Kansas City where his father owned an office supply store, and the university also offered one of the first journalism majors in the country. The college was also where Oakley discovered that, although he had the innate curiosity essential for being a journalist, he totally lacked the ability to put what he might discover in written form.

So Oakley changed his major to American History, studied hard, rooted for the Tigers football team, and dated a few of the girls (and a few of the boys as well) at the school. All the while he remained ostensibly true to his goal and his high school sweetheart, a relationship that finally ended when she, frustrated by his seeming inability to commit to marriage, eloped with his best high school buddy. Oakley's growing awareness that he was attracted more to guys than girls was part of the problem; another was his being what

---

DAVID WALLACE

a later generation would call "a loner" who never seemed to remember to return his ostensible girlfriend's increasingly frustrated telephone calls.

Besides beginning to discover his true sexuality, Oakley was also becoming impatient with Midwestern provincialism. Later, after he made the move to California, he was never really able to articulate exactly why he migrated West instead of moving to New York, the destination of so many young people in the 1920s who, when frustrated with Midwestern culture, found refuge in what was fast becoming the sophisticated world capital of free-thinkers and free-livers. That such an alternative paradise could not last was learned in 1929.

Perhaps part the attraction of California was also spurred by the silent films of Oakley's childhood that nourished a desire among countless thousands of Americans to be part of the escapist glamour of movie making. Certainly, another part of Southern California's attraction was the result of the area's generations-long boosterism; one could hardly buy a single orange in Kansas City or anywhere else without seeing a Southern California–as–Eden illustration of the fruit's origin on the shipping crate from which the fruit was often sold.

Or perhaps Oakley was simply responding to America's centuries-old urge to move westward, stopping only when one reached the land's end. In seeking the answer to California's drawing power during the early part of the twentieth century, author Kevin Starr, later California's Boswell, would write: "Whatever California was, good or bad, it was charged with human hope and linked with the most compelling of human myths: the pursuit of happiness."

People came seeking a new life. People came seeking work. People came seeking happiness. Even God got into the act: the celebrated evangelist and faith healer of the era, Aimee Semple McPherson, came to Los Angeles in 1918 because she believed that the Almighty had told her to do so.

And He may have. Armed with a trombone-like voice that could reach the farthest corners of huge auditoriums and a reputation for making miraculous cures, Sister Aimee would soon build a world-famous career by ministering to thousands of the faithful, many of whom had come west pursuing that "myth of happiness."

She once described her trip as a spiritual quest culminating in a revelation. Arriving in Los Angeles at sunset, she remembered (in the purple prose of the time): "the sun, after leading us ever Westward, laid itself like a scarlet sacrifice on an altar of cradled clouds." Oakley, after his graduation a decade and a half later, was simply following the same siren song when he made his way to the City of the Angels; it was the leitmotiv of an era.

Pursuing happiness in Eden was not easy, however. Until World War II created thousands of armaments jobs in Southern California, happiness was often as elusive as a desert mirage. Homesickness was a problem for many. A fairly primitive infrastructure was another. And work, in particular, was hard to find; among the reasons, there were too many people looking for it, particularly in the first half of the 1930s when California was flooded by thousands of migrants who fled the Midwestern dustbowl for the state's golden promise.

Oakley, however, was lucky. He found work quickly because of a something he never suspected: the homosexual party line. Soon after he arrived in Los Angeles and living in a boarding house, he met—at a bar in East Los Angeles that he still occasionally patronized—and began what turned out to be a short-term relationship with an MGM house lawyer. That lawyer's connections, generously offered, landed Oakley a job in the file room of a downtown law firm, which soon led to a job as an assistant to a private investigator. Within two years, Oakley had the confidence to strike out on his own.

It was also through that job with the PI that he also met and developed working relationships with several detectives employed by the Los Angeles Police Department. Besides providing insider tips and assistance on a number of his cases, the connection also soon made him suspicious that rumors of police and civic corruption were probably true. Although Oakley tended to be cynical about such stories, unlike many of his competitors who adopted a hard-boiled attitude about it (soon to be celebrated in many novels and movies), the knowledge of how things actually got done within the city's establishment was used by Oakley to work effectively on behalf of his clients.

What neither he nor thousands of other Angelenos suspected was the extent of the corruption, the first sign of which would boil over in late 1937 when the revelations of a group called the Citizens Independent Vice

Investigation Committee (CIVIC) appeared. Organized by a locally famous restaurateur named Clifford Clifton, the group's report would accuse civic officials of extensive underworld connections and the police department of accepting bribes and payoffs and spying on anyone who criticized them. It quickly got worse.

The LAPD responded by bombing Clifton's home and blowing up the car of a CIVIC employee and nearly killing him for investigating the mayor's office. The ensuing public and media uproar would force the successful, 1938 recall of Mayor Frank L. Shaw (one of the first big-city recall elections in America), and the resignation of LAPD chief James "Two Gun" Davis and twenty-three of his top officers. However, this was all to take place somewhat in the future; when the scandal was finally exploded, it would taint the image of the LAPD for years.

And in Los Angeles as well as much of America at the time, image was everything.

After a series of scandals in the 1920s, Hollywood became obsessed with its image and created a self-regulating commission to control it, eventually forcing studios to insert morals clauses into actors' contracts as well as having editorial control over movie storylines, scripts, and language (even the expletive *damn* was forbidden until Clark Gable famously uttered it in 1939's *Gone with the Wind*). Gay lovers were forced to separate and marry women, and when bedrooms were pictured in a movie, they had to be furnished with single beds only, even for married couples.

Such propriety was true for individuals (and companies) as well as the movies. When Aimee Semple McPherson wanted to project an image of innocence and purity, she achieved it by wearing a simple, pure white nurse's gown (cost $5), to which she soon added a long blue cape. When Coca-Cola built its new bottling plant in 1937, it was shaped like an ocean liner and painted white to convey the impression of cleanliness. Image was also paramount for professional men like Oakley who dressed formally day or night, hot weather or cold, seven days a week, even when at leisure.

An outfit including a three-piece (or double-breasted) suit, shirt (usually white), tie (usually with a bright geometric print), and hat (usually a fedora) was de rigueur regardless of the weather. Even in the summer heat, Oakley wore a lightweight linen suit or, because it wrinkled less, a seersucker suit following a popular preppy style he had discovered in college.

Men's suits looked different then compared to later in the century; like women's dresses (especially those designed by MGM's legendary designer Adrian for such stars as Joan Crawford), the shoulders were padded to make them appear broader. The waists of men's suits were also cut wider, a reflection of the heavily caloric diet of the era influencing fashion. In fact, Oakley's comparatively slim waist, which forced him to have his off-the-rack suits tailored before they would fit properly, was considered an aspect of feminine allure. All trousers—men's and the newly popular women's trousers and slacks championed by many liberated females of the period—were generously cut and cuffed. All men's shoes were of the lace-up type, some even two-tone white and brown.

Many stores of the era sold preassembled men's outfits often consisting of a suit, a hat, three pairs of socks, two dress shirts, a tie, and a pair of shoes. Sometimes the cost for such a package was as little as $30, but it was usually somewhat more (a suit alone cost just under $20 in New York City; socks were ten cents a pair). So being a dapper dresser, as was Oakley's reputation among his friends and colleagues, was not too serious a financial challenge at the time.

And of course in Los Angeles, there was no need for an overcoat, galoshes, or even a raincoat except occasionally (the trench coat, which would soon become ubiquitous thanks to productions of the socially and physically dark movies now called film noir, usually cost about $2.50).

It was still daylight when Oakley finished his bookkeeping, put several bills in envelopes, addressed them, and fumbled through the stuff jammed into his desk drawer until he found enough three-cent stamps for postage. *Daytime or not*, he thought, *it's time to go home. Better yet, it's time to get a drink.* He pulled on his suit jacket and slapped his trusty fedora atop his Brylcreem-tamed mouse-brown hair.

After exiting the building's birdcage elevator on the ground floor, Oakley dropped the mail in the lobby's ornate brass mailbox and left the building, marveling again at how light-filled the lobby was thanks to the central core of what was beginning to be called the Bradbury Building (for the millionaire who built it) being open to a huge skylight, a design inspired by a building for a utopian society described in one of the first science fiction books, *Looking Backward,* written by Edward Bellamy in 1883.

Today, it's Musso's for a drink, Oakley thought. Also, after deciding that Benny may have had a point about the cigarettes, he spent 20 cents for a pack of Chesterfields at the lobby newsstand. His 1936 Ford coupe (bought for $535), was parked just across Third Street at the Shell garage. "Bambolino Blue"—every time he thought of Ford's name for his car's color, he smiled. "I love it, but where on earth did they get that name?" he said aloud as he started the V-8 engine, shifted into first gear, and drove out of the garage. And he wondered as he had many times since buying the car, *Why did I spend the extra $25 for the damned jump seat out back?* Even though he was secretly proud of the option, he would sometimes complain, "I've never even opened it!"

Sunset and Hollywood Boulevards were already jammed with what was newly being called "rush-hour traffic," but as they were still the best route to Musso and Frank's Grill in the heart of Hollywood, he sighed and resigned himself to the drive. Twenty minutes later, Oakley turned off Hollywood into Cherokee Street and then into the parking lot behind the famous restaurant, patronized since its opening in 1919 by many of the most celebrated actors and actresses of the day. Especially popular was the bar room with its long oak bar, where on any given evening, you could find the likes of Scott Fitzgerald drowning his failure to make much of a mark in the film industry, or even Marlene Dietrich and Greta Garbo, usually with their mutual friend Mercedes da Acosta. Both were usually outfitted in the then-somewhat-scandalous slacks suits which had become a code for lesbianism.

As usual, the bar was crowded and, at least this evening, mostly by movie hopefuls, who for a generation, had come to Hollywood with stars in their eyes but who rarely got any closer to their dreams than to be extras making, maybe, $5 a day. There were also a few publicists in the place and a couple of low-level reporters. "I guess everyone important is next door at Sidney Rose's bookstore," Oakley muttered. The store, because of its physical connection to Musso's bar, had from its opening been a de facto club for stars who sought privacy from their adoring public and, during Prohibition, quietly available hooch.

"Hey, Oakey!" someone behind him shouted. "It's me." Oakley turned as his friend Lester Grady, an agent for a few B movie actors and some non-film Hollywood talents (and sometimes as their publicist when they couldn't afford both), slapped him on the shoulder. "Oh, hi, Les. Nice to see you. How come you're here? I thought you usually hung out at the LA Press Club."

"Jus' checkin' out the scene, Oakey. I had to cover an interview with Sheilah Graham and my client Jean Lamond. Maybe you heard that Jean just got a part in *The Buccaneer*, the new movie that DeMille is producing and directing for Paramount. So it was either the Formosa Café or here, and I hadn't been here for a while, so, well, you get it. Watcha drinkin'? My treat."

"What else? A Martini, and thanks. But tell them extradry, eight to one or better. None of those two to one concoctions like I hear FDR makes at the White House. Ugh!"

"Okeydokey," Grady said as he squeezed his way through the crowd at the bar. He turned and shouted "Twist?" over the genial din in the crowded room.

"Yep, thanks."

It wasn't long before Les, juggling a pair of Martinis high above his head, pushed his way through the crowd. "Don't think I spilled much," he said, handing one of the drinks to Oakley.

"Doesn't look like it. Thanks. What you have to go through just to get a drink!"

"Yep," Les said, leading the way to a less crowded corner of the room. "Beats what we had to go through only a few years back, though."

"The great experiment," Oakley said of the Prohibition era that ended only four years earlier. "What a bust. Just goes to show what damage do-gooders can do." He laughed. "Les, look! Let's grab it!" he exclaimed, noticing that a couple seated at a nearby table were leaving.

"So, watcha been up to?" Les asked after they seated themselves.

"Well, same stuff." Oakley smiled. "Murders, kidnapping, decapitations, rapes, and child molestation."

"OK, OK. I know you don't like talking about your work. I guess that's the 'private' part of 'private investigator.' Sorry." Les continued, "So how's your love life? Haven't seen you around our favorite East LA watering spot lately. Or is that private, too?"

"Well, not really. But not much going on there either," Oakley said as he tore open his new pack of cigarettes and shook one out.

"Maybe it was fate that we ran into each other," Oakley said as he lit his cigarette and took a long drag. "I was thinking of calling you and asking your opinion on something that's bothering me," he added, pocketing the Musso matchbook to use for lighting his gas stove at home.

"A client something?"

"Nope. Something I read in the trades and had a hunch about, so I called your old friend Docky Martin and asked him what Louella thought."

"Good God," Grady exclaimed. "I wish he were an 'old friend.' Every day I work my balls off trying to break Parsons's column, and you call her hubby just to check on a hunch?"

"OK, Les," Oakley soothed. "There's a difference, and you know it. You're a talent agent who, when a client sometimes needs a little polishing, also fills in as a flack, and I'm just a lowly PI. But for someone like Parsons, when you call, she knows you're doing it because someone is paying you to do it. I, on the other hand, am considered a source and might have some hot tip for her that someone isn't paying me to plant. I know it isn't always the case, and you have to constantly come up with legit tips and news for her and all the other columnists, but that's the general impression. I'm legit. You're somewhat suspect. Sorry."

"OK, buddy. So what did you want to ask me?"

"I saw this story in the *Reporter* that Eva Sanderson lost her baby and was so upset she pulled out of *The Matrimaniac*."

"Yep, I saw the same story. Apparently, she caught the measles, and it caused her to lose the child."

"Does that sound legit to you? Not the part about losing the baby—that's sad. But doesn't it sound odd to you that she, a grown adult, would somehow catch a children's disease? That's the part I don't get. I checked around, and no one she knows or has been around caught it, so she is apparently the only one among the thousand or so people at Metro or among her hundreds of friends and associates who was infected. Maybe she wasn't immune, but it seems really odd that if the disease were running around, she was the only one to catch it."

"So what are you saying? And who's paying you to check around?"

"No one is paying me anything," Oakley explained. "I just think that this is a really odd thing to happen, even in Hollywood, and I'm curious. I guess that goes with my job. It seems so odd that I think someone must have deliberately found a way to infect her."

"Wow. Are you sure you haven't spent too much time looking under beds or in closets? Did you say all this to Docky?"

"No, I only asked him if Louella had spoken to Eva and asked what Eva may have told her."

"And?"

"He said that Eva thinks Stan brought the disease into their home from the Disney film he's working on."

"So that's a reasonable assumption. Sounds like that explains it."

"I know. But again, no one whom she or Stan knows has gotten it," Oakley reminded, wondering why Les seemed relieved with the news that his suspicions that Eva had been directly targeted hadn't been mentioned during his conversation with Louella Parsons's husband.

"Mr. Grady, Mr. Grady," someone shouted just as Oakley was about to ask him why he was curious about who might share his suspicions.

"Over here, over here," Les shouted, standing and waving. One of the restaurant's young waiters appeared.

"Mr. Grady? Mr. Lester Grady?"

Les nodded.

"You have a telephone call; they said it was an emergency. You can take it at the phone in the restaurant which will be quieter than using the extension at the bar."

"Thanks," Les said. "I'll be back in a sec." He elbowed his way through the crowd, leaving Oakley to nurse his drink.

Within a few minutes, the same waiter appeared carrying another Martini. "Mr. Webster? Mr. Grady had to leave and asked me to give you this note and bring you another Martini."

"Oh, thanks. I hope it wasn't anything serious?"

"I don't really know, sir. He seemed to be in a hurry, wrote this note to you, asked me to get you another drink, and scrammed. Oh, yeah, he said to tell you the tip is taken care of."

"Thanks, er..."

"Bob Barkley—everybody calls me Bobby."

"So, thanks, Bobby."

"It isn't my real name," the waiter added. "It's my acting name."

"Oh, you're an actor?" Grady asked more out of politeness than interest, thinking that this was more information than was really appropriate from a waiter bearing a simple message and a drink. Still, knowing Hollywood, it wasn't much of a surprise.

"I am. Well, I want to be. Right now, I'm picking up a few jobs as an extra and I do a little part-time work for Mr. Grady, but one day my ship will come in. My real name is Johnny Cleveland. I'm from Rembrandt, South Dakota."

"Glad to meet you, Johnny Cleveland," Oakley said, shaking the waiter's hand perfunctorily. "I'm sure it will all work out for you. You've certainly got the looks for it," he added to be polite, turning his attention to Les's note, which explained that he had a client problem and would call later, while muttering, "You and the ten thousand other dreamers who are standing around on Poverty Row every day hoping to be discovered."

Oakley finished his drink and, elbowing his way through the crowd, left Musso's by the back entrance and retrieved his car. *So what do I do about dinner?* he thought as he dropped the car into gear and edged his way out into traffic. *Pork and beans from a can at home or the diner on Vermont?*

He decided on the diner but was sorely tempted to change his plan as he drove past the Hollywood branch of the Brown Derby restaurant on Vine Street. "Hey, that's Louella's Packard parked in front," he said aloud and slowed down. *Maybe I should stop in and chat a bit more about Eva?* he thought before deciding not to. It was the wrong time of day.

The Hollywood branch of the famous chain that started in 1926 with a place on Wilshire Boulevard across from the Ambassador Hotel (topped with a huge plaster derby hat modeled on that famously worn by New York governor and 1928 Democratic presidential nominee Al Smith) was popular from the day it opened with film stars because it was close to the studios and the food was good. So it was a perfect place for Parsons and, eventually, also her rival gossip columnist, Hedda Hopper, to gather news. *She'll be much too busy to talk with me*, Oakley thought. Better to go on to his favorite diner near his apartment.

Chapter 3

Traffic was, as usual, terrible on Sunset Boulevard. Oakley's stomach was growling, in need of something more filling than gin, as he turned onto Vermont Avenue and pulled into the parking lot of Dinah's Diner. Built in the late 1920s—or rather, "assembled" would be more accurate—what the place lacked in comfort (having been created from an old Atchison, Topeka, and Santa Fe railroad car), it made up for with the sort of fare most Angelenos missed in their sunny, palm tree–framed paradise: substantial, home-style, Middle-Western cooking. Oakley knew that was what he wanted as he seated himself at one of the chrome-and-orange oilcloth barstools at the diner's nickel-topped counter.

"Hi, love!" the counter girl greeted him. "What'll it be tonight? Or d'ja need a menu?"

"What's worth eating today, Olive?" he quipped. "I'm in need of something serious."

"Jus' took a meatloaf outta the oven. How 'bout some? Comes with mashed potatoes and peas."

"That would be great." He smiled. "And some coffee," Oakley added, turning to look around the sparsely filled diner while his order was being prepared. *Not much going on tonight*, he thought.

Just then, someone slapped him on the shoulder. "Hey, Oakey, how ya doin'?" Oakley turned. It was his apartment neighbor, Dave Duncan.

"Dave, nice to see you. Here, sit next to me," Oakley said, indicating the adjoining barstool while wondering why everyone—first Les and now

Dave —thought it was OK to slap him on the back to get his attention when "hello" would suffice.

"Sorry, got a date," he said, reaching for the young blonde next to him. *Well,* Oakley thought, *she certainly fills up anyone's list of must-haves for a 1930s girl.* Jean Harlow, the platinum-blond movie bombshell who had just died at the terrifyingly young age of twenty-six, immediately came to Oakley's mind.

Harlow had always been one of favorite Oakley's favorite stars, probably because of her brash personality and an outrageous lifestyle, which she flung in the face of the bluestockings of the world. It was an attribute that he sometimes wished he possessed.

Oakley also had long felt a connection—albeit tenuous—with Harlow because when she was still Harlean Carpenter, she had been a classmate of Oakley's cousin at a private Catholic girls' school in Kansas City, Missouri. That was long before she married at sixteen and later moved to Los Angeles where she found fame, fortune, two more husbands, and a tragically early death from uremic poisoning. The film community was still reeling from the shock of her death.

In any event, like many young women in Hollywood, Dave's date was doing all she could to copy Harlow's appearance, including the actress's dyed platinum hair, a marcelled hairdo, and an evident disdain for a bra. *I wonder if she also dispenses with panties like Harlow supposedly did?* Oakley thought.

"Dorsey, meet my neighbor, Oakley Webster." Dave said, introducing his companion. "Oakey, meet Dorsey Lincoln. Some doll, huh?"

"You bet, Dave, some doll. You two just out for a bite?" he asked.

"Yep, and then we thought we'd take in the new musical over at the Vista Theater down on Sunset. Say, didja hear that Metro's recastin' *Matrimaniac?* Somebody said that Eva Sanderson has pulled out."

"Yep, I read about it in the trades," Oakley responded without further comment.

"So, I heard somewhere that it had somethin' to do with measles?" Dorsey asked. "Maybe I should try out for it."

"Oh, are you an actress?" Oakley asked, despite already anticipating her answer.

"Sure 'nuff, hon." She smiled. "Doan' I look like one?" she added, flouncing her hair. "Been in a bunch of movies…"

"Really?" Oakley asked.

"Well, no leadin' roles...yet, but that'll come."

"She's been in half a dozen films as an extra," Dave explained, "but she actually had a line in the new *Topper* flick."

"Did she really? Was she cast as a ghost?" Oakley asked, hoping his sarcasm wasn't obvious because he couldn't remember seeing her in the first film based on author Thorne Smith's tale of a man haunted by a pair of friendly ghosts.

"Yep," Dorsey said, completely missing Oakley's dig. "I played a coat-check girl and got to hand Cary Grant a claim check and say, 'You're welcome,' to him. I'm thinkin' maybe I need to change my name...Somethin' more 'zotic...like the big stars of the twenties did."

"I think you're exotic enough as it is," Oakley said. "Don't do anything you might regret later." He realized that so far tonight, he had been batting one thousand meeting movie star hopefuls.

"Hon," she said smiling, "thanks for the advice, but I'm not regrettin' anything. As Mae West says, 'Life's just a merry-go-round, and you might grab a brass ring.' I'm lookin' for that brass ring."

"An' speakin' of grabbin', let's grab that one," Dorsey suddenly exclaimed, pointing to a booth being vacated at the far end of the diner. "Then we can be real cozy," she said, snuggling up to Dave and pulling him toward the booth.

"How's the meatloaf, dearie?" Olive purred as Oakley turned back to his meal. "Or you been eatin' up somethin' else?" she added, glaring disdainfully at Dorsey's swaying hips parading up the diner's linoleum floor.

"It's great, Olive," he said with a chuckle. "I'll be ready for some dessert soon."

"From your expression a minute ago, I figured you already had your dessert."

"No, no, not really my style," he added with a smile. "What's good tonight?"

"I sorta figured. Dessert's the usual—apple pie," she said, indicating the covered plastic display case behind her. "Or lemon meringue. Or chocolate meringue. Or ice cream: vanilla, chocolate, or strawberry. Oh yeah, we also got grapefruit cake—just like the one at the Derby," she said, mentioning the restaurant chain's famous dessert.

"Does that mean that their Cobb salad is going to be on the menu at Dinah's Diner soon, too?" Oakley smiled. "I'll have a piece of the chocolate meringue."

"Comin' up!"

Home was only minutes away from the diner.

Oakley parked in front of the apartment complex at the southeast corner of Alvarado and Maryland where he had lived from the time he got his first real job in Los Angeles. Known as the Alvarado Court Apartments, it consisted of eight once-elegant but now slightly seedy two-story, white-stucco buildings, designed in a faintly Mediterranean style, with each containing two floor-through flats, and situated around a central courtyard. Originally one of the city's most exclusive neighborhoods where stately homes occasionally could still be found amid palm and orange trees near Westlake Park, it was still a respectable location, although not so much so as it was in the early 1920s. Then, residents included the famous director William Desmond Taylor and the silent film star Edna Purviance, Charlie Chaplin's one-time lover and leading lady, who appeared in more than thirty of his films including the 1921 classic *The Kid*.

In 1922, the complex became notorious nationwide when Taylor was murdered in the living room of his downstairs apartment across the courtyard from the building where Purviance's apartment was located, now occupied by Oakley. The scandal surrounding the crime involved stories of drug trafficking; the famous Mack Sennett comedienne (and frequent Chaplin costar) Mabel Normand; the silent film star Mary Miles Minter; her movie mother from hell, Charlotte Shelby, and Taylor's African American houseman (who was gay and disappeared the day after the murder). The murder was never solved.

To Oakley, the history of the place was less important than the comfort of the large apartments, the charm of the apartment complex's courtyard with its ivy-covered pavilion, and the convenience of a Red Line route down Maryland Street alongside the property. Nevertheless, as he entered his flat and punched the ivory-tipped button on the 1920s-style light switch to turn on the living room's ceiling light, he caught himself again wishing that he could afford a more up-to-date place in the glamorous modern style popularized by the movies and located in a more upscale neighborhood farther west—like on Larchmont where Mae West lived, or even in Beverly Hills where Douglas Fairbanks and Mary Pickford lived in old-fashioned but regal grandeur high atop what locally passed for a mountain. Either area would be perfect.

But not on what I make, Oakley thought as he crossed the living room and turned on the tombstone-shaped Zenith radio which was still set from the night before to NBC's Blue network. "Time to find out what is going on in the real world…and it's just in time for Winchell," he muttered as the vacuum tubes warmed up.

Soon, the high-pitched voice of Walter Winchell making his staccato introduction to his nightly broadcast, emerged from the hum. "Good evening Mr. and Mrs. America and all the ships at sea. Let's go to press…" Sponsored by Jergens hand lotion, New York–based Winchell, considered by many as America's first gossip columnist, had become famous for his newspaper "scoops" and thinly veiled innuendos about celebrities that could make or break careers even before he began his popular radio tell-alls.

Tonight's show was no different and led off with the news that was already on Oakley's mind. "Everyone in Tinseltown is talking about Eva Sanderson's sudden withdrawal from Metro's big movie project *The Matrimaniac* after catching the measles and losing her baby," Winchell barked in his breathless, mile-a-minute delivery. "I'm told that she's blaming hubby, Stan Damon, accusing him of being responsible for bringing the measles bug into their Bev Hills manse. Their togetherness has become so bad that insiders say America's girl and boy next door could be telling it to a judge soon. Goes without saying that studio honcho Louis B. Mayer is frantic that the flick, a remake of an old Doug Fairbanks/Connie Talmadge silent comedy caper and budgeted at nearly a million smackers, is done for unless he can find a star to step in for Sanderson. Stay tuned…"

Oakley smiled and then was riveted in place by Winchell's item that followed. "And, folks, I hear that that's not all that Metro's old gray Mayer is losing sleep over these days. Seems like one of his top stars has also been snuggling with a handsome new honey. Nothing new about that except their bath towels are both embroidered *His*.

"Now for some international news. Der Führer is also kicking up some dirt in Berlin…"

Oakley turned off the radio. *Sometimes it's too much*, he thought. Mayer's homophobia is well known in Hollywood. Nevertheless, he hires more "fago-lahs" (as he calls homosexual men) than any person in Hollywood because you can't run a studio without the costume and set designers and musicians, a significant majority of whom had a "touch of lavender" as the phrase went. Plus, the homosexual actors, many of whom, thanks to the new morality clauses in contracts, were unhappily living in name-only marriages.

Oakley knew that Mayer carried his homophobia as far as to actually fire some homosexual actors unless they were too big a star to dump. In that case, he forced them to keep the truth of their sexual orientation from the public with a fake marriage or a heterosexual affair that could be flogged in the fan magazines. "I wonder who he's after this time," Oakley said quietly as he stubbed out his last cigarette for the day and went into his kitchen for a glass of water en route to his bedroom. "At least that's one problem I don't have to solve," which, Oakley little suspected would soon prove that at least in Hollywood, nothing should ever be taken for granted.

The rest of Oakley's week was filled by the bane of all PIs: calls and visits by both men and women—mostly women—convinced that their mate was cheating on them and inquiring how much it would cost to catch them in a situation compromising enough to qualify for a divorce, or perhaps a reconciliation available for a substantial amount of cash.

Oakley usually avoided such cases, although now and then he took them on despite his reluctance to do so—usually when the case was interesting (which was rare because the storyline of most such cases followed similar scripts) or, now, because his bank balance was in serious need of replenishment. There was no time to follow up on his suspicions about Eva Sanderson's loss.

So it was with little or no regret that Oakley sent Benny home early on Friday and was preparing to leave when the phone rang. *Forget it*, he thought, walking toward the door. Inevitably, though, curiosity overcame him, and he turned, retraced his steps to his desk, and grabbed the phone. "Oakley, Oakley, are you there?" a familiar voice shouted from the earpiece. 'I'm here, I'm here," he responded. "Who's this?"

"It's Les, Les Grady," the voice shouted breathlessly.

"Hello, Les," Oakley said, curious why his publicist friend sounded so breathless and why he would call so late on a hot Friday afternoon when it seemed that most flacks habitually stopped working earlier in the day, claiming that they had a meeting to get to in Malibu or the more distant Santa Barbara or Palm Springs, both only two hours away by train or car.

"I gotta see you, Oakey!" he said. "Can we meet somewhere? I don't mind coming down to your office."

"No. I was just leaving," Oakley replied. *What on earth would be so urgent that Les would be willing to drive all the way downtown from his Hollywood office to meet him?* "We could meet at Musso's again," Oakley said, "but it will be a zoo this time on a Friday afternoon. How about we meet halfway, someplace like the Derby—the one with the hat?"

"OK," Les agreed. "Like in a half hour? I'll grab a booth."

By the time Oakley had negotiated his way through rush-hour traffic on Wilshire Boulevard and parked, Les had arrived and found a booth near the front of the restaurant. He was, a surprised Oakley noted as he approached the booth, not alone but accompanied by a beautiful brunette who was about twenty-six or thereabouts he figured. "Hi," Oakley said, as he slid into the booth. "Who's your friend?"

"Oakley Webster meet Rachael Baumgarten," Les said. "And viceyversey." He laughed.

"Glad to meet you. So, Les, glad to meet your friend, but what was so urgent that we had to meet this afternoon?"

"Let's order a drink first," Les said, waving at a nearby waiter. "Rachael, what'll you have?"

"Just a Coke," she said quietly.

"I'll have a Martini, twist, on the rocks," Les added, "and one for you, too, Oakley?"

"Yep, extradry and straight up."

"Rachael is a client of mine," Les said as the waiter nodded and walked away. "Something terrible happened to her the other day, and I couldn't think of anyone better than you to help out."

"I'm sorry," Oakley said, looking intently at the young woman whose eyes were downcast. *Are those tears on her face?* he wondered. "But what is it you need from me?" he asked.

"Rachael is a unique, unusual talent," Les began to explain. "She is a tremendously gifted woman violinist who plays regularly with the Long Beach Women's Symphony Orchestra."

"Good for you," Oakley said consolingly, realizing that the moisture on her cheeks was indeed tears.

"And she just got a big break," Les continued, "one that many musicians work all their careers for. She auditioned and was picked to be the featured soloist tomorrow night at the Hollywood Bowl with the Los Angeles Philharmonic Orchestra—the first woman violinist ever to be a soloist at the Bowl. Maybe twenty thousand people in the audience and probably a big review in the papers."

"My dream is to be a member of Phil Spitalny's all-girl orchestra," Rachael said through her sobs, "and play on his radio broadcasts...you know, the *Hour of Charm* show? I asked Les to invite him, and he is sending someone to hear me, maybe even Evelyn herself."

"Evelyn?" Oakley asked, perplexed.

"Spitalny's soloist who's billed as 'Evelyn and Her Magic Violin,'" Les explained. "One of the most famous female musicians in the country. She also cofounded the all-girl orchestra with him. Big-time lady."

"That's great. Congratulations!" Oakley said. "So what's so terrible?"

"Someone stole Rachael's violin," Les explained. "So unless it's found before then, she won't be able to play, and she will have lost her big break."

"That's terrible," Oakley said, "but can't she just borrow another violin and go on with the show until the police find hers?"

"No," Les said as the waiter set their drinks down on the table. "It doesn't work that way with violinists. The instrument is part of them, and unlike pianists who can't always play on their own piano, string musicians—violinists, cellists—always use the instrument they train with and live with. It's like a marriage—closer than some marriages I know of."

"So what do you want me to do?" Oakley asked.

"I want you to find her violin."

"What?" Oakley exclaimed. "Between now and tomorrow night? I'm complimented that you think that I'm that good, but that's impossible."

"Maybe not. Rachael, tell Oakley what you know," Les said quietly.

"I was at the Hollywood Bowl yesterday afternoon for a rehearsal," the musician said slowly. "I was thirsty, so I left it in the green room—that's what they call the room where the performers stay—and went looking for a Coke or something to drink. It never occurred to me that my violin might not be safe there. When I came back, it was gone. That's all I know. It's a really nice violin, lent to me by the music school that I attended in Illinois."

"What kind of violin is it?" Oakley asked. "You know, do they have identifying brands or something so you can tell them apart."

"It's a good reproduction of an 18th century Guarnerius that was made in the early 1900s by a luthier named Stefano Scarampella of Brescia, Italy. It won a prize when it was made," Rachael started to explain. "But unless you know old violins, about the only way to tell them apart is by their sound and, of course, by their appearance. The finish on a Stradivarius or a Guarneri is unmistakable."

"Luthier?" Oakley injected.

"Violin maker," Les explained. "Go on, Rachael."

"So I didn't know what to do. I found a guard or security person—whatever they call them—and he made a telephone call, and all of a sudden, there were police and security people everywhere. They were asking me over and over what I knew," she said somewhat breathlessly. "But I didn't know any more than I just told you. Then someone called the police, and they questioned me more about who I had seen around the room and if I had any enemies in the orchestra. I couldn't tell them anything more. And I certainly had no enemies. I don't even know most of the people in the Los Angeles Philharmonic."

"So how did you get the booking, gig, or whatever you call it?" Oakley asked.

"In summertime, they can't always get the really top soloists because there is a lot of competition for them at summer music festivals. So from time to time, they look around for local talent to fill in," she explained. "Someone from the Bowl or the Los Angeles Philharmonic apparently contacted the Long Beach orchestra where I play, and they recommended me. Then I auditioned for the concert master and Dr. Klemperer, the conductor, and Les took care of the rest.

"It was so exciting, but now…I was also hoping that if I was good enough, I could play in the George Gershwin memorial concert they are planning for later in the summer."

"I know, Rachael," Les said, hugging her, "it looks pretty bleak now, but Oakley is the best. He'll find it."

"Rachael," Oakley said, pulling out his diary and a pen while Les ordered a second round of drinks, "I want you to give me the names of anyone you think might be jealous of this break for you, like people in the women's orchestra. You have a boyfriend?" he asked. Rachael shook her head. "Was there any mention of someone else in the running for the engagement? Did anyone else audition?"

"I don't know," she murmured. "But you might ask the people who already auditioned me: the first violinist, the orchestra's manager, and Dr. Klemperer."

"I will. But first, who had access to the green room other than you. Was anyone in and out of there that you know of?"

"No," she said slowly. "No one I can think of except, of course, Les here."

"Les," Oakley asked, "did you see anyone or anything odd?"

"No. Just Rachael…and, of course, her violin."

"Les, when Rachael went to get a soda or water, did you see anyone come near the green room?"

"No, Oakey, I wasn't even in the neighborhood of the artists' space. I had gone to my car to get my notebook."

"I thought you never went anywhere without it"—Oakley smiled and pointed to his friend's ubiquitous accessory—"essential equipment for a publicist."

"Well, that's true, but I guess I was so confused with security people arguing over whether I had the right to park in the lot behind the shell that is reserved for performers and press, I forgot."

"OK," Oakley said. "As I said, unless a miracle happens, I see no way of solving this by tomorrow night. So maybe, Rachael, you should talk to the orchestra people and see if there is an instrument that you could feel at least comfortable playing. And for me, I'm going to get on the telephone with whoever I can find tonight. First stop, though, will be the local precinct station. By the way, Rachael, did the police say anything when they showed up?" Oakley said, extricating himself from the booth and offering a hand to the violinist.

"No. I just told them more or less what I told you, and they wrote it down, and that was that."

"Hey, look over there," Les said, nodding toward a familiar woman in a nearby booth as the trio started to leave. "The woman who singlehandedly saved Paramount from bankruptcy a few years back."

"My goodness," Rachael exclaimed, "is that Mae West?"

"Yep. Her three movies did what nothing else seemed to be able to do after the stock market bit the dust. The trades said it was because audiences responded to her characters, most of whom prove they could be successful even though they might come from the wrong side of the tracks. But of course the main reason for the success of her movies wasn't a socially uplifting message like that. It was the sexy stories."

"Hi, Les," a voice shouted from a nearby booth as they started walking to the exit.

"Oh, hi, Mike," the publicist turned and acknowledged.

"Who're your friends?"

"Mike, this is my client Rachael Baumgarten and Oakley Webster, LA's most famous PI," he said with typical Hollywood hyperbole. "Folks, meet John Meiklejohn, LA's most famous talent agent…well, other than me," he smiled. "Who's your friend, Mike?"

"I want everyone to meet my newest client," Meiklejohn said, "just arrived from Illinois—Ronny Reagan."

"Nice to meet you, Mr. Reagan," Oakley said. "Thinking about going into films?"

"I hope so. That's why I'm here."

"You have a background in theater?"

"Nope," the young man said. "Jus' did some high school stuff. Mike here tells me that's less important than looks these days and how well you photograph..."

"We've done a couple tests," Meiklejohn interrupted, "and, as they say, the camera loves Ronny. Great voice for the mic, too. And he's from Dixon, Illinois, right where Louella started her newspaper career. So he has a leg up with her from the start."

"Aren't you lucky," Oakley said, moving toward the door. He hoped his comment didn't sound as rude as he thought it did, but he had heard dozens of similar praises about newly arrived actors, most of whom disappeared as fast as they seemed to arrive in Hollywood or ended up as waiters, waitresses, houseboys, maids, or prostitutes. "I've really got to go," he said.

"Gotcha," Les said, guiding Rachael along. "Me, too. See ya later, Mike. You, too, Ronny. Good luck!"

"That guy will never make it," Les confided to Oakley while they were waiting on the sidewalk in front of the Derby for the valets to retrieve their cars. "A friend of mine called me about doing some pro bono PR for him some time ago, and I said, 'No way!' He's as green as an Iowa cornfield in July. He's only done radio shit—not acting like on a daytime serial but as a broadcaster of sports events. And I hear he is an outspoken Socialist—not the best thing to be in Republican Hollywood. Zero. Zilch. Forget it."

"Well, you may be right," Oakley said, handing his business card to Rachael. "Here's my wagon," he added as the valet brought up his car. "I'll call you as soon as I know something, and you both have my number. Call me if you think of anything."

Chapter 4

Fifteen minutes later, Oakley pulled up in front of the Hollywood precinct station. *Good God,* he thought. *This place needs some fixing up. It's such a dump that it would give any potential criminal second thoughts. And why is it so gloomy in here?* he wondered as he entered the lobby, looking for Sean Doyle, an officer he knew from working on a previous case.

Luckily, this evening Doyle was the night-duty officer. "Greetings, Oakey. What's our favorite gumshoe doin' in this part of town tonight?" Doyle exclaimed as Oakley walked up to his desk. "We got nobody in holdin' yet for you to bail out."

"I need your help, Sean. I was just asked to look into the theft of a violin last night at the Bowl, and as the police were called in, I'd really appreciate anything you can tell me."

"Meddlin' in police work again?" Doyle exclaimed with a smile but in a tone with an edge to it.

"Meddling? I don't think so," the PI replied. "I've been asked to help. You telling me that you folks don't want or need a little help now and then?"

"Hey, Oakley, I didn't mean to ruffle your feathers. It's just that some of your ilk get in the way of people who are actually responsible for solving crimes."

"Does that mean you're about to solve this?" Oakley asked.

"Hell, no. Hardly a top priority. Some tomato lost her fiddle. Fiddle faddle."

"Well, Sean, I agree that she's a nice 'tomato,' but it's no ordinary 'fiddle' we're looking for. This one's worth some thirty or forty thousand."

"What?" Doyle shouted. "Forty grand? No fiddle is worth that much! Six or seven times as much as a new house!"

"Hey, friend, I'm not kidding. This fiddle was made in Italy a few years ago."

"So now we're lookin' for a fiddle made by some dead Dago?"

"Put it any way you want, buddy. That's what you're…we're…looking for. Any ideas?"

"Nawww, nuttin'. Can't say the trail is cold because there ain't no trail. I understan' the fiddle was there one moment and gone the next."

"You check out witnesses?"

"What witnesses?" Doyle asked. "Ain't none. Everybody mindin' their own business. At least accordin' to the couple people we talked with."

"And who might they be?"

"Well, Oakey, that's really none of your biz. But as I know you'll be sniffin' around, I might as well tell you. We talked with whadja call him? Concert master, the numero uno fiddle player in the band. He said he was on stage tunin' up or somethin' like that. And we called the boss, Klemper somethin' or other."

"Klemperer, Dr. Otto Klemperer, the conductor of the Los Angeles Philharmonic."

"Yeah, and his assistant, some broad named Eileen. She said he hadn't even gotten to the Bowl for the rehearsal. Struck out on all counts."

"So you don't mind if I did a little checking around?" Oakley asked. "The lady is really upset because tomorrow night was to be her big debut with the Philharmonic, and now she's out."

"Yeah," Sean said, "so I heard on the radio. They ain't wastin' any time waitin' for you to find the fiddle. Seems that they already have a substitute—some guy."

"Remember the name?" Oakley asked.

"Nawww. Somethin' furrin' soundin'—Dago, maybe. Jewsep somethin'?"

"Giuseppe?"

"Yeah, sounds about right. Hey, Oakey, go ahead and check some if you want, but this sounds like a lost cause to me. But be a lalapazaza and keep us informed."

"'Course, buddy," Oakley said with a smile, thinking that he hadn't heard that term for being a "good sport" since he was a teenager. Out loud (but to himself) he added, "I hope that's no indication of how out-of-touch they are when it comes to doing their job."

Traffic was, as usual for a Friday night, terrible, so Oakley decided to take Franklin Avenue to Alvarado instead of Sunset Boulevard. Normally, it would carry less traffic as it was largely noncommercial, but tonight was an exception; it was a slow-moving traffic jam.

To pass the time, Oakley turned on the radio in his car, a $25 option that he was glad to have ordered. After a short pause, he heard the familiar voice of the biggest recording star in the country, Bing Crosby, crooning his new hit, "Sweet Leilani." "I'd sure rather be in Hawaii than here," Oakley said aloud. "I think it's about time I take a little vacation for myself," he resolved, thinking that he might check on the fares on the new Matson ship he'd seen advertised in the *Los Angeles Times*: the SS *Malolo* that sailed from San Pedro. *Five or six days from here to Honolulu—not bad and on a ship named for a flying fish.* He smiled to himself, remembering that he looked up the meaning of the name. *And maybe I could spring for the new hotel the Matson people built there: the Royal Hawaiian on Waikiki Beach.*

The sudden slowdown of traffic brought a quick end to his daydream. "Shit, better watch what I'm doing," he said aloud, slamming on his brakes just a moment too late to avoid gently hitting the car in front of him. Both cars pulled over to the curb, next to which a gray wall rose like the rampart of a medieval Spanish castle. Both drivers exited and, after seeing that there was no damage, introduced themselves. "My name is Joe Valentine," said the driver of the car Oakley hit.

"And mine is Oakley Webster. I'm sorry I hit you. I guess I was daydreaming."

"My fault, too. I slowed down without signaling," Valentine said. "I live here," he added, vaguely gesturing toward the castle-like structure. "But since there isn't enough parking in the building, some of us park in these garages along Franklin. I was about to turn into mine. I'm sorry."

"So what is this place?" Oakley asked, looking up at the stone wall.

"Well, I'm told it's a copy of a building in Spain, and that's about all I know about the design. It was built about ten years ago by Cecil B. DeMille for New York stage actors when sound came in and Hollywood discovered that lots of the silent movie stars had terrible voices. The place looks like a movie set itself except, unlike movie sets, this one is real. One of the apartments is actually in an old-looking tower, and everything is built around a courtyard with a fountain in the middle."

"Wow," Oakley exclaimed. "So is it still full of New York actors?"

"Not anymore," Valentine said, "but there are a few tenants who want to be, mostly making careers these days as extras. You know how it is..."

Oakley nodded.

"And supposedly Scott Fitzgerald lived here in one of the apartments for a few months. Want to see the building?"

"I'd love to, but I can't just leave my car here on the street now. Give me your phone number, and I'll give you a call when I can stop by. Are you an actor?"

"Nope, just a working stiff, I play—"

At that moment, a car behind Oakley honked loudly. "I guess I better go," he said. "I'll call ya," he shouted, shoving the piece of paper with Joe's phone number on it into his pocket and vaulting into his car, slamming it into first gear, and driving off. *Nice guy*, he thought. *Not so bad looking either.*

The fact that Oakley might be a "pansy" or a "fruit," the usual terms at the time for homosexual men (gay was used as code between homosexuals from time to time but would not be in relatively common usage until the 1950s), may have been suspected by some of his friends but rarely, if ever, mentioned for a good reason: survival. Hollywood had from its beginnings always been accepting, if not exactly welcoming, sexual deviation simply because the film industry couldn't operate without professions that had large homosexual populations.

But a new era of conservatism hit in the 1930s, which brought about such censorship bodies as the Roman Catholic Legion of Decency and the Motion

Picture Production Code and its later manifestation known as the Breen Commission (named for Joseph Breen, its Catholic, anti-Semitic boss) to which all films had to be submitted for review. It ended the sexual liberalism of the roaring twenties, and homosexuality was essentially forced underground.

The new Victorianism was less evident in Hollywood than in the rest of the country, but even in the film capital, there were many actors who were forced to choose between living in the closet, or entering into what were called "lavender" marriages (unions arranged so the ticket-buying public would think they were "normal" people. Among them were former lovers Cary Grant and Randolph Scott, Laurence Olivier, Danny Kaye, and MGM's famous costume designer Adrian and his Oscar-winning wife, Janet Gaynor). Homosexuality was, of course, totally taboo in films, except for making fun of "swish" stereotypes.

Nevertheless, it was inevitable that at least in urban centers, homosexuals found a way to meet one another and even maintain committed relationships. And there was always nearby Palm Springs where homosexuals famously could get away from the bluestockings and party behind the high walls of its estates.

Despite the Friday evening traffic, Oakley eventually arrived home, parked, and let himself into his apartment only to realize that he had completely forgotten to stop at the local Ralph's market to pick up something for dinner. *Maybe there is something*, he thought, opening the door of his "icebox" (as he referred to the art deco–styled General Electric refrigerator he had recently bought) to see if there was anything that could be transformed into a meal. "Not even a God damned egg," he said sourly, slamming the door. "It's tomato soup and a peanut butter sandwich again tonight," he grumbled, opening a can of the popular Campbell's staple and grabbing a jar of Skippy and a loaf of Butternut bread.

Satiated but not particularly happy, Oakley settled back into his favorite easy chair, turned on the nearby floor lamp, and picked up the half-read copy of his favorite author's recent book, Agatha Christie's *The ABC Murders*—not that he thought of himself as an American version of her detective Hercule Poirot. For better or for worse, Oakley was much more direct in dealing with both clients and suspects than was Christie's famous Belgian sleuth. But, as he feared from time to time, he was not nearly as perceptive.

God, I must have fallen asleep while I was reading, Oakley realized, glancing through the kitchen door at the clock on the wall above his small breakfast table. It was 2:00 a.m. *What was it that woke me?* he wondered, and then he heard a shout from outside. "Stop!" God damn you!" a woman's voice screamed. "Stop right now or I'll scream!"

"You're screaming already, you dumb broad," a male voice shouted. Oakley realized it was the voice of his neighbor, Dave Duncan, who had, judging from his slurred speech, clearly celebrated a bit too much. "Scream all you want," he continued. "Who's gonna hear you?"

"Well, jus' the entire fuckin' neighborhood," the woman shouted back. "Find yourself someone else to screw."

"You bet I will," Dave slurred back. "You're nothin' but a flat tire anyway."

"Oh yeah? Screw you! What a fake! You come on like the Sheik of Araby, but you're nuttin' but a bust. Betcha you're a fairy, too! Abyssinia," she said, using a popular slang term for "good-bye," while Oakley, by now overlooking the courtyard from his living room window, quietly watched. *Dave's gonna have a massive headache in the morning,* he thought with a smile as he tossed the book on the chair and went into his bedroom, determined to have a proper sleep, if only at least for what was left of the night.

The next morning dawned clear and warm—a perfect summer Saturday in Los Angeles, but unfortunately not one when he could enjoy himself. Oakley had promised Les and Rachael that he would work on the violin theft, and he had to do so.

Although it was the weekend, his office building was already a busy place when he arrived around 9:30 a.m. He let himself into his office and immediately opened the windows and turned on the floor fan to get some fresh air.

How the hell am I going to find anyone on the weekend? Oakley wondered. "But I have to try," he muttered aloud as he grabbed his telephone book and started checking for the numbers of people who might know something about the loss of the violin.

His efforts were fruitless—well, almost fruitless. The only person he was able to reach was a maintenance man at the Hollywood Bowl who said that one of his buddies said he had seen a man carrying what appeared to be a violin case walking toward the performer's parking lot during the rehearsal. The only reason he noticed the man was because he seemed younger than anyone playing in the orchestra. Calls to the Los Angeles Philharmonic's office provided nothing new other than the name of the violinist replacing Rachael on the program: a studio musician named Giuseppe del Monte.

After trying to find something, anything, for two hours, Oakley realized that he wasn't getting anywhere. "Better to give them the bad news now," he said aloud as he dialed Les's office. "He's not here," a woman, probably his secretary, explained. "Can I take a message?"

"Just tell him that Oakley Webster called, and unfortunately, I wasn't able to turn up anything on Rachael Baumgarten's violin."

"Oh, I understand," she said. "He told me the same thing before he left for lunch—that it looked impossible at this late date for you or anyone to find out what happened. I guess it just vanished into thin air. I'm sure he appreciates your help."

Confronted with the remainder of a Saturday afternoon and nothing else to do, Oakley figured that he might as well take in a movie. As luck would have it, *Saratoga*, starring Clark Gable and his lately deceased idol Jean Harlow, who died while making the movie, had just opened at the nearby Million Dollar Theater. Oakley liked the movie, but it was clear to him where Harlow's double was employed to film scenes uncompleted by the actress when she died.

After stopping in a local delicatessen to pick up something for dinner—in this case, potato salad and a corned beef sandwich—Oakley wondered if his happiness in looking forward to getting home was a symptom of advancing old age. "Damn," he said aloud. "Saturday night, and here I am home alone and planning to stay that way. I should be out at a bar or nightclub or at least going out to dinner." Then the realization hit him: there wasn't anyone whom he would like to be going out to dinner with. "I'm just a tired old man," he growled sadly as he settled into his reading chair, picked up his sandwich in one hand and the unfinished Agatha Christie mystery in the other, and settled back to make the best of the last thing he expected from life at his age: a quiet evening at home.

Chapter 5

Sunday dawned as beautifully as the day before, and this time, Oakley was able to take advantage of it. "No sleeping in today," he said aloud as he jumped out of bed, stretched, and thought about the day ahead. The haze of the evening before had evaporated in the sparkling morning light of a summer weekend day in Los Angeles when there was less traffic to pollute the air.

Maybe I'll call Joe Valentine, he thought. He smiled with the idea but immediately dismissed it. "Too soon, too soon," he muttered sleepily. "So what's to do?"

A rumble from his stomach indicated that his first consideration should probably be to find some food. As another peanut butter sandwich (which was about all that was left in the icebox) wasn't his idea for a Sunday breakfast, it was clear that after a quick shave and shower, Dinah's place was the answer.

"Do you ever get a day off?" He smiled, greeting Olive who was as usual presiding behind the counter at the diner.

"Nawww," she said. "What would I do? This place has all the entertainment I would ever want. An' what can I get you this a.m., darlin'?"

"How 'bout a stack?"

"And real Vermont?" Olive asked, aware of Oakley's preference for maple syrup with pancakes instead of the cheaper substitutes.

"And some Joe?"

"You betcha, hon."

"So," Olive asked when she brought his meal, "whatcha doin' today?"

"Dunno," Oakley mused as he spread a butter pat between the cakes and reached for the small pitcher of maple syrup. "Thinkin' of going to the beach. Looks like a nice day for it."

"I hate you!" Olive kidded with a broad smile. "You lyin' on the sand and me shovelin' flapjacks. Just ain't fair. Where ya thinkin' of goin'? Malibu?"

"Nope, too far. Maybe to that new beach the WPA built by the Santa Monica Pier. I hear it's great. But with all that street work on the Westside, it takes forever to drive out there."

"You mean the one some people are beginning to call Muscle Beach? If you don't wanna drive, why doncha take the Red Car? Goes right there. Lotsa cuties, I hear," she added with a wink.

"Great idea," Oakley said, suddenly realizing that he could catch the Pacific Electric Light Rail car, otherwise known as Los Angeles's Red Cars which crossed the LA basin from ocean to mountains, across the street from his apartment, and with one transfer, go all the way to the beach. "That's what I'll do. Thanks for your suggestion."

After returning home, it took only a few moments for Oakley to shove his swimming suit, the still-unfinished *ABC Murders*, and beach paraphernalia (including suntan oil doctored with a few drops of tincture of iodine to ensure a calendar-art suntan) in a toiletry kit used during his college days, and sprint to the Red Car stop on Maryland Street located just behind Jimmy Duncan's apartment.

While he waited, Oakley realized that the previous night's argument that had awakened him had been rekindled. "You are not leaving me!" Dave's voice, clearly heard through his open bedroom window, commanded. "Fuck you!" a female voice replied. "I'll do what I want. I only came by to get my stuff. And now I have it, and I'm gone."

The sound of a pair of doors slamming was clearly audible over the squeal of the Red Car's brakes as it rumbled up to the stop. *Thank God for small favors*, Oakley thought, happy that his wait for the Red Car, sometimes unpredictable on weekends, was unusually short. "Round trip to the Santa Monica Pier," he told the conductor.

"That'll be fifty cents," the conductor said, punching the appropriate holes in the long yellow tickets. "You'll need to transfer in Hollywood."

"Thanks," Oakley said as he walked toward the rear of the near-empty car and fell into the rattan seat by a partially opened window. "I wonder if that was Dorsey?" he said to himself, realizing that of course it had to be. "Dave's being a sucker."

Undelayed by the usual weekday traffic clogging the Red Line's grade crossings through West Los Angeles and Beverly Hills, the trip to the beach, including the transfer in Hollywood, took only forty-five minutes. Oakley got off, walked over to the beach, rented a locker, and changed into his new, boxer-style swimming trunks he bought the month before in the men's department at Bullocks Wilshire. He was happy to discard his old, bulky two-piece suit now that it was no longer unacceptable or actually illegal for men to appear on public beaches with bare chests. (Notoriously, among the last holdouts against the "no shirt movement" was Atlantic City, New Jersey.)

The beach was crowded. There were sun worshippers chatting among themselves or spread-eagled on towels here and there on the strand working on getting a suntan—a craze first popularized a decade before by the French fashion genius Coco Chanel. Nearby, a small group of men were jumping, swinging, and lifting weights in the part of the beach sectioned off for exercise. Oakley immediately spotted an acquaintance who worked in the same office building as he did whom he occasionally joined for lunch.

"Hey, Donny," he shouted to the handsome blond who was energetically lifting hand weights.

"Oakley, is that you?" his friend replied, blinking through the perspiration running down his forehead as he carefully replaced the weights on their rack. "I'm not used to seeing you without clothes on," he teased. "Whatcha doing here?"

"Same as you," Oakley replied. "Well, not quite the same. Just hoping to get a tan so I don't look so much like a poached flounder."

"Want to try some of this?" Donny invited, waving at the exercise equipment. "That way, you can work on your tan and your body at the same time—not that you look like you need it that much."

"Like with weights and all that stuff you have?" Oakley asked after joining Donny. "You working on a Charles Atlas body? Doesn't look like you have far to go," Oakley said admiringly. "You're certainly no ninety-eight-pound weakling like the guy in his ads."

"Actually, I'm doing that program, the Charles Atlas Dynamic Tension stuff, just like Joe Louis and Max Baer. But I'm never going to be a boxer like them. I do it because it just feels good," Donny explained as he stepped over the short wall separating the exercise area from the sand. "How 'bout a Coke?"

"So, tell me," Donny asked after the pair settled themselves onto towels on the least crowded part of the beach they could find, "how's the Dick Tracy business?"

"Pretty slow right now. Got coupla things working, though."

"Like what?" Donny asked.

"Well, like a musician's violin stolen Friday. A friend of mind called and asked me to help find it for a client of his who was scheduled to perform at the Bowl last night."

"So, ya find it?"

"Are you kidding? Vanished into God knows where. And of course no one was around to do much of what you call my 'Dick Tracy' work yesterday. And I'm still wondering about Eva Sanderson—how the hell a grown woman could get the measles."

"You mean the star of some new Metro movie? I mean the ex-star. She got the measles and then her baby died. Or something like that," Donny commented.

"Well, it was a bit more than 'something like that,'" Oakley said. "She caught the measles and lost her baby and was apparently so distraught that she dropped out of the film. And now she's, I hear, giving up her whole career. I'm trying to figure out what the real story is."

"So, Mr. Tracy," Donny asked, "since you're running a business, who exactly is paying you to find out 'what the real story is'? I read in the trades that Metro is already looking for a replacement—planning some sort of big nationwide search. Here"—Donny handed Oakley a bottle of baby oil—"could you spread some of this on my back, please?"

"'Course, Mr. Wells," Oakley said, somewhat surprised that he was a bit excited by the invitation. True, he realized, Donald Wells was one hell of a good-looking man, but for some reason, physical attraction had never before entered into their knowing each other. "Sure looks like your Charles Atlas routine is really paying off," Oakley said as he began rubbing on the baby oil. "Never noticed before, it was all hidden underneath those Arrow shirts and stuff you wear to work."

"Thanks. I guess it has. Now how about the other side?" he asked, turning over to face his friend. The invitation for a more intimate contact was clear and tempting, but Oakley felt it was much too obvious an interaction between two men in such a public place.

"Hey, you're on your own now." Oakley laughed, reaching for his novel, and laid down, determined both to finish it as well as get his mind off what was a clear attraction.

"Had enough?" Oakley asked a half hour or so later, gently poking Donny in the ribs to wake him from his sun-and-heat-induced lethargy. "Don't want you to burn."

"Gosh, I think it's too late for that," Donny said looking at his sunburned thighs. "You're right. Time to call it a day."

"Hungry?"

"I could eat a horse!"

"Whatcha up for?"

"I think I could really go for some of that chili that everyone is talking about at that joint that just opened up in Beverly Hills," Donny said. "Chasen's Southern Pit—it's more or less on the way to where I live."

"Sounds fine to me," Oakley said as he gathered up his things while trying to remember how to get there on the Red Line. "Where do you live, Donny?"

"Not far from you," Donny said. "Oops, sorry. Didn't mean to pry. I looked up your address the other day after we had lunch at Woolworth's counter."

Mildly flattered, Oakley said, "Well, it's no secret. So you're near me?"

"Yep. In an apartment at the Bryson, on Wilshire."

"I know the place," Oakley said. "Pretty fancy!"

"Well, I got a deal through the owner of my travel agency. And my place is only a one-bedroom apartment," he said as they reached the parking lot. "See you at the restaurant? You know where it is? It's where that old bean field was on Beverly."

"Well, uh, I may be a while. I came on the Red Line."

"No problem, come along with me." Donny said.

Within a half hour, the pair were seated at a table at Chasen's Southern Pit and had ordered the chili that was fast making the place a celebrity and film star hangout.

"I hear that the owner, this Chasen guy, was once a vaudeville star who worked with the Three Stooges and is a friend of the director Frank Capra," Donny said. "You know, the guy who won all those Oscars for *It Happened One Night* a couple years back? Anyway, he didn't have any money, so Capra got the editor of *The New Yorker* magazine to grubstake him—Ross or whatever his name is."

"Harold Ross," Oakley said as the waitress arrived with their chili. "Yeah, I heard that, too. I also read, I think it was in some column in the trades, that in the beginning, Chasen was so broke Capra had to lend him silverware from his own home for his customers. It seems like it was a smart move, though. The place seems to be attracting some stars already and people like Scott Fitzgerald who a friend of mine saw here last week. Too bad he doesn't seem to be making much of a success at Metro. Ever read any of his stuff, like his newest book, *Tender Is the Night?*"

"Naaah. I hear nobody really reads it. Too much about the 1920s, and I'm not a history person. I sorta go for more mystery stuff like that book you were reading at the beach, *ABC*—"

"*The ABC Murders*," Oakley interrupted, "by a Brit named Agatha Christie. She wrote a new one that's just out with the same Belgian detective character named Hercule Poirot called *Death on the Nile*. If you want another really good mystery, there's a new book called *Double Indemnity* by some guy named Cain. Terrific story. Someone ought to make a movie out of it."

The pair ate in silence for a moment or two.

"Can I ask you something?" Donny murmured.

"Sure, anything."

"Well," he said quietly, "I was wondering how you can manage a tough, gumshoe career when, pardon me, I'm pretty sure you're drawn to guys as much as I am. Isn't it hard to act a part like yours?"

Startled by the daring of Donny's question, Oakley immediately realized the gamble that Donny had taken with the question and that there was no reason to dissemble. "Well, Donny, to be honest, I don't think about it much and never have been asked about it—until now."

"I'm sorry," Donny said. "I didn't mean to—"

"That's OK. I'm flattered that you cared enough to ask. Maybe the people I work with most of the time just take for granted that some of the people they work with are not what they seem to be, and not only sexually."

"Oh yeah?"

"So let me tell you how I explain this," Oakley said. "Maybe I'm cynical, but I believe that much of life is based on fiction. The fact that many homosexual people—gay as some of us now refer to ourselves—are married, is a fiction society demands that many people who go for members of their own sex must enter into, especially if they are famous. Most businessmen act confident about what they are doing, but that's often a fiction to cover up insecurity. And speaking of a fiction covering up insecurity, think about religion. Much of what they dish out is reassuring fiction for those who are terrified about what may happen to them when they die.

"And if you doubt any of this, why do you think that, in the middle of the Great Depression a few years ago, while the economy of the country went to hell, Hollywood did just fine. Because Hollywood's happy-time stuff provided, as it always does, a fictional escape from reality. Your Charles Atlas, Dale Carnegie, and the 'every day, in every way, I'm getting better and better' guy, Emile Coue, cash in on the fact that people need reassurance, however unrealistic it may be, that their lives are going to turn out better than what they see going on around them. And that, of course, is fiction. Forgive me for jumping on Mr. Atlas; his stuff actually seems to work—look at you. But I'm pretty certain you're an exception."

"Wow!" Donny exclaimed. "A true cynic. So how do you get through each day?"

"Because I love the sheer adventure of life," Oakley said, lighting a cigarette. "And in my business, it can get pretty adventurous. And I love

Hollywood with its craziness. And I love the unpredictability of life. Take the example of today. When I got on that Red Line car this morning to go to the beach, I had no idea I'd end up eating chili with a great-looking guy like you this evening."

"So," Donny said as they finished their meal, "since you need a ride home, how 'bout you show me your place where, from what I know, the facts contradict your convictions. Seems to me the outcome of William Desmond Taylor's philandering was predictable and Hollywood hasn't provided a neat, audience-pleasing ending."

"Can't be right all the time." Oakley chuckled. "But not this time. Wasn't my apartment but the one across the courtyard. And that's about all that's true about the crime. His name wasn't William Desmond Taylor; it was William Cunningham Deane-Tanner. And before the police arrived, the studio people were already there going through his things to make sure everything looked kosher when the coppers arrived. One of his so-called girlfriends, the actress Mabel Normand, was also there going through everything, too. Who knows what they were looking for? I say 'so-called girlfriend' because he was not as much of a ladies' man as he was portrayed either; apparently, he had been involved for a few years with a young MGM art director named George Hopkins. And I hear his valet, a Negro named Henry Peavy, who may have been procuring young boys for Taylor, hasn't been seen since. Apparently the murder weapon was somehow never found or traced either. Everything was carefully screened or gotten out of the way to maintain a fictional story line."

"OK, OK, I give up." Donny laughed. "Let's go."

Later, after Oakley made Manhattans for himself and Donny, they settled into comfortable conversation backed by the faithful Zenith tuned to Jack Benny's popular show. Inevitably, attraction trumped conversation, was itself trumped by passion, and as one thing led to another, a happy, if somewhat sleepless, night was shared by both.

Oakley woke with a start, realizing that he had failed to set his trusty Big Ben alarm clock. Judging from the light pouring in through his bedroom window, it was clearly later than he normally got up. "And where is Donny?" he grumbled, looking at the empty half of his bed. *Well*, he realized, *this is not the time to worry about that. I've got to get going.* After a quick shower and shave, he dressed, extricated his wallet and change from the pants he had worn the previous day, and left. It was late, but he rationalized, because he was the boss, who cared?

"Benny, were you able to find anything at the library about measles?" Oakley exclaimed moments after he arrived at his office.

"Got it all right here, boss," he said, handing Oakley a pair of medical textbooks. "Been waitin' for you to ask." Oakley settled himself at his desk, reached gratefully for the coffee that his sidekick had gotten at the news counter in the lobby, which despite city and county regulations, managed to provide coffee for office workers in need. He turned to the first book and the page thoughtfully marked by, he figured, the librarian: *"Measles is largely a childhood respiratory disease caused by an as-yet-unidentified infectious agent present in the blood of patients,"* he read in the citation. *"Known also as rubeola and not to be confused with rubella (or German measles, a far less serious disease), it is highly contagious and has, and continues, to yearly kill millions worldwide. It apparently spreads through the air by breathing, coughing, or sneezing and is so contagious that any child who is exposed to it and is not otherwise immune will almost certainly get the disease."*

OK, he thought, thumbing through the information until he found what he was seeking.

"Apparently," the report added, *"unlike children who develop a lifetime immunity after surviving the disease, many women who otherwise gained immunity by having contracted measles when children, lose it when they become pregnant. A recent study of a dozen pregnant women, all of whom had measles, found that one had died, seven suffered pneumonia or hepatitis or both, four went through premature labor, and one lost her child in a spontaneous abortion. Another survey of eight measles pregnancies conducted in California found that three ended in spontaneous abortions or stillbirths while four babies were born with congenital disabilities. And..."*

"That's enough for me," Oakley said. "Listen to this, Benny," he added and began reading the piece to him. "Grab the phone, will you?"

"It's for you, Oakey. Someone named Don something or other."

Jesus, Oakley thought happily, *it's been only a couple hours, and he misses me so much he had to call.* "Oakley! Oakley!" Donny's voice shouted. "Are you there?"

"Yes, Donny. You sound upset. What's going on? And what happened to you?" Oakley asked calmly, completely perplexed by Donny's frantic tone.

"I woke up and had to get to work. But that's not why I'm calling. It's Billy Williams. Haven't you heard?"

"Heard what, Donny?" Oakley asked. "I just got here."

"He got pinched last night. At the Downtown Y. With a bell bottom he apparently picked up somewhere. And I hear he's now in the big house."

"Oh, God. He picked up a sailor? Was he crazy?" Oakley exclaimed, referring to Billy Williams, one of MGM's most famous actors, ostensibly devoted to his boyfriend, Martin Howard.

"Guess so. Hot to trot anyway. I heard about it on the radio and called Marty—"

"You know them?" Oakley asked.

"Yes," Donny said. "Part of my sordid past. Marty is distraught and doesn't know what to do. I immediately thought of you."

"Hey, Donny. I'm a PI, a dick for hire. Sounds to me Billy needs a lawyer."

"I know, and he'll get the best. But I can be really paranoid, which you'll discover, so the minute I heard it, I thought it sounded like a setup," Donny said. "Weird, like the Eva Sanderson thing. I had an idea that maybe you could dig around and see if somebody deliberately framed Billy to get him in trouble. Maybe you could look into that sailor boy...look into—"

"Boss, you'll want to take this call," Benny, who had answered Oakley's second office telephone line, interrupted. "It's—"

"Lemme call you back, Donny. You in the office?"

"Yep. Please."

"Mr. Webster?" the imperious female voice on the phone asked in a demanding tone. "This is Louella Parsons. Docky thinks you could help a friend of mine and gave me your number."

"Yes, Mrs. Parsons," he said, somewhat awestruck by being called by the most powerful columnist in Hollywood. "This is Oakley Webster. What can I do for you?"

"It isn't exactly for me. As I said, it's for some friends. You heard of Billy Williams's arrest?"

"Yes, just now."

"Well, he has several friends, very important friends, who are interested in helping him out of a bad situation. I spoke with a couple of them this morning and told them that Docky suggested that you could be helpful. They are convinced that the whole episode was a frame-up to get Billy in trouble with Mayer, to get him fired from his latest project, another of his Mickey O'Rourke college football movies. Only in this one, he's playing a coach. Makes sense since he's getting a bit long in the tooth to play a quarterback any longer. It's called, I think, *Mickey O'Rourke Grows Up*. And of course Billy living so openly with his boyfriend has been driving L. B. crazy for a long time. You know how he hates homosexuals."

"Yes, I've heard," Oakley injected, wondering where this was going. "Why would some outsider want to get him in trouble with Mr. Mayer if he's done a pretty good job of it by himself?"

"Well, I don't know. Maybe to bring everything to a head and force Mayer to do something. That's a question that may be answered somewhere down the line. All that needs to be done now is to try and see if this was a frame-up and, if it was, that news might slow down or stop any legal action on Metro's part if they realize their dirty laundry was going to be washed in the papers and columns."

"It sounds to me that if this was a frame-up, it would be Mr. Mayer who did it," Oakley suggested.

"I agree that sounds like the most obvious explanation if, indeed, it was a frame-up," the columnist concurred. "But who would ever have the nerve to accuse him of doing that? He's much too powerful. But then again, who knows what L. B. would do? Sometimes, his actions are so unpredictable that I think he simply flips a coin before making a decision, like finding a replacement for Eva Sanderson now that she's off the *Matrimaniac* movie," Parsons said, rambling off the subject. "He's got dozens of top stars on contract, so he doesn't need to mount a nationwide search."

"I think that's for the publicity."

"Of course it is, but he could get all the publicity he wants without going to all that trouble. All he would have to do is give me a call."

Nothing lacking with her self-confidence, Oakley thought. *But of course she's right with twenty million readers in her pocket.* "Of course," he agreed humbly.

"Anyway, I gave your telephone number to a couple of Billy's friends," she continued. "I hope you don't mind."

"No, ma'am, of course not. I don't know if I can be of any help, but they are welcome to call me. Who…?"

"Carole Lombard for one. She's been a friend of his for years."

Oakley gulped. One of the biggest stars in Hollywood. Rumor had it that she was secretly seeing Clark Cable, who was separated but not yet divorced from Rhea Langham.

"And Marion Davies. She has been one of his closest friends for a long time, and the Chief really likes him, too."

Well, that's no surprise, Oakley thought. If Marion Davies, William Randolph Hearst's "companion," has a friend, America's most powerful publisher probably would be one as well. And because Louella Parsons works for Hearst— "the Chief" as all his employees call him—that may partially explain why she's on the warpath to help Billy. There was already plenty of bad blood between Hearst and Mayer, Oakley remembered. After Metro's production boss Irving Thalberg cast his wife, Norma Shearer, in the studio's 1934 *Marie Antoinette* epic instead of Marion Davies, Hearst was so mad he moved his production company, Cosmopolitan Pictures, which had operated from the MGM lot for eleven years, to Warner Brothers.

"And Joan Crawford," Parsons added. "But she probably won't talk to you. She's been Billy's closest friend for years and is, I'm told, inconsolable. She wouldn't even talk to *me* this morning," the columnist snapped. "I think this business about being picked by *Life* magazine as the 'Queen of the Movies' has gone to her head.

"And Michelle Ryder," she added.

"Wow," Oakley exclaimed. "Billy certainly has lots of friends in high places!"

"He does," Parsons said. "And, of course, *me!*"

"Sorry, Mrs. Parsons, I didn't mean to imply—"

"OK, I gotcha. So someone will probably be calling you soon. Dig around and let Docky know what you find. But this is all on the hush-hush now of course.

"And," the columnist continued, "since Hollywood portrays every woman whether they're married or not as presumably available - forever a 'Miss' - and since 'Mrs. Parsons' makes me feel ancient anyway, feel free to call me

'Miss.' Lotsa' stuff in Hollywood is fake anyway - like Billy's name - 'William Williams' for God's sake!"

"Thanks," Oakley laughed. "By the way, Mrs. Parsons...oops, Miss Parsons...does Billy have any enemies you know of? And call me Oakley."

"Oakley, one of the first things you learn in Hollywood is that everyone is a potential enemy. Everything is—what's that term for breakable they're usin' now?—frangible. In Billy's case, the exceptions could be Martin Howard and probably Joan Crawford. As far as all his other friends, friendship in Hollywood always depends on the circumstances. And all this new Puritanism and censorship has certainly turned the circumstances topsy-turvy, and everyone, even those with nothing to hide, is running for cover."

"I understand. Uh, Miss Parsons..." Oakley began.

"Yes? Oh, I guess you're wondering about how you're going to be paid for your time."

"Well..."

"Don't worry. Docky will see that it's sorted out and taken care of. Just keep track of your time and expenses and let Docky know. Gotta go, Oakley. Deadlines, deadlines, my radio show to prepare, and two columns to finish. Jesus, what am I goin' to say about this mess?"

"I'm sure you'll find the right words," Oakley said as they hung up.

Chapter 6

"**Benny, what happened** to my call from Mr. Wells?"

"He couldn't hold, and I said you'd call him back. 'Nother call, boss," Benny exclaimed. "Some skirt named Ryder."

Some skirt indeed, Oakley thought as he reached for his telephone. *Merely the number-one box-office draw last year according to at least one fan magazine.*

"Hello, Miss Ryder," Oakley said, somewhat out of breath as the smoky voice, familiar from a dozen hit films, sounded in his ear. "Miss Parsons said you might be calling."

"Yes, Mr. Webster. Louella tells me that you might be of help to the many friends of Billy Williams. We appreciate that."

"So how can I be of help, Miss Ryder?"

"We firmly believe that Billy was framed because MGM—well, by that I mean Mr. Mayer—wants to bring him down to size. This is all confidential of course."

"Of course."

"Thank you. We think L. B. wanted to humble Billy by kicking him off his new movie," Michelle Ryder began. "To Mr. Mayer, Billy is too popular and can more or less dictate his terms. And Mr. Mayer certainly doesn't like that. He likes his stars to be subservient and do whatever he wants, and, frankly, with the contract system, he really holds most of the cards anyway. But firing Billy off a big movie without a reason is not one of the cards he holds. Billy's millions of fans would scream bloody murder."

"But, on the other hand," she continued, "since Billy's box office has fallen off a bit recently, maybe Mr. Mayer's little pea brain came up with a way of creating a problem—the public scandal of a morals arrest," she continued. "So that is why we, Billy's friends, figure he might be behind this thing—I think you people call it 'entrapment.' So, armed with the new Production Code, he would have an irrefutable reason to discipline Billy. At the least, he could kick him out of the new movie and maybe even reduce him from being a star to just a featured player and cut his salary. People think MGM survived the Depression relatively unscathed, but insiders know that their grosses are way down. This could be his way of killing two birds with one stone. We may be wrong. Someone else may have planned and executed this thing, but Mayer seems the most obvious culprit."

"I understand," Oakley lied, his habitual cynicism causing him to suspect that there might be a lot more to this than anyone, including Michelle Ryder and Billy's other friends, might imagine.

"So we would like to hire you to sniff around and see what you can turn up."

"What would you do if it can be proven to have been a setup?"

"Why, then, if it was L. B.—we'll leave his name out of it of course—we'll give the story to Louella, and she will make so much out of it that L. B. will have to deny any personal involvement in the scandal, and fire some underling to clear the slate. And if it's all about the grosses, he'll have to have the accountants at Metro tidy up his balance sheet. We all know they can be very dexterous about that when they need to be. And Billy remains under contract and goes on to make more films for his adoring fans. And every-one is happy—well, except for L. B. If it turns out that someone else did it, Louella still has a big scoop, names and all."

"I know that Miss Parsons believes Mr. Mayer is too powerful for anyone to accuse him of doing this," Oakley interjected. "Even if it turns out that he did—"

"Don't be naïve, Mr. Webster," Ryder interrupted. "That may be true, but Mayer doesn't know it. If L. B. Mayer is scared of anyone on the planet, it would be Louella Parsons, maybe Winchell, too. Their millions of readers and listeners are also ticket buyers and he knows that all too well. In fact, there is a story running around that he is looking for someone to set up as a rival movie columnist to Louella."

"So what if it turns out that Billy picked up the sailor on his own, that there was no frame-up involved? Then what do you do?" Oakley asked.

"Well, as they say, I guess we'll have to cross that bridge when we come to it," the actress commented. "But I don't think that's possible unless someone at the Downtown Y has suddenly turned into a police informer. And that makes no sense; it would be the exact equivalent of cutting off your nose to spite your face. So someone had to tip off the police. And to do that, that someone had to know about the pickup. And the easiest way of knowing that is to have arranged it in the first place."

"Your logic seems ironclad," Oakley agreed with the actress.

"By the way," she asked, "how much do you charge for your services? Is it by the hour or by the, uh, project?"

"Usually by the day, ma'am," Oakley explained, crossing his fingers as he quoted a fee slightly higher than his usual rate. "Thirty dollars a day. Miss Parsons suggested I keep a record of hours and expenses and route them through Docky. That's fine with me of course."

"Good enough, Mr. Webster. Thank you. We'll talk again soon. Good-bye."

As he hung up the receiver, Oakley was already trying to figure out a strategy of how to discover if Louis B. Mayer had deliberately manufactured a scandal to destroy one of his most valuable assets—a policy that would be laughable in any other business but Hollywood's—and if so, why? Was it to make way for a new star? Was it revenge for a perceived slight? Mayer was notoriously thin-skinned. Was it because of the mounting pressure to control the scandalous lives of many Hollywood stars? Or because Mayer just abhorred anyone who sexually deviated from the straight and narrow. No one, perhaps not even Louis B. Mayer himself, could know for sure.

In 1937, the film industry was essentially still run buy the film pioneers who headed up their own studios. Most were Jewish, and all but a couple were politically and culturally conservative. They were also all relatively uneducated according to the standards of the time, which is why their judgments on what the public wanted (and would buy at the box office) were usually on target.

The studios, most of which had evolved from the storefront operations of a generation earlier, included 20th Century Fox, Universal, Warner Brothers, Paramount, Columbia, RKO, and Metro Goldwyn Mayer, which was the largest and generally considered the best (it was beginning to be called the "Tiffany" of studios after New York's famous jewelry store). Smaller operations included Republic Pictures (which was famous for its Westerns and pioneered what was becoming known as the B pictures) and Disney, who had, in 1928, unleashed Mickey Mouse on the world.

Louis B. Mayer, who ruled MGM, referred to by most of Hollywood at the time simply as "Metro," was a pugnacious, Russian-born, ex–scrap metal dealer from Massachusetts who had early on spotted the potential for film and opened one of the first large movie houses. In 1915, by scraping together every cent he could find (including pawning his wife's jewelry), he bought the exclusive New England distribution rights for D. W. Griffith's *The Birth of a Nation*. It made him a fortune, and in 1918, he moved to what was becoming the site of America's film industry, Hollywood.

Reportedly, Mayer never liked movies, but he knew what the public liked: captivating stories, especially family-oriented spectacle (if religious-themed, all the better), and beautiful people on the silver screen. Although he was forced to tolerate "fagolahs" and lesbians, he disliked them intensely.

To provide the entertainment he felt would be most profitable, Mayer hired the best acting and management talent he could find, the most outstanding of which on the management side was a young filmmaking genius named Irving Thalberg. Thalberg, who eventually married the superstar Norma Shearer, would raise the quality of MGM's output and bring the studio to the peak of its success before his early death at thirty-six (in 1936). His passing was a cosmic shock to the entire industry, and reverberations caused by power, talent, and political realignments would shake Hollywood for years.

"Doan' forget to call this Donny guy back, Oakey," Benny reminded.

"Sorry, Donny," Oakley apologized after getting him on the phone. "It's been crazy here—other people calling me to ask me to look into what happened with Billy Williams."

"So, can you?"

"Of course I can, and I will. I've actually been more or less officially hired to do just that."

"Like by whom?"

"Can't say, Donny. That's why my business card says 'Confidential Investigations.' So, do you know something about this that no one else knows?"

"Well, maybe. I have a friend here at the travel agency who, let's say, patronizes the Downtown Y, and says that this sort of thing goes on all the time."

"That's no secret. Probably at every YMCA in America."

"Well, yes and no. He says that some of the people who actually are running the place are fixing up the guys with other guys. You know, 'rent boys.'"

"You're kiddin'. A male prostitution ring run out of the Y? I don't believe it."

"Believe me. And that's only part of it. My friend says that the coppers have discovered this and that they have bribed a person on the inside to tip them off, and that's what happened with Billy. I think that's crazy. No one would jeopardize their own business."

"The story I got was that he picked up a sailor boy in Pershing Square and brought him to the Y," Oakley said.

"That's the current line that everyone seems to be buying—that it was all Billy's doing," Donny explained. "My friend says he's sure it was a setup. That the bell bottom was hired and dispatched to pick up Billy and bring him to the Y and then the coppers were tipped off."

"So Billy was framed?"

"Seems likely. Can you break for lunch?"

"Nope, Donny. But tonight?"

"How 'bout you come by my place? Park in the lot behind the building, and there is a back door leading into the lobby."

"So we have to be secretive?" Oakley laughed.

"Hell, no. It's just a shorter route and a place to park in case there isn't one on the street. Are you gettin'– what is the word?—paranoid? About us? Already? Back door. Just like the one people use at Musso's."

"OK. I'll be there about six. Will that work for you?"

"Sure. Could you pick up some hooch and coffin sticks."

"Any brand?"

"Yeah, maybe Old Grand-Dad and pack of Camels. I'll make you the best Manhattan you ever tasted."

"Benny," Oakley said as he hung up. "Could I ask you to scoot over to the library again and pick up some stuff on Billy Williams?"

"What could I get that everyone doesn't know. Big star, big pansy I hear, big—"

"OK. Just get me anything new that you can find."

If everyone in Hollywood knew that Billy Williams was a homosexual, it was certainly not common knowledge in most of America, at least not to most of the great movie ticket–buying America.

It was a secret that had been easy to keep outside Hollywood. Williams was a strikingly handsome leading man with an engaging manner, an engaging deep voice, and a boy-next-door likability. And the studio exploited these assets in a seemingly endless series of feel-good films that quickly made him the number-one box-office draw in the country.

The fact that he lived openly with a longtime lover named Martin Howard was unknown outside Hollywood and never touched by the fan magazines. Billy's relationship with Martin was, however, well known and accepted within the film industry, even joked about. Within the closed social world of the film capital, the pair's friend, Joan Crawford, called them "the happiest married couple in Hollywood."

The Hollywood establishment even tolerated Billy's occasionally tasteless behavior—like the time a couple years earlier when he famously goosed both Norma Shearer and Irving Thalberg at one of the famous costume parties given by the powerful publisher William Randolph Hearst and his mistress, the witty, popular Marion Davies, at their 120-room Santa Monica seaside mansion. The Thalbergs were costumed as West Point cadets and Billy and Martin as Tinker Bell and Peter Pan.

But the conservatism that emerged in Hollywood and America at the beginning of the 1930s was increasingly challenging the promiscuous lifestyle of many Hollywood stars, making it much harder to disguise the sexual escapades and unorthodox relationships that were once overlooked.

Soon, even the fan magazines, which since their beginning never said anything negative about anyone in Hollywood even if they had to make up the facts to sugarcoat the truth, had to adapt to the new puritanism if only by editorial innuendo.

Some stars at the very top of their profession, like Greta Garbo, were so famous they could get away with unorthodox behavior and able to make their own rules. But if lesser stars were caught breaking the new rules, especially those involving relationships, their careers and lives could be ruined.

Making the new morals climate even more dangerous was that whenever a star happened to make the inevitable mistake, especially sexual, the press pounced on it, relating all the sordid details to a previously naïve world.

One of the most notorious scandals occurred earlier in the decade when Paul Bern, the MGM producer husband of the superstar Jean Harlow, committed suicide less than two months after the couple's marriage. The press went crazy, especially when the contents of his suicide note found next to his nude body became public; it hinted his suicide was the result of his shame for being unable to perform sexually with his wife, a star who made a career by oozing sexuality from every pore.

Another case involved a party hosted by another MGM producer—described by the people attending it as a bisexual orgy—that got out of hand and the police were called. Then, several people who were present and suspected that Metro had tipped off the police as part of an effort to control their stars' behavior, threatened to give the names of guests at the party—all MGM stars and employees—to the press. Mayer quickly sent the producer/host off to Europe to hide out until things cooled down and, apparently, had a chat with the Los Angeles district attorney, a man generally assumed to be in the pocket of the studios. The DA then managed to convince those who had threatened to go public with the details of the party to remain silent and everything was covered up.

Then, not long before Billy's arrest, Greta Garbo, MGM's biggest star—in fact, the biggest star in the world—was spotted by a reporter in a notorious lesbian bar in Paris in the company with a famous lesbian countess. The press went wild.

Mayer immediately launched an aggressive publicity campaign designed to prove to the ticket-buying world that, at MGM anyway, "men were men," and presumably, women were women.

And then Billy Williams was caught with the sailor.

Oakley spent the rest of his workday trying to organize his investigation into Billy Williams's arrest. Obviously, the most important person he needed to speak with was Billy himself; followed by his lover, Martin Howard; his agent, Phil Berg, and the female superstars Louella had said would call. Oakley, not one to leave anything to chance, decided he couldn't wait for others than Michelle Ryder to call him and needed their telephone numbers himself. He figured that the fastest way to get them was from Louella Parsons's office; she, it was said, had the phone numbers of everyone who counted for anything in the film capital.

A call to her husband, Docky Martin, was promptly returned, and an initial list of people to contact was quickly worked out between them. After speaking with Billy and Martin, foremost on the list, Docky suggested the next should be Billy's agent. As one of Hollywood's most successful talent agents, Docky felt Berg would best know who stood to gain—or lose—the most from the scandal because he possessed the absolutely essential attribute for success in his field, the most cutthroat of Hollywood professions: an all-consuming sense of paranoia.

Along with his telephone number, Docky gave Oakley all the numbers he needed and said that he would vouch for him if anyone wanted to know why Oakley was calling.

After leaving his office, Oakley picked up the bourbon and cigarettes at a Walgreen's drug store near the Bryson.

"Sorry if I'm a little bit late. Here's the stuff you wanted," he said as Donny opened the door.

"Thanks. What do I owe you?"

"Nothing. Well, maybe that Manhattan cocktail you promised."

"Comin' up." Donny laughed as he busied himself making drinks for the pair.

"Nice place," Oakley observed, looking around the small apartment. The Bryson Tower apartments (so named because until the late 1920s, the ten-story building was the tallest on what was then the city's West Side), was an elegant architectural combination of classical and Beaux-Arts styles, built near MacArthur Park in 1913. The top floor, which was devoted to the common use of the tenants, boasted a billiards room, a library, and a view from which snow-capped mountains, orange groves, and in the far distance, the Pacific Ocean and Catalina Island, sixty-seven miles away, could be seen. Unusual for any apartment buildings in the area, because of a hundred-foot setback from Wilshire Boulevard, there was room for tennis courts and wide lawns and gardens in front of the building. The place was popular with the city's "beautiful people" from the day it opened, as was the elegant, art deco–style Bullocks Wilshire department store, built in 1929 only three blocks away.

"That's some lobby downstairs," Oakley said seating himself. "Crystal chandeliers, mahogany furniture, and all that marble! Must have cost a mint. And they certainly didn't stint on the apartments," Oakley said admiringly, looking around Donny's place as his host handed him his cocktail. "All that woodwork everywhere. And the high ceilings."

"Cedar-lined drawers in the bedroom, plus something that was the latest in home furnishings when this place was put up which maybe we can play with later—a hideaway bed!" Donny said flirtatiously.

And so, another happy evening passed between the pair as one cocktail led to another, an impromptu dinner of grilled steak and boiled potatoes was savored, and the hidden bed was opened.

"Gotta go home tonight," Oakley said eventually.

"Why?"

"Same reason you had to leave last night. Have to be at work early in the a.m."

"OK, if you must. Lemme get some clothes on," Donny said as Oakley dressed. "I'll walk you to your car."

The next morning started with, as they said at the time when unexpected happenings occurred, "a bang." Both telephone lines were lit up when Oakley walked in his office. "Get the phone, Benny," he shouted to his assistant who was simply standing in the center of the office with a perplexed look on his face. "I'll take line one. You grab line two."

Oakley punched the button and heard the unmistakable voice of Louella Parsons shouting, "Docky, Docky, are you sure this is the right number? No one is answering."

"I'm here, I'm here, Miss Parsons," Oakley said. "Sorry. Both of my lines were ringing at the same time."

"Oh, hello, Oakley. I'm not surprised what with the news. Did you hear?"

"No, I just walked in."

"Well, the papers don't have it yet, but I have it on good authority that L. B. bailed Billy Williams out of jail. Billy is now in a meeting with him at the studio."

"That can't be good."

"My feelings exactly. Something's going on, and I want to know more about it. If you hear anything, let me know right away. I'll do the same."

"Oakey, Oakey, line two," Benny shouted. "Someone named Martin something."

"Miss Parsons, Martin Howard is on the phone. I'll call you as soon as I find out what he wants. Same number as Docky?"

"Yep."

"Mr. Howard, a pleasure. I wish under happier circumstances," Oakley commiserated.

"I agree, Mr. Webster," Martin Howard, sounding about as miserable as anyone can, murmured. "Michelle Ryder suggested that I call you. She said some of Billy's friends had hired you to look into the possibility that Billy may have been framed."

"Yes, Mr. Howard, that's correct."

"Please call me Marty like everyone else."

"Yes, OK. I am working on Billy's behalf, and I was about to call Miss Ryder to get your number. It would be a big help if you could fill me in on what happened last night."

"Well, I don't know if it was a frame-up," Howard replied. "But I do know that the story which is coming out is wrong. Billy didn't go down to Pershing Square to pick up someone. May I be frank? We're singing in the same choir?"

"Yes, we are. I, Michelle Ryder, everyone I've spoken with, are on Billy's side. I've heard gossip, though, that Billy has sometimes strayed. I heard something about being caught in a raid on an exclusive male bordello a year or so ago?"

"You heard correctly on all counts. By the way, it was a private club, and the cops had no right to do what they did. In any event, Metro covered it all up by fixing it with the DA's office so that the place was simply shut down and the names of the people caught in the raid were never made public. Believe me, there were some pretty big names caught that night and not only stars like Billy. But back to your question. We, Billy and I, have gone down to Pershing Square occasionally in the past to see…well, you know…We've been together for several years, and monogamy isn't really part of our agreement. You understand?"

"Yes."

"But it wasn't Billy's idea to go there this time. About eight o'clock last night, he got a telephone call from someone who asked him to meet at Pershing Square at ten. Said he'd be at the newspaper kiosk. Said he was a young sailor up from Long Beach or San Pedro, somewhere, for the weekend and that his buddies said Billy would show him a good time—"

"Oakey, it's Louella Parsons again," Benny interrupted.

"Hold on a minute, Mr. Howard, uh, Marty."

Oakley punched the other telephone line button. "Yes, Miss Parsons? I was, I mean, I am speaking with Martin Howard on the other line."

"Well, then I guess you can give him the bad news. I just got a call from my person at Metro, and they said that the meeting between L. B. and Billy didn't go so well. Actually, not well at all…"

"Oh?"

"Apparently," she continued, "L. B. told him that he had had enough of his scandalous behavior what with the bordello raid last year and his living so openly with another man. He said he could cover up a lot and has already done so for him and other stars, but things were getting out of hand. And then he demanded that Billy stop living with Marty. And Billy refused. I'm told there was quite a shouting match.

"L. B. then called for his contract and, while Billy was standing there, tore it up—tore up the contract for a star who has made millions for Metro—and threw it right in his face," the columnist said unbelievingly. "I'm told he actually yelled, 'I'll see to it you never work in the movies ever again,' which of course means that Billy is no longer the star of *The Singing Outlaw*, the new MGM movie in the works, and out of the film business."

"Oh God," Oakley exclaimed. "Let me call you back. I don't think it's for me to tell Marty. He'll find out soon enough. This is the first time I've talked with him, and I don't think it's a good idea to start out by being the bearer of bad news."

"You're probably right. I wouldn't be surprised if Billy is trying to call him now."

"Marty, you still there?"

"Yes. As I was saying, this guy called and said he wanted to meet Billy, so Billy hightailed it downtown. And that was it. Mr. Webster, I gotta go now. There's another call coming in on my other line. Good-bye."

Well, Oakley thought with a little shudder, *he's not going to be happy with the news he's about to receive.*

CHAPTER 7

Oakley sat for a while thinking about the information he had just received. *Just because the sailor called Billy doesn't mean that it was a frame-up*, he thought. It could have been someone Billy may have given his number to at a party or at a bar. Or one of Billy's friends, knowing the actor's liking for young men, may have given him Billy's telephone number. And the caller may have been looking for exactly what he said: a little fun and maybe a little extra cash. There were a lot of possibilities other than a deliberate frame-up.

Oakley spent the rest of his workday calling the friends of Billy on his list. Unfortunately, he wasn't able to reach most of them. Joan Crawford's maid answered the phone at her home in Brentwood and explained between her own sobs that the lady was much too upset to speak with anyone. No one answered Carole Lombard's telephone. Marion Davies was up at San Simeon with Hearst, and Docky didn't think to give him that number.

Oakley then called Billy's agent, Phil Berg. His secretary said that he was on the phone and inquired what he was calling about, the usual Hollywood runaround, commonly meant to impress the caller with how important the person being called was. "Just tell him that Miss Parsons suggested that I call him on a matter of mutual concern," Oakley said and then gave her his number. *That should get a rise out of him*, Oakley thought with an ironic smile.

His next call was to Michelle Ryder. Despite her lofty place in the firmament of Hollywood stardom, because she was essentially an employer of his, she could be helpful in helping him reach some of Billy's supporters who otherwise might be reluctant to confide in him. He was right. Michelle Ryder immediately took his call and understood his reasoning.

"I know that Miss Crawford is extremely upset over all this," he said, "but maybe she could talk with you."

"You bet," Ryder exclaimed. "Cranberry adores Billy and despises Mayer."

"Cranberry?"

"Yep. 'Cranberry'—that was Billy's nickname for her when Metro made her change her name from Lucille LeSueur to Joan Crawford. Mayer made her do it because he thought 'Le Sueur' sounded like 'Sewer.' Joan always hated 'Crawford,'" she added. "Still does. She thought that it sounded much like 'crawfish.' So Billy started calling her 'Cranberry,' and he still does. And so do many of her other friends."

"Wow. I've never heard that."

"I'll call her and mention that some of us think that Mayer set up the whole mess as an excuse to get rid of Billy," the actress said. "Joanie loves conspiracy stuff anyway. Do you think that I should mention that he fired him?"

"You might as well," Oakley suggested. "I'm pretty sure that Miss Parsons will have it on her radio show tonight."

"But then, what is it you need from me?" the actress asked.

"Her angle on it. As much as Miss Crawford may dislike Mr. Mayer, does she really think he would actually be behind a frame-up? I know you and some of your friends think Mayer set up the entire thing, but I'm not so sure. It also could have been as simple as the sailor calling Billy on his own because someone told him he was an easy mark.

"Mayer may have had nothing to do with it and fired him after the story broke because, considering the current holier-than-thou atmosphere in Hollywood, he really didn't have any other choice," Oakley continued. "It may have been just a business decision on his part, a decision to protect Metro's box office. He's always had his eye on the dollar. I understand that for years he has been the highest paid person in America, and I don't think he's about to jeopardize that in any way.

"And, Miss Ryder, maybe you could ask what Miss Crawford's husband, Franchot Tone, thinks. And maybe Clark Gable, too. She just made *Love on the Run* with both of them."

"Gotcha. I'll let you know what Joanie thinks, also Franchot. But I don't expect anything from Clark. It's pretty well known that he hates homosexuals and probably will say that if Mayer did it, it was absolutely the right thing to do. Actually, Clark is just the sort of person who would have been behind a frame-up if he had thought of it."

"You mean because of the rumors about Billy and him on some set when Gable was still an extra," Oakley suggested.

"There are stories about every male actor in Hollywood," Michelle cautioned. "It's just the casting couch thing. And if there had been some hanky-panky between Billy and Clark, that's all the more reason for him to have set up Billy for a fall. I'll let you know what I learn."

The rest of the week was frustrating. No one was calling him back. Nothing from Michelle Ryder. Nothing from Phil Berg. Nothing from anyone. And Donny had disappeared. It was only after Oakley put in what seemed like more detective work that he had done for some clients that he discovered that Donny had been drafted by his travel agency at the last minute to attend a seminar sponsored by the Hawaiian tourism people. *Surely he would have had time to call,* Oakley thought in his disappointment.

Late Friday afternoon, the phone rang. As Oakley had earlier that afternoon run through his patience with Benny and sent him home, he grabbed the phone himself after debating for several rings whether to bother with it.

"Mr. Webster?" a fluttery voice asked, barely audible through some odd static.

"Yes, this is Oakley Webster."

"Mr. Webster, the private investigator?"

"Yes. How can I help you?"

"Mr. Webster, my name is Janet Trevalian. I got your name from Betty Barker. She said you might be able to help me."

"Tell me what you need."

"I have a grandson, Michael, and he is an actor," she said in a quavering voice. "Something has happened, and I didn't know what to do about it. So I called Betty, who as you may know is Miss Crawford's assistant. I don't know Miss Crawford, though, but I hear she's a nice Christian lady," she said.

"Where was I? Oh, yes. Mikey, he's only twenty-one, and I call him Mikey, but he hates it. Mikey got a part in a big movie, a Universal movie that was being directed by James Whale…you know, the man who made *Frankenstein?*"

"Yes, I know," Oakley said patiently. He had learned early in his profession that patience was the only way to deal with the frustration over a client's often rambling narrative, especially acute in those clients clearly stressed emotionally as was this woman. And of course he knew who James Whale was. Everybody in Hollywood knew of him and, despite being fairly flagrant about his liking for well-built young men, the director was, seemingly from the moment he arrived from his native England in 1930, a huge success. Whale had not only made *Frankenstein* (which made Boris Karloff a star) and followed that with more successful fantasy/horror films but also directed other kinds of films that were also masterpieces including Universal's top moneymaker the previous year, *Show Boat*, which starred Irene Dunne, Helen Morgan, and Paul Robson. Everything James Whale touched seemed to turn to gold.

"Anyway," she continued, "it was Mikey's first big movie role in this new movie being directed by Mr. Whale," she said proudly. "It was a small part, but Mr. Whale assured him it was important. Then, when the movie came out last month, we all went to see it, but he wasn't in it. Nowhere. His role had been entirely cut out of the movie.

"Mikey called the assistant director and was told that just before the movie was to open, the studio got a letter from someone demanding that all the Jewish actors in the movie be cut out of it. He told Mikey that he was cut from the movie because he was a Jew. But we're not Jewish!"

"That doesn't make any sense to me," Oakley said quietly, trying to calm her down. "I know there aren't a lot of Jewish actors, but that's never been a problem before. Most of the studios are headed by Jews, as you probably know. Who sent the letter? Did the assistant director tell you?"

"He told him he heard that the letter came from the Germans. And since Germany is a big market for Universal films, they had no choice. He also said that they would find something else for him. Despite the fact he is only— what do they call him?—a bit player."

"As I said, Mrs. Trevalian, this makes no sense at all. What was the movie?"

"It's called *The Road Back*, based on a book by someone named Remark or something like that."

"Erich Maria Remarque?" Oakley asked. "The man who wrote the book that Universal's big film *All Quiet on the Western Front* was based on a few years back? Think that was it?"

"I guess so," she said.

"And who did you say wrote this letter?"

"The man told him it was the Germans. He didn't say who. Please help us, Mr. Webster," the woman started pleading. "Please help us. We have some money; we can pay you."

"Tell me what you want me to do, Mrs. Trevalian," Oakley asked.

"I want you to find out who did this to Mikey, and why they did it. We're not Jewish. I don't understand. Please, Mr. Webster, help us. And then maybe he can get his job back."

"I don't think that will happen, Mrs. Trevalian. There is a lot of turmoil at Universal since the founders, the Lemmles, were thrown out recently. But I hope I'm wrong, and the new management will find something for him." Oakley paused a moment and then added, "Tell you what. Give me your telephone number and a day or two, and I'll see what I can find out."

"Thank you. Oh, thank you, Mr. Webster. You're an angel."

Oakley thought wryly that she may be off a bit on the angel part, at least considering his recent nighttime activities, but there was something about this that sounded odd. If for no reason other than to satisfy his own curiosity about an action that was strange and clearly unfair, he leaned back in his desk chair and began to organize a strategy for getting to the truth behind the Michael Trevalian's sudden dismissal.

"Benny!" he shouted before realizing that it was nearly dark and that his sidekick was gone. *I need to get that* Road Back *book*, he thought. *I also need to talk to that assistant director and find out who sent the letter and find out what these Germans are up to and see if there is anything in the papers about all this. Lots of stuff for the weekend,* he thought as he put on his suit jacket, grabbed his fedora, and started for the door.

Just then, his telephone rang. It was Donny, and he wasn't happy.

"Where are you?" he shouted in Oakley's ear.

"I'm still at the office. What are you so upset about?"

"You are supposed to be at my apartment a half hour ago."

"Oh damn," Oakley swore. "I'm sorry. I forgot. Just as I was about to leave the office, I got a call from a person who sounded desperate and begged me to look into something that sounded crazy, and—"

"Like what? What's crazy enough for you to forget a date with me?" Donny whined. "Sorry I was tied up for a couple days with these Hawaiian trip people, but don't you remember I was even going to make special dinner reservations for us? Which I did. And now we're going to be late."

"I'm sorry, hon. I'll leave right now and tell you all about it when I get there. Should be less than a half hour if the traffic on Wilshire isn't too bad," Oakley said soothingly. "Call the restaurant. I'm sure we can come a bit later. I really need one, well, maybe a couple, of your great Manhattans."

I guess getting that book will have to be put off until tomorrow, he thought after retrieving his car and turning west onto Wilshire Boulevard. "Maybe I can find out about this German thing from Bob what's-his-name," he said aloud, remembering the man he had been introduced to by Les at the Eastside bar a few weeks before. *He had mentioned that he worked for the* Los Angeles Times, *and that his name was…what? Bob M-something. Bob Marshall? No. Morris. That's it! Maybe he's on a late shift,* Oakley thought, resolving to call him from Donny's apartment.

As soon as he arrived, Oakley felt even more chagrined over forgetting his date. Not only had Donny stopped and picked up an assortment of tempting hors d'oeuvres, but he had also made dinner reservations for them at Perino's, certainly the city's most famous restaurant when it came to star power. But before he even sat down, Oakley tried to call Morris at the *Times* only to discover he wasn't there but would be at his desk in the City Room the following day.

"So," Oakley said as he relaxed into enjoying his cocktail and took a Ritz cracker spread with deviled ham and topped with a sliced olive from the assorted appetizers. "You're really pulling out all the stops. Perino's! I hear it's now the place for star spotting. Even Mae West has supper every Sunday there. What's the occasion, Donny?"

"Hey, it's nearly our one-week anniversary. It will be in two days anyway."

Oakley smiled. "That's nice of you. And, in addition to the stars, I've heard Perino's is one of the best restaurants in Los Angeles, if not in America," Oakley said between sips of his drink. "What a treat!"

The restaurant's reputation was splendidly upheld by their meal. Oakley chose grilled guinea hen after starting with a wedge of iceberg lettuce topped with the popular green goddess dressing. Donny raved about his shrimp remoulade followed by the traditional duckling à l'orange. The pair shared a chocolate soufflé, the most popular of the restaurant's huge selection of desserts. This didn't come cheaply, though, Oakley realized nervously. Their tab totaled nearly ten dollars plus a two-dollar tip, more than two or three times what a dinner for the pair would have cost in most restaurants in the city. And although Donny wanted to pay for it all, Oakley insisted they split the bill.

"That certainly beat Chasen's chili last Sunday," Donny said as they waited for the valet to retrieve Oakley's car. "Your place or mine?"

"How about mine?" Oakley suggested. "Even though tomorrow is Saturday, I have a heck of a busy day. I'll drop you off on my way to pick up a couple books, and I can do that at Bullocks Wilshire near you and then hit a library for some research."

"Darn," Donny said, clearly disappointed. "I was hoping for another beach day. Got to keep up with my Charles Atlas stuff."

"Maybe Sunday," Oakley said, digging in his pocket for a quarter to tip the valet as his blue Ford was driven up in front of them. "That's always a good day at the beach. Lots of stuff to admire."

"Don't you dare." Donny laughed, slapping Oakley playfully.

The next morning, after dropping Donny off at the Bryson and picking up copies of Erich Maria Remarque's antiwar bestsellers *All Quiet on the Western Front* and *The Road Back*, Oakley drove to the Wilshire Branch Library on St. Andrew's Place to do some background research on the German movie letter. Although the branch, whose spectacular Italianate design was the talk of the town when it opened a few years back, was much smaller than the city's main library near his office, it had an advantage that the older building lacked that was becoming a commercial necessity in Los Angeles: a large parking lot.

Unfortunately, an hour or so of rummaging through old copies of the *Los Angeles Times,* the *Los Angeles Examiner,* and the *Herald Express* proved relatively fruitless. There was plenty of information on the Nazi party that came into power in Germany four years earlier as well as its leader, Adolf Hitler, and his associates, but nothing about any relationship between the movie industry and one of its largest foreign markets allowing the Nazis to censor films; that is if Janet Trevalian's story was to be believed. Somewhat frustrated, Oakley drove home after stopping by Dinah's Diner for a hamburger and a chocolate malt.

After taking Oakley's telephone call the next morning, Bob Morris initially assumed the familiar I-am-a-busy-journalist-why-are-you-bothering-me tone but warmed up appreciably when reminded of how, when, and where they met. "So, Oakey, isn't that what Les said most people call you? What can I do for you?"

"Well," Oakley said, "I have a case where I feel I need to know more about some international film facts before I can figure out how to proceed."

"I don't know if I can help you, but go ahead and fill me in."

"I've been told that, apparently, the Germans, I'm guessing the consulate here, sent a letter to Universal demanding that they edit a recent movie to remove anything to do with Jews, which included re-filming parts of it to cut out any Jewish actors," Oakley explained. "A client of mine was one of those cut.

"It seems crazy to me that the Germans or representatives of any other country would think that they have the right to tell an American filmmaker what or who should be in—or not be in—a movie. I just don't get it."

"Why should you be surprised at anything that the Nazis do?" Morris asked. "They have made it very clear that they consider themselves the master race."

"I know all that," Oakley said. "I read the newspapers and hear the newscasts like everybody else. What I don't understand is why anyone in Hollywood would do their bidding. And I went to the library this morning and looked through weeks of back copies of your newspaper and a couple others and saw nothing about it. Nothing."

"First, Oakey, you have to realize that Germans love American movies. In fact, I've heard that both Josef Goebbels, the Nazi's propaganda boss, and Hitler himself are big fans of Hollywood's films. So, all in all, this has made Germany the biggest foreign market for Hollywood these days, and the money they pay for the film rights is huge. I don't know exactly how much, but it's a lot. So when the German government tells Hollywood something it wants to see up on the silver screen or something it doesn't want to see, the studios pay attention."

"OK, so I didn't know that Germany was the biggest foreign market. But doesn't interference from the Nazis who are, I understand, violently anti-Semitic, bother the studio bosses who are all Jewish?"

"Oakley, dear Oakley, don't be naïve. Never, ever, forget that making money is the reason and the only reason that the studios make movies. And so they overlook issues like doing business with people whom they don't like. And if those people want a few little changes made in a movie or two, and it's probably only a few movies we're talking about, so what? It's just part of the price of doing business."

"So, granted that this is all true, why didn't I find anything about this in any of the newspapers?" Oakley asked the reporter. "You'd think that since, I guess, this has been going on for a while, it would be considered news. But there was no mention anywhere that I could find about Nazis demanding changes in Hollywood movies."

"There are plenty of examples I could tell you about," Morris said. "I've given you the short version. But I really can't go into the reasons why you don't read anything about any of it right now. How urgent is this?"

"Well," Oakley replied, "I have a client who is pretty upset that her grandson was cut out of a movie supposedly because of a letter from the Germans, so to people like her, I guess, it's pretty urgent."

"How about tomorrow?" Bob asked. "Are you free? Maybe we could have a long brunch somewhere so at least we can pretend we aren't really working on a Sunday. And it would be nice to see you again."

"That would work," Oakley said, dreading Donny's reaction to the news that tomorrow would not be a beach day, at least not with him. "Any place in mind?"

"I know a place up the highway a bit from Santa Monica if you wouldn't mind a little drive. It's quiet. They leave you alone if you just want to have brunch, sit, and talk, and we can then have a walk on the beach. So the day won't be totally lost."

Oakley agreed with alacrity.

The next day dawned clear and warm, exactly the sort of day that Donny would love to share with him at the beach. *Well, I'm sorry*, he thought as he dialed Donny's telephone number. *Unlike Donny's travel agency job, mine isn't predictable. People usually plan for trips. Most of my clients have problems that they never planned for.*

Understandably, despite Oakley's promise that he would make up for his disappointment, Donny was hurt and disappointed. *If he ends up going to the beach*, Oakley thought as he hung up the telephone, *I hope he goes to the same place we were last week. It would be hell to pay if he discovered that I was also at the beach*, he thought while filling the coffee percolator and putting it on the stove and pouring himself a bowlful of Kix.

After the ritual shower and shave, Oakley dressed as stylishly as he could afford in what passed for summertime casual wear, also adopted when he was a college student: white slacks, the inevitable shirt and tie, and a sky-blue seersucker sport coat. "Donny would go nuts if he saw me with Bob." Oakley chuckled aloud as he tied his tie. "He'd never believe it was only because of work."

"So, Oakley," Bob said after the pair settled into a comfortable booth at the ocean-side restaurant and ordered their meal: waffles and sausage links for Bob and the newly popular Denver omelet for Oakley. "Let me fill you in on the real story behind Hollywood and the Nazis.

"Let's start with the current story. Next month, Warner Brothers' new movie, *The Life of Emile Zola*, is having its premiere in New York and is slated to open here in September. Zola, as you probably know, was a famous French writer who gained worldwide fame in the 1890s when, after a Jewish army officer named Alfred Dreyfus was convicted of giving military secrets to the German government, he wrote a famous newspaper column claiming Dreyfus was innocent and the victim of anti-Semitism in the French military. Although the movie is more or less a biography of Zola's whole life, the effect of the film, I'm told, is a clear condemnation of anti-Semitism."

"OK," Oakley said, "so where do the Nazis come in?"

"I'm getting to that," Bob said. "Last February, Dr. Georg Gyssling, the German consul in Los Angeles, an ardent Nazi by the way, heard that Warner was making the movie and called the producer, Henry Blanke, to complain about the pro-Jewish aspect of the story line. The last thing they wanted was to have a condemned Jew exonerated of guilt, which is what eventually happened following the uproar over Émile Zola's newspaper story. Blanke assured Gyssling that the Dreyfus Affair, as it was called, played a very small part in the movie. And that was that as far as Blanke knew.

"Then Jack Warner himself suddenly got involved and ordered several changes in the script, completely eliminating the word *Jew* from the script.

"As I mentioned on the phone, American movies are extremely popular in Nazi Germany; actually some forty or fifty movies a year are released there, pictures of American movie stars are on the covers of most of the magazines, and on weekend nights, there are always lines of people in front of the theaters showing them. This has an upside for the Hollywood studios; they make a lot of money from it. But it has a potential downside for the German government because the popularity of Hollywood films can influence what the Germans think. So Hitler's crowd really pays attention to the content of the movies. And the heads of Hollywood studios pay attention to what Hitler wants."

"OK. I understand that much," Oakley said as their brunch order arrived.

"It—the arrangement between the Nazis and Hollywood—all started in 1930, before the Nazis took over, when they staged a riot at the Berlin premiere of the Universal film made from Erich Maria Remarque's book, *All Quiet on the Western Front.* Josef Goebbels, who was there, started the riot when he made a speech from the front row of the balcony asserting that the movie was a deliberate attempt to damage Germany's reputation. Eventually, after more Nazi rioting, the movie was banned in Germany. So, to protect their pocketbooks, every studio began to make films that were carefully edited to please the Nazi regime after it came to power in 1933."

"Later, and I don't know all the details, Gyssling even got to Will Hayes, our friendly movie censor," Bob said sarcastically, "who told a pair of producers who were planning a film that was an attack on the Nazis to forget it; a movie like that would create heavy financial losses for the industry because Germany certainly would probably then ban all Hollywood movies."

"Bob, how the heck has none of this been in your newspaper or any of the other newspapers I looked through?" Oakley asked between bites of his omelet. "And how do you know so much about this?"

"That's what I really couldn't answer when you called me yesterday at the paper," he said. "It's really simple. This is a company town. If you are shocked that the Jewish filmmakers are in bed with the Nazis, why should you be surprised that Harry Chandler, who not only owns the *Times* but more or less controls what we do and say and is a big friend of Mayer goes along with the cover-up? And Hearst, who owns the *Los Angeles Examiner,* clearly knows which side of his bread is buttered. Don't count on ever seeing anything about this in his paper or written about it by his superstar columnist, Louella Parsons."

"I understand." Oakley cringed inwardly, suddenly realizing how expert Parsons had to be to write a column underlaid by layers and layers of Hollywood intrigue, lies, half-truths, scandals, and sometimes actual truths that she could never publicly mention.

"I'm the kind of journalist who hates censorship," Bob concluded. "But I have to make a living. I like the good things my job allows me to have, like this lunch and my yellow Cord convertible outside. "

"Is that yours?" Oakley exclaimed. On his arrival at the restaurant, he was awed by the vision of the new, supercharged, canary-yellow Cord 512 convertible, deliberately parked in front of the restaurant by the valets. "My God, what a beauty!"

"Thanks," Morris said. "In all honesty, journalists don't make that much money, so I had to have a little chat with my family to get it. But to finish what I was saying: 'How do I know so much about this' you ask? Because of my job, I'm privy to a lot of insider stuff. But also, because of my job, I have to keep silent about Hollywood's pact with the Nazis, but one day I plan to write a book about it. But let me go on..."

Oakley nodded. By now, they had finished their lunch, and as there were people waiting for tables at the popular restaurant, Bob paid the bill, commenting as an aside, "An expense account is one of the perks of overlooking some of Hollywood's more egregious sins. This OK?" he asked as he led the way out and onto the restaurant's huge deck overlooking the beach and ocean.

"So to bring you up to date on your question that started this long story about our not-so-holy-and-honorable film industry," Morris continued as the pair sat on a bench. "Your client and the movie he was cast in and then cut from…

"Last April, I'm told, Gyssling went after Universal and *The Road Back*, which was, as you know, the sequel to *All Quiet on the Western Front*, the movie that started all the trouble in Germany. He sent letters to everyone at the studio involved in making the movie who were even faintly suspected of being Jewish or having Jewish ancestors including many of the cast members, even the wardrobe man. James Whale also got the letter. He's not Jewish, but because he was the film's director, in their eyes, he was also guilty. In his letter, Gyssling warned all of them that if the movie was made, any film in which any of them were involved in the future would be banned in Germany.

"This created a major problem for everyone. Although Gyssling, as the Universal people knew, had probably broken the law by using the U.S. mail to threaten American workers who were just doing their jobs, everyone involved was told to keep it all a secret. And then Universal went ahead with the film but cut any mention of Jews out of it as well as editing out a few people like your client. It seemed to be enough to placate the Germans.

"But then some of the people who were fired talked, and the news leaked out," Bob added. "None of this fooled the movie critics who reviewed *The Road Back* badly because of the way it sugar-coated the story. James Whale and the people who were threatened are furious and claim they will never work for the studio again."

"Wow, some story," Oakley said.

"Well, there is a little more," Morris said. "Want to take a walk?"

"Sure."

"Last year, *Three Comrades*, the final book in Erich Maria Remarque's trilogy that began with *All Quiet*, was published," Bob explained as they walked down a gangplank from the restaurant's deck onto the sand. "Let's leave our shoes here," he suggested, as he took off his espadrilles and tucked them behind one of the pilings supporting the restaurant's deck.

"The beginning of this year, *Three Comrades* was serialized in English in *Good Housekeeping* magazine and an English edition has just been published," Bob continued as the pair resumed their walk along the beach. "MGM bought the rights when the book first came out in Europe, and the producer picked Scott Fitzgerald—he was available at Metro at the time—to write the script. I'm told by friends at the studio, the result was a strong attack on the rise of Nazism, just like the book.

"But when Gyssling wrote his letter to the actors in *The Road Back*," Bob said, removing his socks, rolling up his pants, and splashing in the surf, "Metro got scared and thought seriously about dropping the project. Joe Breen, the man who runs Hays's office in Los Angeles who was worried about Hollywood movies being banned in Germany, apparently also panicked when he read Fitzgerald's script.

"Then - I'm guessing Metro made a deal with Gyssling to eliminate anything the Nazis objected to," Bob continued, "they changed their mind and went ahead with the movie. It isn't finished yet, but like Warner and Universal, I'm betting that Metro also sanitized *Three Comrades* to make the Nazis happy. Certainly the cast is as safe as they come: Margaret Sullivan, Franchot Tone, Robert Taylor, and Robert Young."

With that, Morris ran behind several pilings and started removing his clothes. "I'm going for a swim. How about you, Oakey?"

"What about getting wet? We don't have any towels here."

"Don't worry, I've got some in the car," Bob said jauntily as he, clad only in his boxer shorts, ran into the surf. Oakley quickly followed.

As soon as he got home, Oakley heard his telephone ringing from the courtyard of his apartment complex. He ran up the stairs and rushed into his apartment, hoping to catch it before the caller hung up. "Hello, hello," he exclaimed breathlessly, grabbing the handset of the new, modern-style telephone he had recently installed in both his home and office.

"Mr. Oakley?" a man's voice said quietly. "This is Billy Williams. Michelle Ryder gave me your telephone number and asked me to call you."

"Oh yes, Mr. Williams. Thanks for calling. I've been hoping to talk with you."

"What is it you want to know, Mr. Webster? Michelle said that you were involved in helping us find the truth in recent events. I just don't know much more than what she has probably told you already."

"Well, what she told you is correct. She and several of your friends have retained me to try and find out if your arrest was the result of a frame-up or—"

"Or what?" Williams interrupted angrily. "Of course it was a setup! Martin told me he already explained to you that I was called by this sailor who invited me to meet him. This wasn't my doing. Not one bit!"

"I'm sorry, Mr. Williams," Oakley said soothingly. "I didn't mean to suggest that it wasn't a setup. It is my job to try and find out who it was that did this."

"It was that bastard Mayer," Williams snapped. "No question. He did it to have an excuse to fire me."

"Well, now, Mr. Williams—"

"Call me Billy. Everyone else does."

"Thank you, uh, Billy. You are absolutely correct that it appears that it seems reasonable to assume that it was Mr. Mayer's doing, or at least the doing of someone at Metro. But hear me out for a moment. I'm thinking that if Mayer really wanted to fire you, he could have done so when you were caught in a raid a year or so ago at that place on Wilshire."

"It wasn't a bordello," Billy snapped. "It was a private club."

"Mr. Williams, Billy, I didn't say it was a bordello. But it was a club catering primarily to men, wasn't it?"

"Yes, I guess it was."

"But whatever it was, he didn't fire you then. So why fire you now? Doesn't make any sense."

"Does to me," Williams said. "The two movies I made since the raid didn't do as well as the ones before, so maybe I became a bit more, I guess the right word is, well, *expendable*."

"Other actors have had up and down times," Oakley injected.

"But," Billy interrupted, "they weren't homosexual, and he has always hated me for not only living openly with Martin but also for never denying who I am. He was out to get me and so he decided to do so by arranging this little assignation with that sailor."

"Billy, let's change the subject for a moment," Oakley said, finally turning on the light in the rapidly darkening apartment and sitting down. "Tell me about the firing."

"Michelle told me that Louella Parsons told you, but I'll go through it again. He called me into his office the morning after he saw to it that Metro bailed me out of jail and said he had had enough scandalous behavior from me and demanded I stop living openly with Martin and get married—to a woman -- just like Cary and Randy and all the others have done."

"Yes, she told me that."

"And I told him to drop dead."

"Then what happened?" Oakley asked.

"Exactly the same thing happened when he threatened to dump me before. When he eventually figured out that I wasn't going along with his agenda, he then tried another tactic, apparently the same thing he does with every actor and actress he wants to discipline. He suddenly changes into being Mr. Nice Guy and tries to talk you into doing what he wants, not because it embarrasses the studio, but because it might jeopardize one's—meaning my—star status. This time it fell sorta flat because he had already complained that my grosses had dropped and, to him, that automatically meant my star status was eighty-sixing."

"But I guess he didn't make the connection," the actor continued, "so then when that tack didn't get him anywhere, he did what he had always done before when we had a spat. He threw his arm around my shoulders and said, 'Oh my son, oh my son. I never had a son. I always wanted a son. I think of you as my son.' Then he starts to cry. It's all cheap theatrics on his part, and everyone knows it. But before, when he turned on the eye faucets, I discovered a way to stop his crying. I start crying, too."

"Well, that is one way to take control of the situation, I guess." Oakley chuckled.

"Yeah, but this time it didn't work," Billy explained. "This time he got really angry. Maybe he finally figured out I was making fun of him, and that's the last thing a fat, little, two-bit Napoleon like Louis B. Mayer could tolerate.

"So he walked over to his desk and picked up some papers. He said it was my contract. Maybe it was. Maybe it was a prop. You never know for sure with him. And then he tore them in half and screamed, 'You'll never work in Hollywood again.' You'd think he could come up with a threat more original than an old chestnut like that, which has been around for ages and probably came from some silent film title card."

"So what did you say, Billy?"

"I told him he was a greedy bastard who claimed to be a loving father to his employees but ruthlessly brutalized and exploited them when it came to his and Metro's pocketbook. Since he has, I hear, an income of several hundred thousand dollars a year, which makes his and Metro's pocketbooks one and the same thing. Then he threw the torn-up papers, or whatever they were, at me. So I gave him the finger and walked out."

"Well, that was a pretty loud-and-clear way to tell him how you felt about the situation." Oakley laughed. "But seriously, do you think anyone else could have had it in for you, someone else who might have arranged the frame-up?"

"Sure, I can think of a lot of people who hate my guts, if for no other reason than for being America's number-one male star for years," Billy said. "I made a lot of enemies then. That's Hollywood. As much as everyone pretends to love everyone else, everyone is numero uno in their own book. Even if someone gets a less-than-rave review, someone who was your best friend yesterday often jumps in for the kill today.

"One reason I refused to do what Mayer demanded and dump Martin is that even after all these years together, I love him. He's my guy. Another reason is that he is the only person in this fucking town who I trust. Well, I trust Cranberry, too. And I guess Michelle Ryder. And she says I can trust you, otherwise I wouldn't be talking with you now," Billy asserted.

"Well, Mrs. Ryder would be right. You can trust me," Oakley said. "May I ask what your plans are now?"

"Well, some of my so-called friends have suggested that I have a chat with some of the other studios, but all these bastards stick together like glue—well, except for Republic. But I'd rather beg for pennies on the corner of Hollywood and Vine than work for them. You know everyone in town calls the place *Repulsive* Pictures, and they're right. Yates, the guy who runs it, is a real scoundrel."

"I've heard that."

"So I think I'm going to walk away from this whole movie-making business," Billy added. "Hollywood has certainly been good to a poor boy from Pennsylvania like me, but it's clearly time for a change. You've maybe heard that I am a collector of antiques and also have a bit of a reputation for designing interiors for people? I've actually done a couple houses for friends like my agent, Phil Berg, and Cranberry."

"I think I saw something in the trades some time ago that you did a bedroom for Miss Crawford—all in white I think it was."

"No, that was Lombard's. Anyway, a couple years ago, I opened an antique store on La Brea Boulevard, and thank God it's fairly successful. So that's what I'm going to concentrate on now. Bye, bye, Metro; hello, muslin. Hey, Oakley, you oughta drop by the shop someday. Never know when you might decide to do some redecoratin'. By the way, where do you live?"

"Alvarado Court Apartments."

"Really? Isn't that the place—"

"Yep. I guess you know your LA history, Billy."

"Everyone knows the history of that place," Billy said. "Doesn't it keep you awake at nights?"

"Not really," Oakley said. "I'm not in Taylor's apartment. I'm across the courtyard from his in the one where Edna Purviance once lived."

"One of the great ones," Billy said. "I can never get through watching *The Kid* without crying my eyes out."

"Me, too," Oakley agreed. "I just might take you up on your invite to drop by the shop someday. Then I can meet a real movie star," he said playfully before adding in a serious tone, "I'm certainly going to need to talk with you again, probably as soon as I've nosed around a bit more. Should I call you at the same number I called when I spoke with Martin?"

"That'll do, or you could call me at the shop on La Brea. Bye."

Oakley sat back in his reading chair and thought quietly for a while. Little that Billy Williams had told him was new except for Louis B. Mayer's theatrical crying jag. But by being told the story first-person by the victim, it became far more tangible. *There is little question*, Oakley thought, *that Billy was set up. But if it was Mayer who did it, how the hell would it be possible to get the goods on him, the most powerful man in Hollywood?* The only way to do it was to try to work backward to get into the plot, if there was one. He had to find the sailor.

Oakley dialed Billy's number. After apologizing for bothering him again so soon after they had spoken, he asked if Billy remembered the sailor's name.

"Of course I do," Billy said, sounding somewhat irritated. "I never forget a face or a name. Why do you need it?"

"I need the name of everyone involved in this," Oakley said somewhat weakly, suddenly realizing that now that the story of his arrest and firing was beginning to die down, probably the last thing that Billy Williams wanted was for the scandal to be reignited. Clearly, he was worried that by now involving the sailor, whose part in the whole mess had been overwhelmed by Billy Williams's fame, it could do just that. Scrambling to reassure the actor, Oakley added, "I just need to tie up some of the loose threads."

"Does this mean that now you're going to want to talk to the people at the Downtown Y also?" Williams asked, his voice dripping with sarcasm. "How do you know that the bell bottom—his name is Carl Andrews, by the way—isn't going to be terrified that his name is going to be everywhere in the scandal sheets? It hasn't been mentioned so far because I am the big fish that got caught, and he's probably scared to death that his mommy and daddy back in Iowa or wherever he's from might find out their darling boy is a pansy in bell bottoms hustling older guys. That'll go over really well in Des Moines, won't it?" Billy said in the same sarcastic tone. "And he's probably in enough trouble as it is with the navy. I don't think they're overly happy having one of their sailor boys involved in a scandal like this, or seeing the story in the headlines again."

"Billy," Oakley said, exercising his patience, "I know all that. But I have to find out if someone put him up to it or if it came about as simply as Martin said it did—that someone he may have met at a party or a bar may have mentioned your name as a person who could show him a good time. And he saw a chance to do exactly that. And never forget that within our community, you're a big movie star and that lots of kids from the sticks would do anything just to boast that they slept with you. Especially these days when they can then boast to their friends that they did it with a famous male movie star when so many queer actors in Hollywood are now pretending that they are straight like, well, Cary Grant. Or really straight like Errol Flynn."

"Honey, like Errol Flynn? For all his sashaying around with girls like Dolores del Rio and marrying Lili Damita, everybody knows that he swings both ways. And don't get me on the subject of Cary! But I get it, Oakley. I get it. Go ahead and see if you can find him, but please be careful," Billy said. "Carl Andrews."

"Do you know what his outfit or, uh"—Oakley racked his mind for other information he might want to find a sailor—"the name of his ship? Did he mention anything about that? And do you remember what his rank was?"

Then an idea struck from the blue. "Are you certain, Billy," Oakley asked before the actor had a chance to answer, "that he was a real sailor, and not just a hustler with a sailor costume rented from some prop shop?"

"Of course he was a real sailor. At least I'm pretty sure he was, but the cops arrived before I got past the uniform to be able to check out his dog tags," Billy said. "Rank? I don't know what rank he was and never asked. He had some stripes on his uniform, but I have no idea what they meant, and I was more interested in getting him out of uniform than counting stripes. Then, with the arrest and all, there wasn't time to go into all that anyway. I do remember he mentioned the name of his ship, but don't remember it, and that he said he was up from San Diego."

"OK, thanks, Billy," Oakley said. "Sorry to bother you again, and be assured 'careful' is my middle name. So don't worry. Night."

Chapter 8

Oakley managed to make it into the office more or less on time the next morning. It looked like it was going to a busy week, and he wanted to get ahead of the tide.

"Benny? Weren't you in the navy?" Oakley asked his sidekick when he walked into his office.

"Yep, I lied and signed up when I was sixteen. Wanted to get out of Buffalo. Wanted to see the world. But all I saw of the world was the recruiting station in Wichita. Seen more of the world right here at the corner of Third and Broadway in LA than in two years in the navy. So why do you ask?"

"Need to find a bell bottom."

"Like the one that Billy Williams picked up?" Benny asked.

"Jesus, Benny, I guess I can't hide much from you. How does one go about locating a sailor?"

"Well, it ain't goin' to be easy, but a good start would be to call the personnel office at the navy station in Long Beach and see what they say."

This was the beginning of one of the most frustrating mornings Oakley had ever experienced—a seemingly endless round of repeating his question to one navy clerk after another. The problem, as it soon became apparent, was that the personnel records included the names of only the people stationed at the Long Beach navy station or, as he was soon directed, to the headquarters of the navy's Pacific Ocean operations in San Diego. "Who's payin' for all these long distance calls?" Benny asked as both he and Oakley were holding on separate lines for personnel clerks in different departments at the San Diego base. "Don't worry," Oakley said. "No one is concerned about the expenses on this except you"—he hesitated a moment—"and me. Just make sure we keep a record of everything and that I remember to bill it all out."

Just then, the clerk Oakley was holding for, seemingly the hundredth to whom he had described his need, came back on the line. "Mr. Webster," he said, "I've gone through everything we have, and I finally found two Carl Andrews. One is employed at the naval air station in Manila, and the other is a welder at the naval headquarters in Pearl Harbor. Would one of them be your man?"

"I don't think so. The Carl Andrews I'm looking for was in Los Angeles last week."

"Have you checked the crew rosters?" the clerk asked.

"The what?" Oakley asked. "I've spoken to dozens of people, and no one said anything about crew rosters. I guess I assumed that you folks were able to check everything."

"Not necessarily. If a ship is in port for a day or two, there is no way or reason we would have or need their roster."

"So how do I do that?" Oakley asked, waving for Benny to hang up.

"I can transfer you to the port master who should be able to check with the personnel officer of each of the ships that are in port."

Jesus, he thought, *yet another person to deal with. If this is the way these people fight wars, we're in trouble.* "Well, if that is the only way..."

"Sir, that is the only way. Hold on a moment."

Needless to say, dealing with the port master's office was initially an even larger challenge than he had encountered with the personnel clerks. The last thing anyone he spoke with wanted was to deal with a "civilian" like Oakley looking for a sailor who may or may not be on one of the warships in port, especially for reasons that Oakley himself wasn't sure sounded entirely legitimate. Finally, after being switched from one clerk to another, he ended up being transferred to the port master himself.

"What was it you wanted?" the gruff voice of Commander Eric Soloway demanded impatiently. "Who are you, and why do you want to contact him?"

Oakley patiently went through his now well-memorized script again, adding (with fingers crossed) the clearly fabricated story that he was acting on behalf of Andrews family to convey an urgent message.

"Well," Commander Soloway said with a more friendly tone, possibly affected by Oakley's sincere-sounding concern, "maybe you're in luck. We have only two ships in port at the present time. Both are heavy cruisers: the *Indianapolis* and the *Astoria*. Both ships will soon be on their way to join the Asiatic fleet, and if your man is on either ship, particularly the *Astoria*, he's probably been run pretty ragged."

"Run ragged?"

"As in 'busy as all get out.' The war that began a couple weeks ago between Japan and China has everyone worried," Commander Soloway explained. "In fact, both of the cruisers were in Pearl last month for a simulated operation against the Imperial Japanese Navy, just in case. Then the *Astoria* sailed here, refueled, and then went on to San Francisco where it was part of the opening ceremonies for that new bridge on May 27. They're calling it the Golden Gate; I hear it's quite a sight to see," Soloway added.

"Then…I'm reading from the port log," he continued, "after returning here for a while when many of the crew had a short leave. Then the *Astoria* sailed to Portland, Oregon, where she was a featured ship in the Pacific Fleet Festival that began on July 16. Part of the damned PR stuff that we all have to do all the time. I play golf now and then when they're in port with the *Astoria*'s captain, Chuck Gill, so I'll give him a call," the port master said. "You said his name was Carl Andrews, right? If we locate him, what do you want us to tell him?"

"Ask him to call me. He can reverse the charges. Tell him—"

"I know, an 'urgent message' from his family. We'll give it a shot."

Oakley turned to Benny and shrugged his shoulders. "Dunno if that will do the trick," he said, "but I don't know what else to do to find this sailor. What do we have on the docket today?"

"Just a coupla messages I took before you got in. Your friend Lester Grady wants you to call him back, so does someone named Joe Valentine."

Oakley called Les Grady who wanted to bring him up to date on what was doing with his client Rachael Baumgarten. It was good news—well, considering past events, relatively good news. Because it seemed that despite the work of Oakley and the Los Angeles police, her own violin had apparently disappeared for good, she had accepted, albeit reluctantly as Les earlier explained, the loan of another. Arranged through the Los Angeles Philharmonic, the loaned instrument, a Stradivarius, was one of several violins owned by the famous radio comedian (and little-known violin virtuoso) Jack Benny who, after his show began originating in Los Angeles instead of New York in 1936, had become a patron of the orchestra.

"Let's have lunch or dinner soon," Les said after relating Rachael's news.

"That would be great," Oakley exclaimed. "I'm really behind the eight ball right now, but give me a call next week."

"Joe Valentine? Joe Valentine? How do I know the name?" Oakley asked Benny after ending his conversation with Grady.

"I dunno, but he said he met you a coupla weeks ago when you rear-ended his car."

"Oh yes, now I remember," Oakley said, recalling his encounter with the handsome Italian and his recent resolution to call him. "He lives in this strange building in Hollywood built by DeMille a few years back. Looks like the movie set of a medieval castle."

"Whatcha expect from DeMille?" Benny asked. "I hear he even decorates his place in the Valley with props from his movies. This guy an actor?"

"I dunno," Oakley said, his interest in Joe Valentine suddenly reawakened. "I never got around to asking him. Give me his number."

As Valentine's telephone was busy, Oakley put the message aside to remind him to try later, and turned to more of the business at hand, deciding that he needed to bring Michelle Ryder up to date on his progress with the Billy Williams case. Her number was also busy, so she joined Joe Valentine on his to-do list. "Time to go to lunch," he said to Benny, who usually brought his lunch in an old, battered Red Ryder lunchbox. "If you decide to go out, just lock up," he said.

Coincidently, Donny was also lunching at the popular dining counter of the Woolworth's Five-and-Dime store near his office. "Hey, Oakey, surprise, surprise. Sit here next to me," Donny shouted as Oakley walked in. Like many, Oakley appreciated the quick service and quality of the fare, even if it meant eating while perched on a frequently wobbly barstool.

"This is a nice surprise," Donny added, patting the seat next to him.

"Ditto. I was going to call you after lunch. What's up?"

"Nothin' much new. Lotsa people booking trips to Hawaii for later this year. That *Malolo* ship is already full up for all the sailings in October."

"Oh?" Oakley observed as he seated himself and grabbed one of the mimeographed menus encased in slightly greasy cellophane covers. "Wish I could sail off to Hawaii. What looks good today?"

"I had my usual. Toasted cheese sandwich and a chocolate malt," Donny said. "Jeanie"—nodding at the counter waitress—"always gives me extra pickles."

"I'll have a BLT and a Coke," Oakley ordered as the waitress set a glass of water at his place.

"So when am I going to see you again?" Donny asked. "I'm feeling a bit left out after you stood me up this weekend."

"Didn't stand you up," Oakley said. "I had to work. I'm drowning in it."

"The Billy Williams thing? How's that goin'?"

"It's a problem. You're not the only one to think the whole thing was a frame-up. The problem is, if it was a setup, finding out who did it is a tough call. You don't survive in Hollywood as long as Billy has without a lot of people having a motive to get rid of you. And I think it's clear, at least to me, that someone found the perfect way to do it. To the world, it looks like something caused by Billy's bad judgment. A perfect crime."

"Shouldn't be that hard to find some suspects other than the people who hated him for his success," Donny said. "I'd start with the pansy haters."

Why is it that everyone always calls when I'm out of the office? Oakley wondered, shaking his head in disgust after returning from lunch and seating himself at his desk. Benny had just gone off for a lunchtime walk, but before he left, he had skewered a half-dozen messages on the lethal-looking message holder (basically a huge nail mounted vertically on a fancy base) on his desk. Oakley lifted the lot off the spike and dealt them from the bottom to begin with the oldest call. *It was from Donny who must have called before I ran into him,* Oakley figured, tossing the message in his trash basket while wondering how he was going to handle their mutual urge to get together with what was becoming a rapidly mounting demand for his time from anxious clients whose needs were beginning to converge.

The other calls were from Michelle Ryder, Docky (twice), LAPD sergeant Mike Maloney, and Donny again, who had called just before he got back to the office, as the time on the message memo indicated. *Let's find out what was so important for him to call me only minutes after we had had lunch,* Oakley thought while dialing his number.

"Hey, Oakey," Donny exclaimed, virtually shouting into the telephone. "Guess what? I got back to the office and right on top of my messages was a cancellation for the *Malolo* on its sailing to Honolulu the middle of September. Want to go? My boss wants me to go on the trip as hand-holder for all the people we already booked on the ship, but if I move quickly, I could rearrange the cabin assignments, and we could share one. So it could be sort of a honeymoon for us. And we would then have a few days in Honolulu before we return. I have to escort another group we booked back to the States on the *Lurline*. Three weeks in all. Maybe a couple days more."

Oakley was tempted. Although he didn't consider his relationship with Donny anywhere near something that would deserve a honeymoon, he really liked him, and the idea of a couple of weeks at sea and in a tropical paradise was tempting. "And how much?" he started to ask.

"Next to nothing. Just a small part of the Matson Lines fare and half the hotel bill in Hawaii. But I gotta know now."

"Well, I..." Oakley hesitated, then realized that if his current cases weren't solved by then, they probably never would be. And, hell, going to Hawaii was what he'd been wanting to do for a long time. So why not? "OK, Donny. Sign me up. But I gotta go now. I'll call you later."

His next call was to Docky Martin who explained that he had called when Louella had asked him to get Oakley on the telephone between her own calls. He immediately passed the call to her.

"Oakley? Oakley?" Louella Parsons's husky voice commanded. "I just heard from Metro that they picked someone to replace Billy in *Mickey O'Rourke Grows Up.* Ron O'Bannon, of all people!" she spat out. "I think L. B. has finally lost his marbles!"

Oakley thought a moment before responding. He knew what she meant. O'Bannon's appearance fit the bill perfectly. He, like Billy Williams early in his career, looked like a boy-next-door type ordered up from Central Casting: open-faced, Irish-cute, tousle-haired with a snub nose, freckles, and a smile that seemed pasted on his face. And he had been in a number of college romance films like the ones once made by Billy Williams. But whether he could step into *Mickey O'Rourke Grows Up*, a movie where Billy's signature character was no longer a collegiate football player but an older football coach, a role that was written for a new, more mature Billy Williams, seemed uncertain at best.

"I think you're right," he agreed. "It sounds to me that Mr. Mayer has cast O'Bannon for the roles played by the old Billy. I've only seen a couple of O'Bannon's movies, but all he seems to share with Billy is that Irish-boy-next-door look and, as I read in *Photoplay*, a talent for interior decorating."

"Jezzus!" Parsons exclaimed. "I'd forgotten that. Thanks for reminding me. I wonder whose places he decorated? Besides his own, of course. And if they're any good? That would make a good item for my column. Anyway, how you comin' on the frame-up?"

Oakley reviewed his recent work for her, recapped his extensive conversation with Billy Williams, and announced that he had found, but not yet spoken with, the sailor himself who, luckily, had apparently not yet shipped out.

"Great," the columnist said. "Keep me informed. "Now I have another bit of news for you. I heard that measles has struck down another actor, like Eva Sanderson."

Oakley's attention was immediately seized by the news, and he wondered if Parsons was also suspicious that Eva's measles and the subsequent tragedy may have been caused deliberately. Apparently not, he realized, when she continued, "Now I'm told by people at Paramount that John Wayne has contracted measles and that the studio has suspended production on the remake of *Born to the West*, the Zane Grey story that he's making with Marsha Hunt and Johnny Mack Brown. Now, that's the person Metro should have grabbed to replace Billy."

"Wayne?"

"No, of course not!" she barked. "Are you crazy? Johnny Mack Brown! He was once a football player, and he certainly had those boy-next-door looks and a great career going until Mayer screwed him when he dumped him for Clark Gable in some stupid film. Damned idiot!"

Oakley assumed it was Mayer who was the idiot, not Gable, but the way Louella Parsons rambled from one subject to the next as if she was constantly writing footnotes to her conversation was beginning to make him a bit seasick. "I thought John Wayne worked at Republic," Oakley said, trying to steer the subject back to the measles.

"He does. Lately, he's been making a lot of B movies for them and before that for the Poverty Row studios that merged into Republic—Monogram, Majestic, Mascot, the cheapo operations. But Marion works for everyone. Everyone loves him. Marion Williams Morrison, that's his real name," she rambled again. "He hates it when anyone calls him Marion. I always do." She giggled.

"Oh, I'll bet that really peeves him," Oakley said.

"Gotta go," the columnist said breezily. "Radio show tonight and nothing to talk about—well, except measles. Hope I don't get 'em."

Oakley then called Michelle Ryder, and as she also wanted to know how his investigation of Billy Williams's troubles was coming along, he recapped his work as he had done for Louella Parsons.

He then returned the call from Mike Maloney, an LAPD contact he had previously worked with, to see what he could find out about Billy's arrest from the other side.

"Hey, Mike," Oakley said. "How you getting along?"

"A voice from the past. Wow!" the seemingly always-exuberant Maloney exclaimed. "A call from my favorite private dick!"

"I know, I know," Oakley said apologetically. "I never call except when I want something, right?"

"I didn't say it; you did. What's up, buddy?"

"Just want a little inside buzz, like who fingered Billy Williams the other night."

"Wow, Oakey, you don't want much, do ya? Just inside dope on our operations."

"Come on, Mike. I know you know these things don't just happen. Someone had to tip you off. I just want to know who it was."

"That, I don't know, and with the things the way they are right now, I don't dare to check into it too deeply. Everyone is runnin' for cover right now," Mike said, clearly sounding wary of who might be overhearing their conversation at his end.

"Why?" Oakley asked. "What's going on?"

"Well, it seems that there's a committee been organized to look into rumors that there has been some funny business goin' on around here, and ever'one is bound and determined to cover their ass. So…"

"Look, I've also heard something about a citizens committee being organized to look into Shaw's office as well as the LAPD, but that could all be journalistic noise," Oakley explained. "And it has nothing to do with this. All I want to know is how you ended up raiding the Downtown Y at exactly the right time to nab Billy Williams."

"Well, since I wasn't involved in the raid, all I can tell you is what the story is around here. Someone called the Hollywood station and tipped them about Williams pickin' up this sailor in Pershing Square and said they then went to the Downtown Y for more than a little canoodling. And then the tip was relayed here since any raid on the place would have to be done by this division. I don't have access to Hollywood's call records, so I can't say who it was who called, and I don't have access to our call records either, so I don't know if Hollywood said who called them. Probably never did. Sorry, buddy. That's all I know."

"Thanks, Mike. We gotta get together soon."

"That would be great. Any time. Depends on what is happenin' with this citizens committee crapola, though."

"I know. Let me know. Bye."

Oakley thought for a moment and realized that another visit to the Hollywood station would be appropriate, but that would have to wait. The afternoon was already shot. He picked up the phone and called Donny at his office. "What about dinner in a couple hours? I'll pick you up at six thirty. Meet you in front of your place? You'll be home by then? You can fill me in on the trip to Hawaii, and we can do some catching up."

"Sure, I'll be there," Donny replied with barely contained enthusiasm. "Where we goin' for dinner?"

"Surprise. See ya later."

"So, where we off to?" Donny asked the moment he got in Oakley's car.

"Thought we'd 'eat in the hat,' as their slogan goes. The Brown Derby OK with you? I was there for drinks the other day. Come on, it was business," Oakley said as he noticed the obvious question forming on Donny's lips. "And Mae West was there. You'da loved that."

"Great," Donny exclaimed. "Never been there."

The evening was the hit Oakley hoped it would be. Donny had a steak and Oakley the restaurant's classic liver and onions. They shared the Brown Derby's signature Cobb salad and each had the restaurant's equally famous grapefruit cake for dessert. (As the menu reminded all Brown Derby diners, the Cobb salad was invented by the Brown Derby's owner who, having not eaten at midnight one evening a year or two earlier, created it from kitchen—not customer—leftovers, adding bacon prepared by the line chef. The grapefruit cake was created for Louella Parsons when she requested a "less fattening" dessert.)

During dinner and afterward at his apartment, Donny described the Hawaiian vacation he had arranged for the pair, to Oakley's obvious delight. They would share an outside cabin on the *Malolo* for the five-day voyage to Honolulu and the same accommodation on the Matson flagship *Lurline*, a ship especially popular with Hollywood stars, for their return. In Honolulu, they would be staying at either the Royal Hawaiian Hotel or the Ala Moana next door. It was the perfect trip right out of a promotional brochure: a romantic, tropical vacation. "Do you think I can take some surf-boarding lessons?" Oakley asked of the new craze, becoming more and more popular in California.

"Depends," Donny said with an evil smile.

"On what?" Oakley smiled, knowing where this conversation was headed.

"On whether I let you out of the room long enough to find the beach."

When Oakley arrived at the office the next morning—a bit late as was getting to be the case when he and Donny spent the night together—Benny had just picked up the telephone. "He's not in yet," Benny was saying, then caught himself the moment Oakley walked in. "Oh, here he is. Hold on a minute."

"Who is it?" Oakley asked as Benny handed him the telephone.

"Dunno, someone named Andrews."

"Great. It's our sailor boy," Oakley said. "Benny, could you go downstairs and buy me a pack of Chesterfields?" he added, knowing that he wanted as much as possible of this conversation to be private. Benny nodded. After he saw Benny close the office door behind him, Oakley returned to the telephone.

"Hello, Mr. Andrews. Thank you for calling. I guess you got the message that I was trying to reach you before you sailed."

"Yes, I did," the voice on the other line said in a clearly suspicious tone. "The exec on my ship said Captain Gill got a call from the port master asking me to call you. What is it you want?"

"I'm sorry, Carl. May I call you Carl?" The sailor grunted an affirmation. "There is some information about the unfortunate incident the other night that would be helpful."

"Helpful for what?" Andrews said, his previous suspicious tone now sounding distinctly hostile.

"Helpful for getting any record of this matter to go away," Oakley lied, knowing that the potential erasure of the incident could be the only bait that might interest Andrews at this point.

"How the hell is that going to happen?" he snapped. "I was booked just like Mr. Williams and then was sprung from the brig by the MAs. I'm in a pack of trouble, and it's all thanks to this 'unfortunate incident' as you call it. And, of course, everybody on my ship now knows I'm a pansy."

"MAs? I don't know the term."

"Master at Arms, navy police."

"Well, Carl, I'm sorry you're in trouble, but from what I hear, you brought it on yourself."

"Shit, no! This guy I met at a party said I should call this big actor Williams, and he would give me a good time. Look, I kinda go for older guys, and what the hell...who the hell are you anyway?"

"I understand," Oakley said soothingly. "My name is Oakley Webster, and I'm a private investigator who has been retained by some of Mr. Williams's friends to see if there might be some way to, as I said, make all of this go away—to expunge the incident from the records."

"OK, but how's that going to help me with Uncle Sam?"

"Well, I'm pretty sure that once any record of the incident is removed from the official records here, the navy could be convinced to do the same. After all, if there is no record of the incident, then the arrest and all must have been a mistake on the part of the LAPD. So your people would have no choice but to erase their record of the incident, too."

"And just how is that going to happen?"

"Well, Carl, let's just say that there seem to be a number of ways to induce the LAPD to overlook things."

"You mean they're on the take? I don't have any money for that."

"I didn't say anything about anybody being on the take, did I?" Oakley said. "But there are ways. Let me ask you a couple questions. I understand that you called Billy, inviting him to meet you."

"Yep, I did," Andrews confirmed. "As I said, there was this guy at a party—"

"Do you remember his name? And whose party was it?"

"I never got the name of the guy who gave the party. It was at a big house in, I seem to remember, a place called something Park."

"OK. How did you know about the party? Were you invited?" Oakley continued.

"A friend of mine had been invited and asked if I would like to go to a party. It was as simple as that. Then, as I said, at the party I was talking to this guy, and he acted real friendly, like he was comin' on to me. When I said that I'd like to meet a real movie star, he gave me Mr. Williams's telephone number and suggested I call him. I did and suggested we meet in this big cruising place downtown, and he seemed to know exactly where I meant. We met, he liked me, I liked him, and he suggested we get a room at the Y. Couldn't take me home 'cause he said he had a boyfriend there."

"And that was that?"

"That was that," Andrews said, then hesitated. "Well, except for..."

"Except for?"

"When this guy at the party gave me Billy's telephone number, he asked me to call him if we hit it off. So I did. I called him from a phone booth in the park. He asked what we planned, and I told him we were on our way to the YMCA. I also called the navy to make sure it was OK for me not to get back to my ship until the next afternoon."

"Do you remember the telephone number you called?"

"Nope. But I think it started with…I couldn't figure out what it was. I thought it was strange. *Y-O* something, I think, and the number. I sorta remember the guy's name, too. Something like Ronny or Donny. That's all I know. I gotta go now. I don't know where we're off to, but the scuttlebutt is that it's the Philippines. So I don't know how you'll be able to reach me."

"When I know more I'll contact the port master, and he'll certainly know where to contact you or your ship. Good luck, Carl. By the way, how old are you?

"Thanks. Sorry I was angry at first, but all this has really thrown me for a loop. All I want to do is forget the whole mess. I'm nineteen goin' on twenty."

CHAPTER 9

So we know for sure that it was a setup, Oakley realized as he hung up, *and we have a phone number—well, sort of a phone number:* Y-O. "Benny, do you know what the telephone exchange starting with *Y-O* is?"

"That's an easy one, Oakey. York. I got an aunt who has a York phone number. Lives near Wilshire and Crenshaw."

"Thanks," Oakley said, realizing that his search was narrowed to, maybe, ten thousand people. Well, 9,999 to be accurate…York plus four numbers. And sailor boy's recollection of "something Park" could be Hancock Park, the walled enclave in the area.

Oakley spent the next couple hours on the paperwork that had been piling up on his desk. "We gotta get a secretary type to do this stuff," he complained to Benny. One letter in the unopened mail, oddly addressed to "Oakey the PI," immediately caught his attention.

The message inside was terse and composed with letters cut from a newspaper and glued to a piece of brown wrapping paper, clearly planned to appear anonymous. "Mr. oaky," it read. "beWARE, Jewlover, you are NEXT! Unless you stop NOW on ROAD Back investigation." It was signed "a REal AmeriCAN."

Well, Oakley thought, *nothing subtle about the anti-Semitism here. I wonder if the writer realizes that Michael Trevalian—was that the name?—wasn't Jewish.* Or were Michael and his grandmother lying? There were a lot of people in Hollywood who, despite there being so many Jews working in the film industry, were changing their names and trying to pass as gentiles, like his buddy Ed Rogerson who now exclusively went by the name of Rogers. Of course, because Ed was in the PR business and had to work with both Jews and non-Jews, maybe he figured that it was just good politics to appear neutral.

And how did the writer of the letter know he was working to find the reason that Michael Trevalian was cut from the final edit of *The Road Back*? Only with that knowledge could the writer have mentioned the film. If he or she knew that, he or she certainly knew that Oakley probably was aware of the letter that Gyssling sent to stars and workers on the movie.

It was time to have a conversation with Mikey.

Janet Trevalian was as talkative as Oakley suspected she would be, wanting to know everything that Oakley had done on her grandson's behalf. "Nothing yet" should have been his answer, but knowing that would be something she didn't want to hear, he mumbled something indistinct about "doing research" before coming to the point of his call. "I need to talk with Michael."

Predictably, she offered to set up a meeting, but Oakley, knowing that he had to get the story relatively unvarnished from Michael himself, said that he would prefer a one-on-one conversation. So it was with obvious reluctance that she gave him Michael's telephone number.

"Who did you say you were?" the woman who answered his call asked.

"Oakley Webster," he said. "I'm a private investigator. Michael Trevalian's grandmother asked me to try and find out what happened with his role in *The Road Back*. Is he there?"

"Yeah, just a minute. Mike," she shouted, "someone named Oak-something on the phone for you."

Following introductions, explanations, and Michael's apology for his girlfriend's seeming abruptness, Oakley got to the point.

"Michael, I really need to sit down with you and learn everything you know about what happened to you on *The Road Back*. I'm sure you realize that you weren't the only person that the Germans wanted out of the movie, so there is a lot more to this than meets the eye."

"Great," Michael said. "Tell me when and where. I obviously am pretty free right now."

"Someplace relatively quiet where we can talk," Oakley suggested. "Do you know Lucy's El Adobe Café on Melrose across from Paramount? How about drinks there around five?"

"Sure, I know it. Hangout for actors and pretty good Italian food, too. I'll be there. How will I know you?"

"I don't know…standard PI outfit maybe. Fedora hat, boring brown suit. You?"

"Dirty blond, five feet ten. I'll be wearing a light blue shirt and a tan jacket. See you then, Mr. Webster."

"Hey, you don't have to 'mister' me. I'm only a few years older than you. Call me Oakey like everyone else." *That should make him feel comfortable*, Oakley thought.

"Hey, Benny, since you're not part of the furnishings, get the damned telephone when it's ringing," he shouted as he answered his second line.

"Hello, Mr. Webster? This is Janet Trevalian. Did you reach Mikey?"

"Yes, I just talked with him," Oakley said soothingly, thinking that because they had spoken only moments before, she was turning out to be a bit of a handful.

"Was he helpful?" she asked.

"We're going to meet later," he said. "So—"

"May I be there? Don't you need me in the meeting?"

"No, Mrs. Trevalian. As I said earlier, I think that a private visit with your grandson is best for now," he said, biting his tongue at having to repeat himself.

"Well, I just want you to have all the information you need."

"Mrs. Trevalian, do you know anything that your grandson doesn't know about this matter?" Oakley spoke firmly, knowing that unless she was removed from the dialogue, the entire investigation, hardly begun, could easily end up overwhelmed by chatter.

"Well, I guess not," she said, sounding somewhat chastised. "But Mikey tends to forget things now and then. That girl he's seeing—"

"And who would that be?" Oakley said, remembering the voice that had answered his call.

"Her name is Laurel—Laurel Fox—and she's all wrong for my Mikey."

"How so?"

"Well, for one thing, she's a year older than he is. And she's, well, I found out that she's really...uh...Oriental."

"Oriental? Like Chinese?" Oakley asked, suspecting that he already knew what Janet Trevalian was really getting at.

"No, she's, well, uh"—Trevalian hesitated for a moment—"she's Jewish."

Got it, Oakley thought. "And you don't approve?"

"Well, no, of course not. Too grasping. Too pushy. Pushed herself right at my Michael. Like she knew we aren't Jewish, and she wants to pass for being non-Jewish and going with Mikey was a way for her to do that. Maybe the Germans have the right ide—"

This has gone too far, Oakley thought, his anger building. "Mrs. Trevalian, I must tell you that although I haven't met the young lady, Laurel. Whatever she's like," he forcefully interrupted, "she could never be as offensive as you are right now. In fact, other than, from what you told me, I think a real injustice may have been done to your grandson, I would prefer not to have anything more to do with you or your bigotry!" he shouted, slamming down the receiver.

Within minutes, his phone was ringing again, and as Oakley was clearly still seething over his conversation with Janet Trevalian, Benny answered it. "Boss," he said, "it's someone named Michael. He sounds—"

Oakley grabbed the telephone. "Yes?" he snarled into the mouthpiece. "And now you?"

"No, no, no, Mr. Webster, Oakey. I just heard from my grandmother what happened, and I'm so sorry. I'm so sorry and very embarrassed. I share none of her racial opinions, and I really never knew how deeply her anti-Semitism went until her views sort of exploded when I started dating Laurie. I think she thought she was Scottish or something because I always referred to her as Laurie. I don't know where all this came from. Maybe it's a generational thing with my grandmother. I can't explain why she is so anti-Jewish. I love my grandma, but I despise this sort of bigotry.

"But, please, may we still meet? I would be so grateful if you would please, please still consider working with me so we can find out what happened. I can pay you. One of the good things about the job on *The Road Back* was, besides all the wonderful people I met and all I learned about filmmaking, is that I did get paid for my work. So I can pay you. Please, Mr. Webster."

"All right, Michael, but we have to leave your grandmother out of it. I'm not known for having a short fuse, but when it comes to crap like this—pardon my language—like hating people just because they may be a different color or race or religion"—Oakley nearly added *or being queer like me*—"I get really angry."

"I'm with you," Michael said. "Still on for five at Lucy's?"

"Make it six, and we'll have dinner, too, that is if you're free," Oakley suggested. "And bring Laurel along if you want," he added.

"I'll ask her, thanks. But considering what's been said to you by my grandmother, there is something else you should know."

"Oh?"

"I'm Jewish—well, some people might consider me partly Jewish."

"What?" Oakley literally shouted into the telephone. "Your grandmother said that the big irony of your being cut out of the film is that you aren't Jewish. What the hell?"

"Let me explain," Michael said. "As you may know, since the Middle Ages, Jewish heritage has been traced through the mother's line, not the father's line. The reason is that you always knew who the mother of someone was, but there was no way of proving who the father was. My grandmother's father, my great-grandfather, was Jewish, but as no one else in the family was, and it's not totally the mother's line, I guess she is comfortable with saying that we're not Jewish. But as far as the Germans nowadays are concerned, I'm at least one-thirty-second or some fraction Jewish. Which is why I figure I ended up on the list."

"Good God," Oakley exclaimed. "These people must be obsessed with this to go so deeply into everyone's genealogy. And someone like you who they never knew."

"But my name was on the cast list of *The Road Back*, and they didn't want that film made, at least not made in any way that resembled the book. So they went after the people who were making it. Maybe someone who knew about my great-grandfather tipped them off. Probably it was someone at the studio because they had our personal information and knew where to start looking. Anyway, that's the story."

'OK, Michael. I don't know what I'll be able to do since we know who sent the letter, and we now know why they wanted you out of the cast. But we don't know who the culprit was: the person or persons who did the research on you and the other people named in the letter. And this is really important because they had to take the time to check out everyone whose names weren't clearly of Jewish origin. Some job. Maybe some clerk at the German consulate did it, but somehow I don't think so. I think it had to be someone actually working within the industry or at the studio itself who could check personnel records and then tip off the Nazis. But I gotta go now. I'll see you at six. We can continue our conversation then."

It was just a couple minutes after 6:00 p.m. when Oakley walked into Lucy's El Adobe. As he was giving his name to the host, a young man at a booth near the front door jumped up and approached him.

"I guessed it was you, Mr. Webster, since you seemed to be looking for someone," he said as he shook Oakley's hand. "I'm Michael Trevalian. Thank you for coming. Come meet Laurie."

Based on appearances alone, there was no question in Oakley's mind about how Michael's grandmother was able to claim that her family wasn't Jewish. Both of them, Michael and Laurel, were twentyish, slim, blue-eyed, and very blond—Michael's hair cut stylishly short and Laurel's worn long in sexy, soft waves like the new style sported by such stars as Joan Crawford and Carole Lombard. *In fact*, Oakley thought cynically, *the pair could have been models for Mr. Hitler's pure-bred Aryan ideal—proving again how absurd the entire practice of racial profiling and its stepchild, bigotry, was.*

The visit with Michael evolved more or less as Oakley surmised it would. The actor repeated his chagrin over his grandmother's remarks, his disappointment in being cut from the film, and his hope that Oakley would be able to discover who took the time to research his genealogy and their motivation. Laurel's comment surprised him, though. After mentioning that she never made any effort to hide the fact that she was Jewish, she suggested it might have been her relationship with Michael that caused his being removed from the film.

"You might have something there," Oakley agreed. "Do you think anyone you dated before meeting Michael was jealous or angry enough to have executed such a complicated and time-consuming scheme to hurt him?"

"I can't think of anyone," Laurel replied. "Of course there is always an element of disappointment and sometimes anger when you break up with someone, but I've not done that more than a couple times, and none of the guys seemed angry—more like unhappy."

"What about you, Michael? Anyone you previously dated may have been angry when Laurel took her place?"

"Nope, can't think of anyone specific," he said. "A couple of them may have said something to my grandmother, and that may have been the way she found out that Laurel is Jewish. Beyond that, I don't have a clue."

"So let's eat," Oakley said, picking up the restaurant's extensive menu listing classic Italian dishes that had made the place famous within the film community. "I'm having the scaloppini. What do you kids want?" Oakley then realized again that the term *kids* wasn't particularly appropriate; he was, as he had earlier remarked to Michael, more or less a contemporary. "Oh," he added, "I wanted to ask you to be sure and call me if you remember anything else, especially any anti-Semitic or pro-German comments made by an ex-girlfriend or ex-boyfriend who might have then gone and tipped off the Nazis."

"That's fine," Laurel said. "And I guess we should ask something else... how much are you going to charge for helping us?"

Good girl, Oakley thought, realizing that Laurel was as modern in her outspokenness as contemporary women like Eleanor Roosevelt and Mae West were in their own but very different worlds. "Why not get that out of the way," he said. "Michael, how much did you make for your part in *The Road Back*? That's what you suggested using to finance this project."

"You're right. Three hundred."

"Well," Oakley explained, "as is fairly clear, I'm in this with you and Laurel less for making money than for helping to right what was clearly a completely immoral act on the part of the studio or somebody. Why don't we say fifteen bucks a day? That's about half my normal fee. And when I reach fifty bucks or so, we'll have a chat about going further."

"That seems fair," Michael said as their dinners arrived. "What do you think, Laurie?"

"Sound's reasonable to me. It's your money anyway," she said adding, "Mr. Webster, don't people in your business add expenses? What about that?"

"Yep, that's normal—messenger services, postage, telegrams, travel, that sort of thing. But I don't see much in the way of expenses being incurred for this case. Let's say a top of twenty dollars unless something major comes up, and then we'll talk."

"Sounds fine," Michael said. "And dinner is my treat."

"Nope," Oakley said. "How about getting things off on the right foot? Let's go Dutch tonight."

An hour or so later, as Michael walked into the courtyard of his apartment after parking his car, he noticed with some alarm that the light was on in his living room. Worse, after ascending the stairs to his place, he saw that the door to his apartment was ajar. *What on earth is going on?* he wondered as he pushed the door fully open and walked in. It was apparent from the noise being made that someone was in his kitchen. "What…" he started to say aloud when the apartment superintendent, Luis Baragon, walked into the living room. "What's going on?" Oakley demanded. "Why are you here?"

"I'm sorry to have surprised you, Mr. Webster," the super said, "but I got a telephone call from Mr. Duncan saying that he had seen someone going into your apartment this afternoon and tried to call you. I guess you weren't in your office, so he came over to see what was going on and found a man from the gas company in your kitchen. I knew about it because this gas man had come to me and asked for the key to your place. He said you had called this morning and said you had smelled gas. He said you had to leave for the office and to get the key from me. I guess I should have called you, but I didn't because this guy said he had to get into the apartment right away because a report of a gas leak is always treated as an emergency. So I let him in. I never heard anything more, so I assumed everything checked out OK. I guess Mr. Duncan called you because he didn't know what was going on."

"So why are you in my place now?" Oakley asked, his irritation clearly evident in the tone of his voice.

"Well, after dinner, I realized that the gas man would have had no way to lock up after he left, so I came over a little while ago to check things out and lock up."

"I guess," Oakley said, "you did what you thought was right, but please, Luis, never ever let anyone into my place unless you clear it directly with me.

And I'll bet the gas guy didn't show you any identification, did he? So the excuse of an emergency could have been a passport for anyone with a rented uniform to go into my apartment. And if that happens ever again, always stay with them when they are working in my place. The fact is, I never called the gas company about a leak, which you would have known right away if you had called me. So whoever it was got into my place with a lie, and I'd like to know why," Oakley said, anger slowly building. "Did anything look like it was out of place?" Oakley asked before realizing that the superintendent wouldn't know.

"Everything looked fine to me. Sorry," Luis apologized. "I did what I thought was right because it might have been an emergency that could have endangered everyone."

"And I appreciate that," Oakley said soothingly. "Just remember to demand identification in the future and stay with them," he repeated as he escorted Luis out the door, which he then closed and locked. *Now let's have a look-see around*, he thought.

At first glance, everything seemed in order. But then, Oakley noticed a couple of things that were clearly out of place, things that no legitimate gas company repairman would have had a reason to move. For one thing, the copy of *The ABC Murders*, which Oakley had finished, was no longer on the floor alongside his easy chair where he had dropped it; it was now on the side table next to the chair. The ashtray on the side table, which Oakley distinctly remembered emptying and cleaning that morning before leaving for the office, now contained a cigarette butt. These weren't accidental mistakes made by an intruder, Oakley realized. Both were changes in the way he had left the apartment which had to have been deliberately done by whoever had entered his place. The question was why? Did someone want to unnerve him by making it clear that he had access to him even in the presumed security of his home? Or was it a warning? But a warning about what? And from whom?

Well, Oakley thought, philosophically muttering the old maxim, "Time will tell." Nevertheless, before going into his bedroom he made certain that the kitchen door leading to the apartment's back stairs was also locked, and he blocked both doors by wedging dining chairs under the doorknobs. "Call me paranoid," he said aloud, wondering if he should also close and lock his windows. Because it was a warm night, he decided that would be carrying security a bit too far. He was on the second floor, and a locked window wouldn't stop anyone who was determined to enter the apartment. All they needed was a ladder.

Maybe, he thought an hour or so later as he put down *Death on the Nile,* Christie's newest book that he had started reading in bed, *I might invite Donny over tomorrow night. Strength in numbers in case someone tried to enter this place again. And I'm sort of longing for him, too.*

"Hey, Oakley," his neighbor Dave Duncan shouted as Oakley was walking to his car the next morning. "Got a minute?"

"Sure, what's up?"

"Is everything OK? I tried to call you yesterday when I saw some guy going into your apartment."

"I guess so," Oakley lied. "He said he was checking for a gas leak, and Luis let him in. Turned out there was nothing to worry about. Thanks anyway."

After the relative turmoil of the past few days, it was a relief for Oakley to enjoy a somewhat uneventful day at the office where he was able to focus on routine chores. There were few calls other than one that turned out to be the highlight of the day: a call from Docky Martin who, after inquiring how matters were, proceeding on the Billy Williams case and being reassured that all was moving along, told Oakley that he was sending a check for $250 just to keep things more or less up to date. *Good news,* Oakley thought as he thanked Docky, *I won't have to worry about the bank account on top of everything else.*

His nervousness of the previous afternoon's invasion of his privacy by a fake gas company employee had lessened somewhat but not his curiosity about it. A call to the gas company confirmed what he already suspected: that no call had been received from anyone claiming to be him, and no employee had been dispatched to his address. *Just another case to be solved,* he thought, but he still called Donny and suggested he pick up some food for dinner at his place and "bring your toothbrush." Donny was delighted.

Feeling more than a little overwhelmed by the demands suddenly put on him in the last couple of weeks, both professionally and personally, Oakley realized that the most important thing he had to do at this point was not to worry about solving any of his cases but to organize what was on his plate.

"Benny, why don't you take the afternoon off," he said. "I need to spend some time doing homework."

"OK, boss, but you sure I can't help?"

"No, thanks. Go home."

Oakley, who was by nature inclined to organize his life, strangely found it easier to prioritize responsibilities not in the order of their importance or urgency but chronologically. This of course ran contrary to all logic. It was like putting the purchase of more Lipton teabags—even if he had several left—ahead of paying an overdue electric bill despite Consolidated Edison's threat to turn off the power unless payment was made immediately. Perversely, it somehow worked for him—most of the time anyway.

So, at the top of his list was the first of the current cases that were piling up on his desk: the strange saga of Eva Sanderson's measles and subsequent loss of her child, which, of course, wasn't really a case in the traditional sense of the word. That would be a project that generated income for his agency. It was solely an issue based on Oakley's innate curiosity. Better businessmen wouldn't have wasted time on it; that, however, wasn't Oakley's way. In fact, by following his curiosity rather than the dollar in the past, he occasionally ended up actually making money and, often, because his motivation was clearly unselfish, making new friends and contacts.

But what came next in seeking an answer to the Sanderson enigma? Obviously, if there was any case at all, he had to assume that she was deliberately infected. Given that assumption, he had to find out who might know that she was not immune to the disease, that she was so emotionally fragile that any damage done to her unborn child might cause her to quit the film, and who and how that unknown someone would benefit. Probably the best place to start would be with people close to Sanderson to see if he could dig up more than Louella Parsons knew. Oakley decided to start with Eva's husband, Stan Damon; her secretary; and her agent, whoever that might be.

I guess the violin theft is more or less past history, Oakley thought. Even though Rachael Baumgarten now had Jack Benny's violin, we still don't know what happened to her own instrument, but because it was no longer as urgent a matter, he decided it could be kept on the back burner for now.

Next on the agenda would be what seemed to be Oakley's biggest case and the one most likely to bring him an income commensurate with the time necessary to hopefully solve it: the Billy Williams frame-up. For indeed he knew that it was a frame-up; if for no other reason, the conversation with Carl Andrews had proven that. So finding who benefitted most by his being fired from Metro was probably the best path to finding out who framed the actor. This would have been—on the surface anyway—Ron O'Bannon who was cast to replace Billy in *Mickey O'Rourke Grows Up*, maybe the producer of the movie as well, whoever that might be.

"I wonder who I know might know Ron O'Bannon?" Oakley asked himself aloud. He knew it would certainly be more effective, as it always was in Hollywood, to reach him through friends instead of through the smoke screen that most studio publicity departments erected unless it concerned the news they manufactured themselves. *And what's this story Louella told about O'Bannon's interest in decorating? Is he a member of the choir?* Oakley wondered. *And because it appears being openly queer was the reason that Billy was finally fired, if O'Bannon was also gay, why were L. B. Mayer's rules different for him? For the hell of it, maybe I should call Howard Strickling, the head of Metro's publicity department.* "I won't get anywhere," Oakley said aloud," but he might squirm a little, and he might accidently spill something helpful."

And Mike Trevalian? This is getting to be weird, Oakley thought. *We'll know more about that soon.*

And then there is this strange coincidence, if it is a coincidence, with John Wayne coming down with the measles, he thought. Because it would probably be impossible to reach John Wayne by storming the privacy walls normally erected by the Paramount publicity department, this called for a conversation with the folks at Republic, Oakley decided. *Enough of list making,* Oakley thought and reached for his telephone.

Chapter 10

Republic Pictures, as everyone in Hollywood knew, was ruled with an iron fist by a cunning, cigar-chomping, five-foot-four-inch former tobacco salesman named Herbert Yates, who founded it in 1935 by merging several Poverty Row studios—the small, often fly-by-night operations that were clustered on Sunset Boulevard near Gower Street. Most of Hollywood also felt that Republic remained little more than a cheap, Poverty Row studio but bigger and in a new location. As Billy Williams had reminded him, many people in Hollywood called it Repulsive Pictures.

Westerns and serials were Republic's early stock in trade (the original *Three Musketeers* series was made by Mascot Pictures which became part of Republic when it was formed). And it was in eight of those early Westerns that a young cowboy actor began his climb to fame as one of the most popular stars in Hollywood: the now measles-struck John Wayne.

After looking up Republic's number in the telephone book, Oakley dialed the studio's number and asked the operator to speak with Mrs. Yates. When, as expected, he was asked who he was and why he was calling, Oakley, who knew well that as name-dropping was a basic element of Hollywood's social communication, he might as well take a chance that would resonate with Petra Yates, the wife of the studio's boss. "My name is Oakley Webster," he said. "Michelle Ryder suggested I speak with Mrs. Yates about a matter of mutual interest."

"Oh yes, sir, just a minute. I'll see if I can find her for you."

It seemed only moments before the Brooklyn accent of Petra Yates boomed in his ear. "Mr. Webster?" she asked. "I don't think we've ever met. But you say my dear, dear friend Michelle Ryder asked you to call me?"

"Yes, Mrs. Yates. I'm working on a separate project with Mrs. Ryder, and she thought you could be helpful in my contacting John Wayne. It's always such a nightmare dealing with the PR people at the big studios, and she felt that you knew him better anyway."

"Yep, I know what you mean by them big studios. We try and maintain a family atmosphere around here. Why, two of our kids are workin' here now."

"That's wonderful," Oakley said, wondering if he was laying it on too thickly before realizing nothing he said would probably seem outrageous to Petra Yates. So he might as well drop another name. "Louella—"

"Ohhhh, dear Louella," Petra Yates interrupted, "I adore her!"

"So do we all," Oakley said coolly. "As I was saying, dear Louella told me that Mr. Wayne had come down with the measles, which she understands is very dangerous for an adult, and she wanted to know how he was getting along, And Michelle is worried sick about him. So she wanted me to ask you for his telephone number or to call him and ask him to call me."

"So why didn't Louella call me herself?" Yates snapped, her voice sounding very different—more like Oakley imagined her husband would sound in a contract negotiation.

Oakley thought for a moment and figured that he was in so deep now that a little more lying couldn't do any harm. "Well," he said soothingly, "Louella has her daily column to write and her radio show to prepare, and Michelle, being a great friend of Eva Sanderson, as you certainly know, has been spending all her spare time with her since her tragic loss. So they asked me to help out and call you."

"Tragic, tragic," Petra Yates chimed in. "I unnerstand. Lemme get his number for you. Lois!" she screeched, practically breaking Oakley's eardrum. "Gimme Johnny Wayne's telephone number! Here it is, Mr. Webster," she said, giving him the number.

Oakley thanked Petra Yates, who added, "Be sure to give Louella, Eva, and Michelle all my love."

"Only in Hollywood," he said to himself with a wry smile as he hung up.

By the time Oakley got home and parked his car, Donny, carrying a large bag, was already waiting at the door of his apartment.

"Let me show you what I brought," Donny said happily, as he started to empty out the bag on Oakley's dining table. "First and foremost," Donny announced, "a bottle of Old Granpappy since I wasn't sure if you had any. Thought we'd switch from Manhattans to Old Fashioneds tonight. And I brought along some oranges and a bottle of maraschino cherries from Ralph's market down the street for making them.

"And before I went to Ralph's, I drove down to Jee Gong Low in Chinatown and had them make up a special dinner for us including their sui gow, egg rolls, rice, and all the trimmings. I even remembered some soy sauce and fortune cookies."

"All I can say is 'Wow!'" Oakley exclaimed. "You even remembered the cigarettes."

"You bet. You goin' to make the Old Fashioneds, or am I?"

"You do the honors. You're the drink expert. Bar glasses are in the cabinet under the radio, but you know that by now anyway. While you're doing that, why not turn on the radio and see if you can find a little music?"

After taking a moment or two for the tubes to warm up, the first sound from the radio was a rebroadcast of a big band performance by Guy Lombardo and his Royal Canadians, one of the most popular bands in the country. And they were playing their hit from several years before, "Love Me or Leave Me." *Perfect for the mood of the evening*, Oakley thought. "They say this is the 'sweetest music this side of heaven,'" he said to Donny, grabbing his hand. "Come here. Not many places where we can dance together anymore, so let's make this our own Cocoanut Grove for a while."

"You know, I could get used to this—and you," Donny said as the pair embraced and moved to the seductive swing music. "I always tune into Lombardo's New Year's Eve broadcast," he said. "And I have dozens of his records, even this song with his brother, Carmen, singing, which I've played until the groves are worn out. How did you know?"

"I had nothing to do with it." Oakley smiled. "You turned on the radio. Must have been fate, just like our meeting at the beach a couple weeks ago. And I'm not about to fight with fate." He laughed as the pair danced slowly into the evening as the band segued into another of their hits, "You Made Me Love You," followed by the Lombardo band's famous song "Street of Dreams."

"Now, about those drinks?" Oakley asked.

Back to business, Oakley thought the next morning as he was finishing his second cup of coffee. Donny had left, but only after he had convinced Oakley that they should get together that evening and hopefully spend the weekend together. Normally, this would be a bit too much togetherness for Oakley, but still nervous over the break-in of his apartment, he found it somehow comforting that he wouldn't be alone. This led to a resolution to try and find out who had invaded his privacy in the guise of a gas company employee. But as experienced as he was, he couldn't figure out how to start unless he would involve criminal investigators who could, perhaps, begin tracing the intruder through fingerprints. But then, Oakley realized, Donny and I have probably already compromised that possibility by thoughtlessly rummaging throughout the kitchen and the rest of the apartment without any thought of preserving evidence. So bringing in the big guns—effectively making him the victim in a criminal investigation instead of the person who is hired to solve crimes against others—would clearly complicate his own investigations. "Oh well," Oakley sighed as he was dressing, "whoever it was wouldn't have moved things around as a warning if they wanted to attack me. Why bother? But I need to pay better attention," he resolved, falling back on another ancient proverb: Forewarned is forearmed.

"Benny," he said after arriving at his office, "I've decided that I'm going to play my first telephone call of the day the Hollywood way. I want you to call John Wayne at this number," he said, handing him the note from the previous day's conversation with Petra Yates. "Pretend to be by assistant, which you are anyway."

"So whatcha want me to say?"

"Just call, and when someone answers, it will be Wayne's assistant," Oakley speculated. "Just say 'Oakley Webster calling at the suggestion of

Mrs. Harold Yates,' and I'll bet that will do the job. The idea is to get John Wayne on the telephone; he is getting to be such a big star that like most of them, probably thinks that being difficult to reach means that they are important. Same thinking that causes the studio publicity departments to be such a pain in the ass to deal with. All it really is is a way to regulate traffic; the more popular you are, the more people want to reach you. I doubt this is true of Mr. Wayne who, based on what I know or have read about him, seems to be a straight shooter. But you never know about the people around stars who sometimes think they are as important. So the answer is to drop a name as big as theirs or bigger. Anyway, let's try it."

It worked out exactly as Oakley had guessed. Within moments, John Wayne, his already-famous drawl unmistakable, was on the telephone. "Mr. Webster, I think your man said? Do I know you?"

"No, Mr. Wayne, you don't. I'm a private investigator looking into the matter of the Eva Sanderson tragedy, and Louella Parsons told me that you had come down with a case of the measles, which forced the suspension of production on *Born to the West*. It seemed odd to me that so soon after Miss Sanderson contracted the disease that you would then come down with it."

"Well, you'd be right," Wayne said as Oakley crossed his fingers hoping the star wouldn't ask who he was working for. "You said Louella told you? I wonder out how she knew?"

"It's my impression that Miss Parsons knows everything that's going on in Hollywood, even before the people it is happening to know it. You know they say that she knows when a star is pregnant even before the future mother does."

"I hadn't heard that." Wayne laughed. "Sure sounds like our Lolly, though."

"So about your catching measles. It's true then?"

"It's true, and lemme tell you, it ain't somethin' that you want to catch as an adult, an' thank God I'm just about over them…no longer infectious anyway. I heard that's why Miss Sanderson lost her baby because of measles. I dunno why I never contracted it when I was a kid…Maybe it was the heat when we lived in the desert. And my pop was a druggist, so maybe he gave me somethin' that made me immune. I got no answer for you."

"So, Mr. Wayne, do you have any idea of how you might have been exposed? Were you around children?"

"I've been tryin' to figure out just that, too, and I can't. I've only been at the studio, and there aren't no kids in the movie, and no one in the movie caught 'em either. And no one at Paramount that I can figure. Jus' me. It's a mystery."

"Well, indeed it is a mystery, just like Miss Sanderson's case. No one in her movie, or at Metro, or anywhere around her caught them, not even her husband, but then I think he had them when he was a child. Some people have speculated that she was deliberately infected with the disease."

"What? Can you do that?" Wayne asked.

"I really don't know, Mr. Wayne. Maybe, but no one can figure out how. Or how to even get the germ or whatever it is that can be used to infect a person. Maybe it will stay just a mystery. I would appreciate your thoughts about something else, though. Pardon me for asking, but do you think there is anyone, any actor, who could profit by your contracting the disease? Someone who might step into your role in *Born to the West* if you were going to be out for so long that Paramount might feel some financial pressure and need to move ahead with someone else in the part?"

"I don't mind answering that because it also occurred to me," Wayne said. "What I'm gonna say may sound egotistical, but there isn't anyone like me who could step into the role. Who they gonna ask? Tom Mix is runnin' a Western circus now. Buck Jones's career is over the hill. Poor Ken Maynard is a drunk. Tim McCoy is making ten grand a week at Ringling. Making movies has always been a sideline for Hoot Gibson; he's really a rodeo rider. Bill Cody, who I personally like—we both started on Poverty Row—made the worst Western you ever saw which sorta finished him."

"What was that?" Oakley interrupted.

"A real stinker called *The Border Menace*. But lemme continue," Wayne said. "Bill Boyd is too identified as Hopalong Cassidy. Gene Autry is too young and who wants a singin' cowboy in a real Western anyway? And Leonard Slye? He may have rebranded himself as Roy Rogers a year or so ago, but he's just another damn singin' cowboy posin' on a white horse. These days,

Paramount isn't exactly short on money either. Mae West's sexy movies that snuck in before this goddam code took effect in '34 bailed them out of their financial troubles. So there ya are. That's why they'll hafta wait for me—on this movie anyway."

"Got it! Thank you, Mr. Wayne," Oakley said. "Please let me know if you hear anything more, and I'll do the same."

"Gotcha."

Oakley hung up the telephone, pleased that he had reached the actor but also uncertain if he had really learned anything. John Wayne had indeed caught the measles, but that wasn't news. Like Eva Sanderson, the Western star had no idea how he might have caught the disease. So, Oakley admitted to himself, there seemed little reason to suspect foul play, certainly not in the case of John Wayne because there wasn't a problem with postponing the film. The fact that two prominent stars contracted a childhood disease within a few weeks of each other may have been only a coincidence.

So why was he still uncomfortable with it? Because it was simply too much of a coincidence.

It wasn't as if Eva Sanderson and John Wayne had caught the flu or even broken a leg about the same time; that would have been a coincidence. But for two prominent stars to be forced out of major film roles at more or less the same time because they had each contracted a childhood disease to which most people were immune kept ringing Oakley's alarm bells. And it wasn't just due to his innate cynicism; the main reason was simply that he had encountered too many hidden agendas in his career not to suspect deliberate action the moment he read about Eva Sanderson's odd illness and its sad outcome. And suddenly, John Wayne came down with the same disease.

As Oakley picked up the telephone to finally return the call from Joe Valentine, a racket erupted at the front door of his office. "Mr. Oakley? Mr. Oakley?" a woman's husky, highly accented voice commanded as she caromed through the door. "Is this Mr. Oakley's office?"

"Yes, ma'am. It's the office of Mr. Oakley Webster," Benny said, emphasizing Oakley's last name.

"I've got to see him!" she commanded and then spotted Oakley seated at his desk. "That can't be you!" she exclaimed. "You're nothing but a kid!"

"'Fraid it is me." He smiled. "I'm Oakley Webster. What can I do for you?"

"You don't look like you're old enough to buy a drink. And Michelle tells me you're the best PI in town?"

"I don't know about that," Oakley said soothingly. "But it's flattering to hear that Michelle—I'm assuming you mean Michelle Ryder with whom I'm working on a case—said that. Please have a seat," he said, indicating the chair next to his desk. "And tell me what I can do for you. And you are?" he asked as she seated herself.

"My name is Maria Karinopolis," she said. "And Michelle said I should see you because of something terrible that happened to my husband, Ari—that's short for Aristotle—and the talent agency he founded fifteen years ago."

"So…"

"It's called the Corinthian Talent Agency; everyone in Hollywood calls us simply CTA. After many years, we had a going business representing the great, the semigreat, and the simply grateful—like most management agencies in Hollywood.

"Ari started the company on a shoestring, and for years, I was his only employee—secretary, Girl Friday, even the janitor when he ran it from our house on Selma Avenue. But he worked hard and got results for his clients. He launched the careers of some of the biggest stars of the silent era and now the sound era: Louise Brooks, for one. We represented her from the day she arrived in Hollywood from a Broadway chorus line. Claudette Colbert was another he helped start, and Jack Warner, who has been a friend of Ari's for years, got my husband together with Al Jolson when Jack cast him in the role that made him famous, *The Jazz Singer*, and we got him the films he made after that like *The Singing Fool*. Doug Fairbanks was a star long before CTA represented him, but Ari helped him make the transition into talkies, getting him the starring role in the part-talkie *Mr. Robinson Crusoe*. And many more. We've been around."

"Impressive," Oakley acknowledged. "So what brings you here today so upset about something?"

"Well, Ari isn't getting any younger. So about a year ago, he brought in a person who was once an assistant to Howard Strickling, you know, the boss of Metro's publicity department. His name is Henry Graber, but a better name would be Grabber," she said angrily. "After learning the ropes from us, he recently quit and started his own talent agency, and took a couple of our most important clients with him—our bread-and-butter clients, the bastard."

"Unfortunately, that's not a new story in Hollywood, but that doesn't mean it is any less painful," Oakley said consolingly.

"And the latest is the worst," she said. "A few months ago, we signed a very pretty brunette named Carole Martin. She was from Colorado and because he knew her family from when he was raised in Denver, Doug Fairbanks suggested we take a look at her. She seemed to be a bit of a light-weight in the acting department and a little too serious for her own good, but Ari saw some possibilities. So we decided to take a chance on her and bring her along slowly so she could learn as she went and build a reputation. Well, she was one of our clients that Henry 'Grabber' stole when he left. I'm told he convinced her that Ari's plan was all wrong and that she was talented enough and ready to go for the brass ring, and she did. She probably slept with God knows how many people, but God damn it, it worked. It hasn't been announced yet, but she's the person who's been picked to replace Eva Sanderson in *The Matrimaniac!*"

"You're kidding," Oakley exclaimed, again in awe of yet another coincidence to come his way.

"And," Maria snarled, "that was after Mr. Grabber changed her name to Viola Pearl, made up a new biography, and erased any reference to her representation by CTA and Ari!"

"So what can I do for you and Ari?" Oakley asked.

"I want you to destroy him!" she shouted. "I want you to ruin Henry Graber after what he did to my Ari and our business."

"Well, Mrs. Karinopolis," Oakley said, "destroying people isn't my business. But I'll tell you what, I'll do what I can to find out all I can about Henry Graber—where he's from, his past actions, everything people know about him—and give it to you. Whatever use you make of anything I may discover is your business. Does that work for you?"

"Well," she said, "it's not as direct as putting a chunk of lead in him, as much as I'd like to do that along with a little torture on the rack before I shot him, but I guess that's the only thing to do. But I want you to discover something that I can use to destroy him, to ruin him in Hollywood forever."

"I'll do my best," Oakley said as she gathered up her purse and left.

"Whew," Benny exclaimed, "that was certainly one for the books."

"I guess it goes with the territory," Oakley said, reaching again for the telephone to try making his call to Joe Valentine. "But mum's the word, as always."

"'Course, boss," Benny said as he picked up a call on the second line. "Hey, Oakey, you may want to take this call first—Michelle Ryder."

Damn it, Oakley thought to himself, flattered that the superstar would be calling him but still frustrated by being interrupted every time he tried to return Joe's call.

"Hello, Miss Ryder," he said cheerily as he switched telephone lines.

"Hello, Mr. Webster." "I know from Docky where you are on Billy's case, but as I seem to be the person in the middle, don't you think it might be valuable for us to get together and trade information?"

"Good idea, Miss Ryder," Oakley said, mentally kicking himself for not taking the lead by meeting with the players in what seemed to be his biggest case instead of assuming they could work together by simply exchanging telephone calls. "What would work for you? By the way, I was visited by Maria Karinopolis who you sent my way. Many thanks."

"You're welcome. She's a bit emotional, but I'm sure you've encountered emotional people before in your profession. Back to getting together. How about tea—well, let's be honest about it, drinks—this afternoon. Maybe the bar at the Beverly Hills Hotel?"

No way, Oakley thought. *It will take me an hour to get there through rush-hour traffic.* "I'm all the way downtown," he said. "Anything closer that would work for you?"

"Oh, I didn't know where your office was. Then how about the Tea Room at Bullocks Wilshire?" she suggested. "I'm sure they could mix up a Sidecar for me and whatever you like for you. At, say, five thirty?"

"Perfect. See you then," he said. "You won't know me, but I won't have any trouble recognizing you." *And*, he thought happily, *it's virtually next door to Donny's place at the Bryson Apartments...for later.*

Oakley, like most Angelenos, considered Bullocks Wilshire to the most famous department store in Los Angeles, probably in America, both because of its design and its revolutionary rethinking of a department store. And although he had previously shopped there a couple of times, like most people, much of what knew about the store, he learned from the publicity its PR department relentlessly churned out. It was hardly possible for a movie star—or even a movie hopeful—to walk into the place without an item appearing in a *Hollywood Reporter* or *Variety* gossip column the next morning.

Opened in 1929, the copper-accented architectural masterpiece resembled an art deco church with a flashing light at the top of its tower that spelled out "Hollywood" in Morse code, which could be seen for miles. The building had been deliberately designed to cater to the new automobile culture; shoppers (called "guests") drove through wrought iron gates into a porte cochere decorated with a fresco titled *The Spirit of Transportation*, where valets took and parked their cars. Mae West, a frequent customer, took the store's design concept to heart by refusing to get out of her car (double-parked in the porte cochere) and doing her shopping from its back seat, thus forcing salesgirls to scurry back and forth with samples of lingerie, dresses and furs for her to choose from.

This was not as easy as it sounds, as the store was one of the first to organize its inventory in specific boutiques strewn throughout several floors. Among them were the first floor's mirrored Hall of Perfume; the Louis XVI room where designer dresses were modeled by live models; salons devoted exclusively to Coco Chanel and Irene Lentz's designs (the future MGM costume designer's creations sold for a staggering $400 to $700); a "Doggery" for canine accessories; and the city's first leisurewear merchandise sold in the Playdeck.

The crown jewel of the store was the Tea Room on the fifth floor, decorated in soothing tones of pale green, salmon, gray, and blue. The food was as soothing, too. None of the heavy, calorie-laden dishes of the era were to be found on the menu; instead, there were light sandwiches, salads, and their signature Cantonese chicken salad with strawberry dressing.

Besides Los Angeles socialites, the Tea Room was popular with figure-conscious stars like Gloria Swanson, Norma Shearer, Clark Gable, Carole Lombard, and even John Wayne, all of whom often ordered from a "stream-line menu," which included a vegetable platter of grilled tomatoes, mushrooms, string beans, asparagus, squash, and celery. On Tuesdays, for $1.25, there was a fashion luncheon where ladies could nibble healthful goodies while viewing models wearing the latest fashions. For male shoppers, there was an adjoining, wood-paneled suite where they could enjoy cocktails while bow tie–wearing salesmen provided gift suggestions, a service Oakley had previously taken advantage of while Christmas shopping.

Chapter 11

It was just 5:30 p.m. when Oakley drove his blue Ford under the porte cochere, handed it off to the valet, entered the store, and walked across the rich travertine floor to the stainless steel-and-copper-sheathed elevators. Exiting on the fifth floor, he immediately spotted Michelle Ryder seated in the waiting area outside the main dining area, surrounded by an eager, autograph-seeking crowd of fans. After waving to her and pointing to himself, he walked over to Humberto Lara, the Tea Room's longtime maître d'. After nodding toward the crowd surrounding the actress, Oakley suggested that because he and Michelle Ryder were there for a business meeting as well as the hospitality of the restaurant, it might be easier on everyone if they could be accommodated in one of the private dining rooms. Lara immediately extricated the actress from her admirers and escorted the pair to the unoccupied Salle Moderne, the restaurant's main private room.

"Could you ask someone to bring me a Sidecar," the actress asked the waitress who had followed them. "Actually, better bring along two. I'm getting thirsty just from looking at the decoration," the actress sassed, nodding at the paintings of desert animals in their arid habitat that adorned the room's walls. "And for my friend here," she said, indicating Oakley, "bring him whatever he wants."

"A Martini, very dry," Oakley said, "straight up with a twist."

"Two of them for him, too."

As mesmerized by her presence as any fan, Oakley loved her directness, just like his late idol Jean Harlow and Billy Williams's close friend Joan

Crawford. But Michelle Ryder's openness wasn't the secret for her success nor, entirely, was her acting, as accomplished as it was. It was clear to Oakley that whether she could act or not, she would have become as famous from her looks, but more particularly, from her magnetic presence.

Slim and of medium height, Ryder seemed to move on screen—and as he now saw, also in real life—just as Rudolph Valentino did a decade and a half before: like a cat always ready to pounce. Hers was a taut, coiled presence that translated instantly to film. Combined with her stunning, faintly Italian looks and a sensual voice that resembled aural honey, even when she was secondary to the action in a scene, audiences couldn't take their eyes off her.

She also was quite well aware of the way she affected people and immediately sensed Oakley's awkward shyness in her presence. "Hey, Oakley—may I call you that?" She smiled, making an effort to help him relax. "Since we have this entire fucking room to ourselves, we might as well be less formal, right? Come on, big boy, I'm just a girl from the Kansas sticks."

Her profanity, as she intended it, did the trick. "Why not?" he asked. "I guess that makes us neighbors. I'm from Missouri."

"So, Louella and Docky tell me that you're on top of the Billy Williams mess," she said, deciding that getting directly to the point would also help reduce any shyness on his part by raising the conversation from the personal to the professional level. "'Course he was stupid to pick up that sailor and play right into Mayer's hands. But he can't change that now. Have any luck with tracking all that down?"

Oakley explained how he had found the sailor, Carl Andrews, and described his conversations with both him and Billy Williams, which made it clear that the episode was a deliberate frame-up. "And now," he added, "all I have to do is find out who rigged it."

"Well, at least any doubt about it being a frame-up is behind us. That's a start," Michelle said as a waitress entered bearing their drinks, all four of them.

"I don't see how it could have been anything else. The fact that the person who suggested Andrews call Billy also asked him to report in on his success is a clear giveaway. Poor Carl, he's young and apparently pretty naïve and didn't see that he was just a pawn in a bigger game," Oakley said.

"And our problem—your problem—is finding out who is playing the game."

"Actually, it's more than that," Oakley added. "The problem is not just to find out who set this up, but what the game itself is. There had to be a reason for someone to go to all this trouble, but God knows, I can't figure out what it is—not yet anyway. It sure would have helped if sailor boy Andrews had written down that phone number. But it is what it is. I'm sure we'll find the answers soon."

"And that's why we hired you," the actress said. "How's your drink?"

As they visited, Oakley reminded himself that as it had been a mistake not to meet with Michelle Ryder earlier on the Billy Williams case, he had also erred in not digging more deeply into the Eva Sanderson mystery sooner. Obviously, a conversation with Eva herself was out of the question as it could be taken for granted that she would still be too upset to think objectively about how she may have contracted measles or, if it were a deliberate act, who might have done it and why. So it was time for a visit with her husband, Stan Damon.

As soon as Oakley escorted Michelle Ryder to the elevator, he found a pay telephone and called Donny. He was, of course, elated that Oakley was in the neighborhood and could come right over. "I don't have much in the icebox," Donny said happily, "but there are the remains of a roast chicken and some succotash and of course an Old Fashioned to wash it down with."

"Sounds great," Oakley said. "But I'd better skip the drink because I'm feeling what I just had on an empty stomach. Well…maybe a Martini so then I won't be mixing drinks. But I do need to make a couple telephone calls if that's OK with you."

"Of course, lover. I'm getting used to that. And I might even find us a little Guy Lombardo again."

While waiting for his car to be extricated by the store's valet and then driving the three blocks to Donny's apartment, Oakley tried to figure out the best way to approach Damon. It had to be gently done, that was clear, and it had to be done in such a way that Eva's husband would feel comfortable talking with him about such a personal tragedy. It was, after all, his child, too, that Eva lost. So Oakley decided to seek the advice of a person who, in only a few minutes in his office, had impressed him as being thoroughly ethical and a straight shooter—both rare commodities in Hollywood. He would call Maria Karinopolis.

"What is it, kid?" she asked after answering the telephone when Oakley called her following the exchange of dutiful boyfriend greetings with Donny.

"I need some information, Mrs. Karinopolis," he said. "I need to talk to Stan Damon, and since he doesn't know me from Adam, I need someone to open the door with him in a way that won't scare him off. Do you have any idea who represents him? I think that would be the best place to start."

"Do I have any idea?" she exclaimed. "Maybe I wasn't clear about why I was so angry about Grabber stealing Carole Martin from us. Didn't I explain that both Eva Sanderson and Stan are clients of ours?"

"I'm so sorry," Oakley said. "I had no idea."

"No hard feelings, honey. And call me Maria, please. Since we consider our clients as part of our own family, Eva's loss of their child was devastating to Ari and me—not as devastating as it was to Eva and Stan but terrible. We love them both. Which is part of the reason we're so angry with Grabber. We pride ourselves in our professionalism, and our clients have always respected that fact and have hardly ever gone against our judgment. That is until Grabber sweet-talked Carole into leaving the agency. We never would have put her up for Eva's role because there is no way she's going to be able to fill her shoes, but that's for Mr. Mayer and his production crew for the *Maniac* movie to find out for themselves. And of course, Carole—I mean Viola now. She's going to drive them crazy. She may be as pretty as Connie Talmadge who played the part of Marna Lewis in the original *Matrimaniac*, but Dutch—a lot of people hereabouts still call Connie by her nickname—had a sense of comic timing, which neither Ari nor I discovered in Miss Martin. People said Connie sparkled. Carole barely flickers. So I don't see how the hell Carole can do it. So what do you need to talk with Stan about?"

Oakley explained how he had been puzzled by Eva Sanderson's tragic bout with measles from the moment he learned of it and was determined to discover the truth. He added that there was no client involved, no reason to be doing this except for his experience-driven suspicion that such a thing could rarely happen to someone unless there was some sort of deliberate, malicious action behind it. He was determined to discover what that was and how it was accomplished.

"I guess that puts you on the side of the angels," Maria said, "at least on our side anyway. Let me talk with Stan and explain to him what you're about. I think he'll do it mostly because you have no ulterior, financial motive, like moving in a client to replace Eva. I also think he'd feel more comfortable with getting together if I were to sit in on the conversation since you're a complete stranger. Would that be OK?"

"Of course," Oakley agreed. "That way, I wouldn't need to repeat everything that took place to you later."

Within an hour, Maria called him back, and it was agreed that they would all meet in his office the next morning.

"Saturday," Oakley complained with a smile after hanging up. "There goes another beach day."

"What was that about the beach?" Donny asked. "Did you say something about the beach? It's time for another Charles Atlas tune-up for me. And you're looking a bit pale, too," he said, handing Oakley his drink. "Despite your partying with a superstar at Bullocks Wilshire, you seem sober as a judge. I went out and splurged on some gin for you so you can damn well drink this." He laughed. "I even bought some of your darn Chesterfields. You need to come off the PI stuff now."

"OK, OK." Oakley laughed. "Just doing my job. Actually, I'm not really doing my job; I'm bird-dogging a scent I can't get out of my nose. On my own, no client, nothing but a conviction that something bad was done to some nice people. And I want to find out why."

"Tell me all about it," Donny said, sitting down on the sofa next to him. "How's your drink?"

The next morning, following a hurried trip to his apartment to freshen up and get clean clothes, Oakley arrived at the Bradley Building just as Maria Karinopolis and a man he assumed was Stan Damon entered from the opposite end of the building's lobby. After introductions, Oakley, as had many observers of the phenomenon of movie stardom had done before him, was struck by how short most leading men were. True, Stan Damon was not as small as such male silent film stars as Ramon Novarro or Charlie Chaplin, but he was still short compared even the swashbuckling he-man himself, Doug Fairbanks (five-eight on a good day), whose role Stan was slated to reprise.

After Oakley seated the pair in his office, he explained why he suspected foul play was involved in Eva's tragedy, and why he was determined to get to the root of it. The explanation seemed to relax Stan sufficiently for Oakley to start digging. And he figured he might as well start with the tough stuff.

"I have heard, Mr. Damon, that some people, perhaps even your wife, suspect that you might have brought the infection in your home, and that you may have picked it up when you were doing the voice-over work at Disney."

"Absolutely not!" Damon shouted, "I never—"

"Stan, relax. He's only trying to get to the facts," Maria soothed.

"OK, " Damon said. "Sorry. You're right. Eva figured out that Disney was the most likely place for it to be picked up since there were a lot of people around me there, and she was virtually housebound and rarely saw anybody except family and our staff. So there is no proof that I wasn't the carrier—is that the term? Other than the fact that no one else at the entire Disney studio contracted the disease."

"Just like Metro, where no one but your wife contracted measles," Oakley observed, "so she couldn't have picked it up when she was there for a couple *Matrimaniac* meetings."

"Right," Damon agreed.

"Unless she was deliberately infected somewhere," Oakley interrupted. "And I think it was done by someone when she was at Metro for meetings. It's the only place that makes sense to me."

"So who do you think that it was who did the deed?" Damon asked. "And why the hell would anybody do something like that? And where would they get the measles germs or whatever they needed to infect her? And how would they do it?"

"Which are all questions that I'm trying to figure out," Oakley said. "Did she have any enemies that you know of, any people who were so threatened or angry or jealous about her getting the lead in *The Matrimaniac* that they would go to such an extreme?"

"Well, no one can really be trusted in Hollywood," Damon said, echoing the opinion Louella Parsons had earlier expressed to Oakley. "Except Maria and Ari, of course," he quickly added.

"Of course!" Oakley and Maria echoed in tandem.

"Eva doesn't have any real enemies…like Louella who hates all the other Hollywood columnists whether they are real competition or not, or Joan Crawford who despises Bette Davis," Maria chimed in. "At least nobody that I know of that you could describe as an 'enemy,'" Maria added. "And of course there is the long-running feud between Olivia de Havilland and her sister Joan Fontaine, but that is more of a sibling rivalry."

"How about you, Mr. Damon?" Oakley asked gently. "Anyone you know of who would want to harm to you so badly they'd do this?"

"I don't dislike anyone, and no one I know of dislikes me," Stan said, contradicting the opinion he had shared only moments before. "So I don't see why anyone would do this to her, to us."

Stan has a problem, Oakley was beginning to realize. Doug Fairbanks, whose old role Stan was stepping into, possessed an innate comedic sense shown in the thirty movies—among them *The Matrimaniac*—that he made before moving into the swashbuckler genre that would make him world-famous with the 1920s *The Mark of Zorro*. To make his new screen persona work, he took his talent for comedy along with him; Douglas Fairbanks's genius was to realize that his new, over-the-top macho characters would have seemed ludicrous even to the least sophisticated audiences unless they were also likable. And the best way of being likable was for the audiences to know that he wasn't taking all the daring-do action seriously, and he was letting the audience in on the fact that it was all a big joke.

It was becoming clear to Oakley that Stan, unlike Fairbanks, took himself much too seriously, although, he admitted, with the loss of his child, he had a good reason to seem humorless. Nevertheless, although he was no film critic, Oakley simply could not see Stan, even after he mended emotionally, playing a lighthearted character in a comedy. *I wonder of Maria and Ari realize this?* he thought. But with Stan sitting not ten feet from him, this wasn't the time or place to ask Maria.

"So, Mr. Damon," Oakley asked, more to keep what seemed to be an aimless conversation going than to find out anything significant, "are you planning to remain in the role."

"Of course he is," Maria said. "Why wouldn't he?"

"Well," Oakley said carefully, "it doesn't seem to me that anyone like Stan would be particularly comfortable playing opposite a person—a nontalent according to you—who replaced his wife in a plum role."

"So much you know about actors!" Maria exclaimed, actually rising several inches out of her chair. "A professional can act anywhere with anyone. And Stan is a professional!"

"I never meant to infer that he wasn't," Oakley said. "But you have to admit that this situation is different than casting, say, Bette Davis and Joan Crawford in a film together, who won't even speak to each other. Mr. Damon has no reason to hate or even dislike Carole, I mean Viola Pearl. It's not the actor which I suspect may be painful; it's the situation."

"I spoke with Eva about this," Damon interjected. "And she said it would be all right with her if I stayed in the film. I haven't decided if I want to, though."

"Stan!" Maria interrupted. "The last time we spoke about this you said you were going to go ahead with it. What's changed?"

"Nothing, Maria. Nothing other than that I've had time to think about it ever since Parsons predicted in her column that I'd drop out of the movie both because being around the production day after day would be a constant reminder of what happened and my responsibility to care for Eva as she recovers. So I'm not sure it would be a good idea."

I'll bet, Oakley thought, *that was Lolly's way of warning Stan to get out of a film in which the public and critics were likely to eat him alive when his performance was inevitably compared with that of the young Doug Fairbanks in the same role. And she was also telling him how to do it in a manner that everyone would respect.* The problem, Oakley knew, was how to tell Stan what it was that Parsons was actually suggesting he do.

"You, and I, and Ari," Maria said firmly to Stan, "need to have a conversation about any decision to leave the movie."

"I think that's enough for now," Oakley said as he stood, interrupting what had suddenly become a tense moment between Maria and her client, "and thanks for coming all the way downtown on a Saturday morning. Mr. Damon, and Maria, of course, if you have any new ideas about what might have been behind this tragedy, please call me right away," he added, handing his business card to both of them. "And, of course, I'll do the same. Stan— uh, Mr. Damon—I can always reach you through CTA, right?"

"Of course." Maria nodded.

"Call me Stan," the actor said, seeming to relax a bit. "And you can call me directly at any time. Here, I'll write my home number on your desk calendar. Thanks for your time."

"Bye, Oakley," Maria said. As they left, she quietly muttered, "Stan, don't ever give out your and Eva's number, certainly not to private eyes and people like that. That's what Ari and I are here for!"

Well, Oakley thought, *So now I'm a 'people like that?' I didn't think Maria was so insecure, but you never know.*

He then sat again at his desk and reached for the telephone. "Now," he said aloud, "finally time to call Joe Valentine back."

Valentine was clearly happy to hear Oakley's voice on the line and invited him to come by his place for drinks that evening. "If you like movies, you're probably going to love this place," he added, mentioning, as he had begun to during their earlier encounter, that the Hollywood apartment complex where he lived had been built by Cecil B. DeMille in 1927, when sound was coming into films, to house New York theater people who were needed because of the new demands of the medium.

Many film professionals thought theater-trained actors had voices that would record better than those of silent film stars, although, in practice, that didn't always turn out to be true. Many silent film stars made the transition to sound easily, among them Doug Fairbanks, despite possessing a relatively high tenor voice, which common wisdom claimed was wrong for sound. John Gilbert, already one of the silent era's great romantic leads, soared to superstardom costarring with Greta Garbo in the film that made her a star, 1926's intensely romantic silent *Flesh and the Devil* (off screen, the pair fell in love as well). But when sound arrived, his career essentially ended overnight. Several reasons have been speculated for his precipitous fall, the most common being that his voice recorded badly.

"Look at all this. Isn't it amazing?" Valentine enthused after opening the wrought iron gate to the complex for Oakley and escorting him past the star-shaped fountain at the center of the palm-and-flower-filled inner courtyard of the building to his apartment.

"My God," Oakley exclaimed on entering the soaring, twenty-two-foot-high living room boasting a fireplace that seemed large enough to walk into and a balcony running the entire width of the room. "This is amazing," he said, taking in the architecture of the apartment as well as Joe's furnishings which included a grand piano and a Venetian-style sofa.

"Told you." Joe smiled. "Not many places like it anywhere. Looks like a movie set itself."

"May I go upstairs and look around?" Oakley asked.

"Sure, feel free, anything you want. What would you like to drink?"

"Can you do an Old Fashioned? Or a Martini if you have the makings. Either will be wonderful," Oakley suggested as he walked up the steep stairs—each riser fronted with colorful Malibu tiles—to the upper level of the bedroom.

"Jesus!" Oakley exclaimed, leaning over the railing of the balcony. "How did you ever find a place like this?"

"Gotta be honest," Joe said, "I didn't. My agent found it after I arrived in Hollywood a couple years ago. He knew the town, knew where I needed to be; remember, I'm only a few blocks from the studios, the studios that aren't in the Valley anyway. And I make pretty good money recording soundtracks for films."

"So that's what you do," Oakley said. "I was wondering, what with that terrific Steinway and what's in that case sitting on it—a violin?"

"That's right. I play both although my main instrument is the violin. You play anything?"

"Only the radio."

"Come back downstairs. Here's your drink. I'll be just a minute," Joe said after Oakley sat himself on the sofa facing the large fireplace. "I need to fix something to nibble on from the stuff I picked up at the deli over on Ivar."

Oakley had just raised his glass to his lips when the telephone on the side table next to the sofa rang. "Get that, would you?" Joe shouted from his kitchen.

"Hi, is this Giuseppe?" a slightly accented male voice asked.

"Who?"

"Who is it?" Joe shouted.

"Dunno. Someone asked for a 'Giuseppe.'"

"That's me, silly," Joe said, wiping his hands on a dishtowel as he walked into the living room. "Joe…Giuseppe…same name," he said, taking the receiver. "Hi, it's me."

Oakley walked into the dining room and then the apartment's small kitchen to allow Joe a semblance of privacy. From the kitchen, a back door opened onto a small patio separating the building from busy Franklin Avenue. "Doesn't the traffic noise drive you crazy?" Oakley asked, sensing that Joe had finished his call and walked into the kitchen behind him.

"You get used to it, but it can be a bit of a racket in the summer when the windows are open, and everyone seems to be driving up this street to the Bowl; it's only five blocks away. And anyway, if it hadn't been for the traffic, you wouldn't have rear-ended me, we wouldn't have met, and you wouldn't be here now."

"Can't fight with that logic," Oakley said, turning just as Joe kissed him.

"Now get back in the living room, and let me finish fixing some food for us."

So that's the agenda, Oakley realized as he reseated himself on the sofa. *Not that Joe isn't appealing. He's very attractive, but there's something that seems a bit off kilter about this,* he thought. *Maybe it's because it's so new.* Just then, Joe walked back carrying a tray of crackers, an opened can of pâté, and a jar of cornichon pickles.

"I thought you were fixing something."

"I did," Joe said with another of his infectious smiles. "It's called opening cans and jars."

"What's this 'Giuseppe' business?" Oakley asked as he spread some pâté on a cracker. "I thought only people on movies or show business used other names."

"Well," Joe said between bites, "I'm in show business, aren't I? Playing music for all those movies? And 'Giuseppe' isn't 'another' name. It's my own name, only in Italian. And I'm Italian, as if you can't tell. Giuseppe Valentino."

I use a different last name professionally," he added. "Otherwise, it would sound like I was aping the star."

"Was that your idea?" Oakley asked.

"Nope, it was my agent's—or at least my old agent's. I've just switched agencies. And I liked the idea anyway. And it's sorta my name anyway. Unlike Lucille LeSueur which had no connection with Joan Crawford."

"There's a difference," Oakley interrupted. "I was told it wasn't her decision to change her name. Louis B. Mayer decided to do it because he thought 'LeSueur' sounded too much like 'sewer.' You're a musician, right? So are there a lot of agents in Hollywood for musicians, in addition to all those for actors and actresses?"

"I don't know," Joe said, spreading the last of the pâté on a cracker and handing it to Oakley. "I think that many agents handle both. At least in my case they do. It's all part of the same industry after all."

"So who is your agent?"

"Well, my old agent was Les Grady."

"Oh, I know him. Good guy."

"I know. I like him, too, but he had this younger guy in his office who, basically, did all the work for me. He got me my biggest studio orchestra job. So when he left and went to another agency, it sorta made sense for me to go with him."

"What's the name of the new agency?" Oakley inquired, still surprised at the coincidence of Joe Valentine being Lester Grady's client. He also suspected that Joe's departure, at least to Les Grady's thinking, probably was more like client raiding than "making sense."

"It's named the New World Agency, but everyone calls them simply NWA."

Just like CTA, Oakley thought. *These Hollywood talent agencies are sprouting more abbreviations than all those new government agencies Roosevelt created a few years back.*

"So, how about a refill?" Joe asked. "Then maybe we can go out for a quick bite."

"That's a deal," Oakley said. "But only if you promise that you'll play something for me on your violin."

"Thought you'd never ask," Joe smiled. "After dinner," he added coyly.

The rest of the evening turned out more or less as Oakley surmised. Joe suggested they keep dinner simple and informal, which was fine with Oakley. There was a branch of the popular Carpenter's Drive-In nearby on Sunset Boulevard, and because it was an easy walk, they soon found themselves there enjoying the restaurant chain's signature $1.25 special: fried chicken with honey and mashed potatoes. An impromptu concert followed back at Valentine's apartment with Joe playing Nikolai Rimsky-Korsakov's virtuosic *Flight of the Bumblebee* followed by the sentimental *Liebesfreud.*

"That was amazing," Oakley said. "I had no idea that you could play like that, especially the *Bumblebee* piece—all those notes flying by like bullets from a machine gun. Where did you learn how to play so well? And your violin itself sounds amazing. Where did you find it?"

"I've played the violin since I was six and started on a miniature instrument," Joe said. "So sixteenth notes like those in the *Flight of the Bumblebee* don't terrify me like they once did."

"I think I've heard the *Bumblebee* music before, only with an orchestra," Oakley observed.

"That's how it was originally composed, but a lot of violinists play it as a solo piece. And you may have heard it on the radio. It's the theme music for a new serial called 'The Green Hornet.'"

"Maybe that's where I heard it," Oakley said. "You're great, and as I said, the violin sounds amazing. I'm sure part of the reason is that you know how to play it well, but does it have a story? It looks sorta old, and a lot of old violins seem to have stories."

"Well, as I said," Joe replied, "I've been doing this since I was a kid. But you're right, the violin is special. It actually belongs to Fritz Kreisler, the famous violinist who also composed the second piece I played for you, *Liebesfreud,* which means 'love's happiness' in German. I met him through mutual friends, also violinists, when he was in Los Angeles for a concert at the Hollywood Bowl a couple years ago. We got to talking about my career, and when he heard how well I was doing with only a cheap violin, he offered to lend me this one from his collection. It's not a famous old Italian instrument like his Stradivarius but was good enough for him to sometimes use in concert. It was made by a French luthier (*there's that word again*, Oakley thought) named Jean-Baptiste Vuillaume in 1860. I don't know how long I'll be able to have it, but every day I have it to use is a joy. And hear this: I met Mr. Kreisler when he was playing at the Bowl, and last month I played his violin at the Bowl. Small world, right?"

"You played at the Bowl?" Oakley asked, clearly impressed with his new friend's talent. "How did that come about?"

"Well, the person who was scheduled to be the soloist with the Los Angeles Philharmonic last month got sick or something happened—I never found out exactly what it was—and Les got me the job. It was amazing to be standing there playing the Beethoven concerto for fifteen or eighteen thousand people, and then afterward, just as I did for you, I played Mr. Kreisler's *Liebesfreud* as an encore. Wasn't that great?"

"Great," Oakley said, thinking it was certainly convenient for Lester Grady to be able to substitute another client of his for Rachael Baumgarten after her violin mysteriously disappeared. *Maybe a little bit too convenient*, he thought. "So, thanks for the concert," Oakley said. "I think I ought to take my leave. It's getting late."

"Oh," Joe said, his disappointment clearly evident. "I thought…"

"Give me a rain date," Oakley said. "I was in the office all morning and have to work out a lot of stuff tomorrow," he fibbed, hoping that Joe wasn't planning to spend the day at the beach in Santa Monica, which was where he was planning to suggest to Donny that they head tomorrow; to disappoint him again could spell the end of what was, to Oakley's thinking, getting to be a pretty nice relationship. And he certainly had to think out this new revelation involving Lester Grady. "But soon," he said, giving Joe a quick hug and a good-bye kiss. "It's been a wonderful evening."

'What about tomorrow night?" Joe asked, following him out into the courtyard of the apartment building. "Remember I mentioned that I played for the orchestra at the Angelus Temple, and I think you might be interested in seeing one of Mrs. MacPherson's sermons, which are acted out like plays. It's going to be a special evening, too. You ever heard of Anthony Quinn?"

Oakley shook his head.

"Well, one day you might. He's an actor trying to break into movies who just married DeMille's daughter," Joe said. "Anyway, he plays the saxophone in a small dance band that he formed, and he also plays in the orchestra at the Angelus Temple. He's doing a jazz set with his own band tomorrow night, and it should be terrific. I think you'd like it."

Actually, Oakley was interested, less in hearing the music of a young actor than in watching Aimee Semple MacPherson performing one of her famous "illustrated sermons" as she called them—a sort of sacred theatrical production that often resembled musical comedy or vaudeville more than a solemn church service. He remembered hearing that on one memorable occasion, MacPherson, dressed as a football player, ran down the main aisle of the temple along with a dozen staff members also dressed as football players, pretending to score a touchdown for Jesus.

"Don't know what she's planning for tomorrow night, but it's bound to be good." Joe said as he walked Oakley to his car.

"Let me see how things go tomorrow," Oakley said. "What do I do, just show up?"

"Well, yes, but I'll go ahead and reserve a seat near the front. We usually have more than five thousand people on Sunday nights."

"And if I can't make it? Should I call and cancel the reservation? Does it cost anything?"

"No." Joe said. "Just throw something green in the collection plate when they pass it around. Sister Aimee always says she likes 'quiet money,' meaning greenbacks and not coins. And don't worry about the reservation. It's such a madhouse, no one would know what to do if you called. I'll try and block a seat near the orchestra, and if you don't show up, someone will grab it anyway. If you can come, just get there before seven when the illustrated services start and tell the ushers that you're in the reserved section… they'll show you where it is."

"Thanks, Joe. I'll probably be there." *So if I show up with Donny*, Oakley thought as he started his car and pulled out into traffic, *I'll just yell and scream that there were supposed to be two seats reserved. They're not in the business of turning people away.*

Chapter 12

As Oakley expected, Donny was delighted when Oakley suggested they spend Sunday at Santa Monica Beach, although he was hesitant about Oakley's further suggestion that they then attend one of Aimee Semple MacPherson's "illustrated services" at the Angelus Temple of the Four Square Gospel Church she founded.

"I'm not all that religious, Oakey," Donny said.

"Donny, I'm not either. You don't have to be religious; it's more of a show than a church service anyway. I'm told that even Charlie Chaplin, who is as big a nonbeliever as they come, goes to her Sunday evening performance and gives her pointers on how to make her shows better. A friend of mine who plays in their orchestra said that they're going to have a jazz band this Sunday, and according to newspaper ad today, it says her sermon this week is titled 'The Shepherd and the Flock,' which means she's probably going to have a bunch of sheep running all over the place. Hell, Donny, it's an LA experience."

"Well, OK," Donny said. "Your place afterward?"

"Where else?"

The day at the beach was as delightful as anyone could wish. The weather was perfect, the waves were just right, and the crowd working out at the new exercise area—"Muscle Beach" as everyone seemed to be calling it—provided attention-getting visuals. Donny got in his Charles Atlas exercise time while Oakley, despite his attention being frequently diverted by the passing crowd, managed to get through a couple of chapters of his Agatha Christie mystery.

After a fast hamburger at a greasy spoon at the beach and a stop at Oakley's apartment to freshen up, the pair arrived at the Angelus Temple just as most of the crowd also arrived.

"Where the hell are we supposed to park?" Oakley yelled in frustration when it was clear that despite the fact most of the crowd arrived on chartered buses, there were no spaces left on Glendale Boulevard nor on the adjoining streets.

"Come on, Oakley," Donny said. "Why are you getting all worked up? Because you might be late for a church service? If we're a few minutes late, God—and presumably Miss MacPherson—will forgive you," he joked. "There!" he shouted when they turned into Echo Park Boulevard as someone was pulling out. "There's a place."

Oakley grabbed it, and it was only a short trek around the corner to reach the gigantic, gold-domed auditorium surmounted by a pair of towering radio antennas, both bearing the initials KFSG, the call letters of MacPherson's Four Square Gospel radio ministry.

As it turned out, Oakley didn't have to make an excuse for bringing Donny along: there was plenty of room in the reserved section. Their arrival also coincided perfectly with the start of the service. "There she is," Oakley said, pointing out MacPherson who was walking ahead of the large choir singing "What a Friend We Have in Jesus." After several more hymns were sung to the accompaniment of the large orchestra in which Oakley immediately spotted Joe seated toward the rear of the violin section, Quinn's dance band launched into a short jazz concert. Then the choir sang another upbeat hymn. It was time for Sister Aimee to take charge. Suddenly from the rear of the auditorium, a baa-ing and shouting erupted as a herd of sheep and goats began to wander down the main aisle of the temple, followed by MacPherson herself who had, during the hymn singing, left the stage and changed into a sheepherder's costume complete with a shepherd's staff with its crooked end for capturing strays—lambs or, presumably, sinners.

"Well, so much for reserved seats," Oakley said as the livestock was assembled directly in front of him and Donny. "Who knew they would be in a stable? I guess that might be appropriate for Christmas, but it's a bit much here. And how many of them anyway? Twenty? Thirty?"

"Just part of the LA experience," Donny added sarcastically, repeating Oakley's original invitation to attend the service, as he wrinkled his nose at the pungent barnyard smell that suddenly enveloped them. "Can we move?"

"I don't think so. I don't think there is any other room now," Oakley said, turning and scanning the rows of nearby seats. Suddenly, he spotted a familiar face at the end of the row behind them. *I've met that guy*, he realized. *Who the hell is it? Blond, crew cut, Scandinavian appearing. I know him but from where?*

"See any other seats?" Donny asked, following Oakley's gaze. "Oh, I see you've spied something else. Who's he?"

"That's what I'm just trying to figure out," Oakley said. "I've met him, but for the life of me, I have no idea who he is or where it was."

"Well, keep it only to looking," Donny said. Just as he spoke, the unknown man turned, looked at Oakley, and waved.

"Damn, this is going to drive me crazy."

"Forget it," Donny said. "It'll come to you eventually."

The rest of the service was pretty much as Oakley expected, with MacPherson drawing the obvious parallel between the animals she had shepherded down the aisle and the flock of church members. Also as expected, most of the huge audience applauded wildly, at least those who weren't so emotionally overcome by the power of MacPherson's oratory that they were reduced to tears. "This lady knows more about involving an audience than most actresses in Hollywood will ever know," Donny observed. "She ought to be teaching acting classes on the side."

"Tell me!" Oakley said. "Let's scram and get ahead of the crowd."

About the same time that Oakley and Donny were appraising Sister Aimee's thespian skills, some four miles away, a stately, sleek, midnight-blue Packard V-12 sedan was being waved through the gates of Los Angeles's Hancock Park community. From the 1920s when the one-and-one-half-square-mile area was developed by the Hancock family with profits from oil drilling near the La Brea tar pits, it was popular with many of the city's most affluent and powerful people. Among the reasons was the privacy assured by its being walled off from the neighbors, a central location with a low population density as a result of zoning (most of the houses had to be set back at least fifty feet from the street), and that it was built adjoining a private golf club.

After entering the enclave, the Packard turned right, entered the driveway on the side of a huge, ornate, Beaux-Arts mansion, and pulled to a stop under a porte cochere. The passenger, a beefy man in his midforties with a Nordic crew cut, emerged and was escorted inside by the mansion's major domo. He briefly noted the rich, walnut paneling of the entrance hall, which also featured a bust of the mansion's owner on an ormolu-encrusted credenza. It led to the building's music room, reportedly brought intact from an Austrian castle, which boasted hand-painted silk panels set in intricate wood paneling and a provenance claiming that Mozart, while a child prodigy, played a concert in it when it was still in its original setting.

In any event, the room's furnishings as well as the Steinway grand piano at which the home's owner was playing Beethoven's "Für Elise" when his visitor entered were at least two centuries newer than the room's decor. The piano, the visitor recalled once being told, was previously owned by the legendary pianist Jan Paderewski and left behind when sold his two-thousand-acre wine ranch near Paso Robles, California, in the early 1920s.

"So?" the man at the Paderewski Steinway asked while continuing to play. "I see Kurt picked you up on time. What have you learned?"

"Well, sir, only that the information we have is correct. This man Oakley Webster is a private investigator and apparently has been hired by friends of Williams to look into how he met that sailor and who then tipped off the police about the assignation."

"How do you know that much?"

"I took advantage of Webster's being away from his apartment and entered disguised as a gas company repair man on an emergency call. When I was in his apartment, I discovered some notes he took during a conversation with Mr. Williams in which he described how he met the sailor, a Carl Andrews. I believe it was a telephone conversation."

"Have you found the sailor? It would be helpful if he were to disappear," said the pianist, who had finally stopped playing and turned on the piano stool to face his visitor.

"No. Apparently, as they say in the American navy, he has 'shipped out.' I have no idea where he is now or any way of knowing if Mr. Webster ever spoke with him."

"What about Webster? Have you learned anything else about him?"

"Only that he apparently knows many top Hollywood stars and that he is a homosexual."

"Oh, that explains the Williams interest. How do you know that?"

"I was following him on Sunday when he went to the beach in Santa Monica with another male. They were very affectionate with each other, very unseemly."

"Do you think that through his Hollywood connections he is looking into any of our other activities?"

"I have no way of knowing that, sir. If there was a way of tapping his telephone, perhaps we could learn more. But only the FBI or perhaps some of the people at the Los Angeles Police Department could order that."

"Which is a possibility. What about the measles disease agent we obtained from the laboratory in Munich where it was isolated from patients? Do you still have some?"

"Yes, a little. Probably enough even if we need to deal with more people. I also have a small supply of the pneumonia bacteria. I used some of that recently on the people who are making trouble for me. All of it is carefully stored in a deep freezer at a restaurant owned by my cousin."

"It sounds like you disobeyed my order never to use any of our weapons for personal reasons."

"No, no, never, sir. The person, a talent agent involved with one of our solutions, made several comments to a supporter of ours that sounded like he suspected what our objective is. I knew this had to be stopped quickly and, hopefully, with finality. I was able to infect him at his place of business."

"Good. But if a similar situation arises in the future, please do not proceed without speaking with me first. Come, follow me. I have something to give you besides your retainer."

The mansion's owner led his visitor into the living room where he pushed a decorative carving on one of the room's oak-paneled walls. It opened into a smaller room, which housed a table and chair next to the steel door of a large safe. After a few turns of the dial, he opened the safe's door, revealing a room the size of a large closet, walked in, and returned with an envelope.

"Here is your retainer for this month. It is urgent that you make every effort to learn if Mr. Webster is looking into our other activities. Also, it might be valuable if you were to look into the activities of his male friend—what he does, where he lives, what he does in his spare time. Do you have a gun?"

"No, sir," the visitor said, surprised.

"Here," the mansion's owner said, after walking into the safe again and returning with a large, blue pistol and several small boxes of ammunition. "I'm assuming you are not too experienced in the use of a weapon like this?"

"Correct."

"Here is my card," the man said. "Go to the Hollywood Gun Club and ask for the owner. Give him the card, and tell him I would like him to teach you how to use it. He will bill the training charges to us. Get proficient in the use of this weapon as soon as possible, and try to keep it near you at all times—in the glove compartment of your car, in your briefcase, wherever you can access it quickly."

"Why, what are you expecting me to do?"

"I'm not saying that I want you to do anything with this—not yet. Now go and do what I have asked you. It is very important that we find out if Mr. Webster is up to more mischief," he said, pushing a button on a desk, which quickly summoned the major domo. "Erik will escort you out, and Kurt will take you home."

Chapter 13

Monday morning dawned hot and clear, a condition that would soon be replaced by ever-growing pollution from the burgeoning number of automobiles. Oakley decided that regardless of what the day would bring, he would dress for the climate and not for appearances. So he donned a short-sleeved white shirt and his cream-colored linen suit. *Forget the tie*, he thought with a smile. *If I need one, I have one at the office.*

Benny had arrived ahead of him and was ensconced in Oakley's desk chair with his feet on the desk. "Hey, Benny, it's a new day and a new week!" he exclaimed on seeing his relaxed assistant. "If you made yourself any more comfortable, you'd be asleep. And get your ass out of my chair!"

"Sorry, Oakey. Jus' a bit slow getting movin' this morning. You look like a vanilla ice-cream cone."

"I guess that was the idea," Oakley observed as, just then, both telephone lines rang. "God!" Oakley exclaimed. "Not even time to sit down. I'll get line one. You get two."

It was Joe Valentine on Oakley's line. "Any chance of my redeeming your rain check this week? Saw you at Sister's show last night and tried to find you afterward, but I guess you scrammed early."

"We did."

"We?"

"A friend of mine I brought along. As far as my rain check? Fine. What did you have in mind?"

"Thought we could go to a movie and dinner. Oh, yes. I'm playing with the LA Phil for the George Gershwin memorial concert at the Bowl next month, and I have a few box seats to give to friends. You're my guest if you can make it. Looks like a great event. The famous soprano Lily Pons is singing, and José Iturbi, Oscar Levant, and Fred Astaire are also on the bill. Wednesday, September 8. I hear CBS is going to broadcast it, but hearing it on the radio is nothing like being there."

"Count me in," Oakley said. "Sounds great. And if you want to get together this week, how about dropping by my place? I can whip up something. Friday?"

"I'll be there. Oh yes, where exactly is your place? Sort of essential."

God, Oakley thought after giving him directions, *a personal life dry as a desert for a year and now two in a row. Guess I should be grateful—*

"Oakey, you got this woman Karinopolis on the other line," Benny interrupted.

"Sorry," Oakley apologized, picking up the line. He was immediately assailed by sobs.

"Oh, Oakley, I don't know what to do," Maria Karinopolis cried. "Ari has come down with something that seems like influenza—I know the symptoms because I lived through the great epidemic twenty years ago—but then it got worse, and now the doctors say it's pneumonia. But the doctors at LA County Hospital, where the ambulance took him, say that his is the only case they've seen for weeks.

"I know they are doing everything they can for him," the hysterical woman sobbed, "but there doesn't seem to be any medicine that can cure pneumonia. Only time and good care and natural resistance they say. I'm so worried," she cried. "This is just like Eva who got the measles when no one else got them. It's like someone is targeting Ari."

"This is terrible news," Oakley commiserated. "Maybe he just caught it naturally? We don't know enough yet to be suspicious that there was foul play." Nevertheless, like Maria, Oakley was struck by the similarity to the recent measles contracted by Eva and John Wayne; to consider it another coincidence strained credibility. However, Ari contracted pneumonia; it seemed clear that, as with the measles cases, the infection seemed to have been deliberately delivered—out of the blue—with the accuracy of a bullet. "What can I do to help?" he added.

"Help me find out who is trying to kill my Ari."

"Maria, we don't know that someone is trying to kill your husband," Oakley explained calmly. "All we know for certain is that he contracted pneumonia, and it seems to have been deliberately done. Who and why anyone might have done this to Ari is uncertain. And there are two other questions, as in the case of Eva: how anyone managed to secure the virus for measles and for pneumonia, and how the hell they infected them. That is, as I said, if it was deliberate.

"Can he have visitors? Could I see him? Maybe he might have an idea of how he contracted the disease and who might have done it if, as I said, it turns out that it must have been deliberate."

"He's not allowed visitors now except for me," Maria said. "But if you're there with me, I think it would be OK. Could you meet me at the hospital at three?"

"I'll be there."

Oakley hung up the telephone and leaned back in his chair. It was time to put on his Sherlock Holmes hat again but not just to try and figure out who was committing these crimes. These were certainly crimes unless everything from Billy getting caught in an assignation to Eva Sanderson, John Wayne, and Ari contracting diseases no one else in Los Angeles had were all accidental—a conclusion, Oakley felt, that would have required the naïve credulity of an angel. This time, however, he needed to look into another aspect of the cluster of incidents, accidents, or crimes that landed on his desk. Why him? Were similar incidents being encountered outside of his immediate orbit? It seemed odd at the very least that he was suddenly being called upon to solve a number of incidents involving actors and performers. Or was it mischief aimed at homosexual actors? Or Jewish actors? Or heterosexual actors? That didn't seem to be a common denominator: Billy was homosexual actor and a gentile. Eva Sanderson was a gentile heterosexual actress. Rachael Baumgarten was a presumably heterosexual violinist and a Jew, and it wasn't clear if the loss of her violin was a hostile act anyway. John Wayne was a heterosexual actor and also a gentile. Ari Karinopolis may be Jewish - *I never asked* Oakley realized. And Michael Trevalian was a heterosexual who some might consider partially Jewish,. *And I*, Oakley thought, *am a homosexual goy. Does that make me a potential victim too?*

The more he tried to find a common thread, the more frustrated he became. Time to have a heart to heart with the LAPD, he realized, reaching for the phone to call Mike Maloney, his acquaintance at police headquarters.

"Hey, Mike, it's Oakley. Got a minute?"

"Yeah, for you. Still looking for more about dirt about the Williams arrest?"

"Nope, much more. Need to have a chat about a whole raft of cases I suddenly have and learn if anyone else in our lovely city is fighting crime these days. Got time for a drink or two?"

"Sure. You're sorta in the neighborhood. How 'bout we meet at five at Chris Lyman's joint— the place on South Spring. Good beer on tap."

That worked for Oakley, who decided that he'd better also touch base with Docky Martin and the people who were paying him to solve the Billy Williams frame-up. It was Docky's wife, Louella Parsons, who answered the phone.

"Hellooo," she crooned as soon as Oakley identified himself. "How's Sherlock Webster getting along?"

"Well, enough, Miss Parsons. Actually, I'm getting somewhat buried in cases that, unlike Billy's case which has turned out to be a fairly straightforward setup by culprits I'm looking for, seem to have no motive that I can decipher. I've come to the conclusion that I need someone with a really objective mind to talk to about this, and I couldn't think of anyone better than you," he explained. "Would you happen to have any free time in the next day or so to advise me for a half hour or so?"

"Well, I think I'm the last person in Hollywood anyone in their right mind would consider objective," the columnist hooted, "but it's nice to hear someone say so. And free time? I don't know what that is anymore. But I'm flattered that you think my view of your cases—I'm assuming that we are talking about cases other than Billy's, which Docky assures you are moving on just fine, right?"

"Right. A handful of them that seem to have no common thread, yet I suspect there is one."

"Aha!" she shouted into the telephone. "A conspiracy—nothing I like better! But I warn you, my terms are stiff. If I help you sift out the facts from fantasy, and remember most of everything that goes on here is pure fantasy, I have my price."

"And that would be?" Oakley asked warily.

"Whatever you find out, I get to scoop it. Even if it's as big as my Fairbanks-Pickford divorce scoop. No one but me gets to touch whatever you find. And I'm assuming what you are looking into involves some nasty doings."

"Could be. Maybe very nasty or maybe nothing. And, of course, you'll know about whatever I discover whatever it is—even if it's nothing—before our friends at the LAPD, or Miss Sheilah Graham, or anyone else does."

"Good. You free this afternoon around six?"

"Sorry. Meetin' a friend from the coppers at Chris Lyman's."

"Oh, goodie. Talkin' to him about what they know—good plan. You can tell me what he has to say when we get together. How about a late lunch tomorrow? Like at the Derby in Hollywood, the one on Vine? Around two after I finish writin' my column? They always put me toward the back where we can be private. Or at least as private as I can ever be. Don't really want to be too private, if you get my drift. Mind if I bring Docky along? Saves the time it takes to repeat everything later, and since he's sort of involved in the Billy business, makes sense."

Whew, Oakley thought. *Does she ever stop talking long enough to breathe?* "Fine with me," he managed to fit in at a pause. "Two at the Derby on Vine."

"An' don't worry yourself if Docky boy has a couple drinkies. Even when he's three sheets to the wind, he doesn't repeat anything. Just goes to sleep. I'll have Dorothy Manners, my assistant who you should meet one day, make the reservations."

"Sounds perfect, Miss Parsons. It will be a real treat to actually visit with you in person instead of over the telephone," Oakley said, knowing that she was clearly susceptible to flattery, which, of course, cost nothing. "See you tomorrow. Thanks."

After reminding Benny that after lunch, he would be out of the office for the balance of the afternoon, first visiting Ari Karinopolis at the hospital and then meeting Mike Maloney at Lyman's saloon at five, Oakley left for lunch. Today, it was again at the nearby Woolworth's lunch counter, and again, he opted for a BLT and a Coke. It then seemingly took forever to drive to the hospital situated in the congested Boyle Heights community and even longer to find Ari's room in the huge, crowded, six-hundred-bed facility. Thanks to the directions offered by a friendly volunteer on the third floor, he finally found the room. However, Maria Karinopolis's loud complaints mixed with despairing shrieks, which could be heard the moment he got off the elevator, would have easily led him there anyway. Ari, whom he hadn't met before, looked terrible—sweating and gasping for breath inside an oxygen tent. Maria, who barely stopped her wailing long enough to introduce him by lifting the corner of the oxygen tent, was nearly incoherent.

This will never work, Oakley realized, *unless I get her to calm down.* With that, he put his arm around Maria's shoulders and whispered for her to relax, adding that he understood how worried she was but that he had to ask Ari a couple of questions. Finally, she relaxed sufficiently for Oakley to raise the oxygen tent, reintroduce himself, and ask Ari if he could answer some questions. After he nodded, Oakley, knowing that his time was limited, went directly to his most important question: "Mr. Karinopolis, do you have any idea where and how you might have been infected?"

Ari shook his head violently, muttering in a barely audible gasps: "No. How do you know how you catch a cold? All I know is about a week ago—the time a doctor here told me that it took for this to develop—I had a delivery from the deli. It must have been from that."

"Do you remember what you had?" Oakley asked.

"He had his usual," Maria interrupted. "A chicken salad sandwich on rye bread and a Nehi cream soda."

"Did they taste OK?" Oakley asked. "And if you had ordered previously from the same deli, was it the same delivery person?"

"He told me that it all tasted fine but that the delivery person was someone new," she added while Ari shook his head. "He told my Ari that the other delivery man was sick."

That should be easy enough to check out, Oakley thought.

"Around the same time, did you order food from any other sources or go anyplace unusual?"

Ari shook his head. "No," he whispered. "The rest of the week, Maria brought me my lunch."

"Thanks," Oakley said. "I think I have enough to start looking into this. I'll call you later, Mrs. Karinopolis. And Ari—may I call you Ari? You're in good hands here at County."

With that, Oakley bade the couple good-bye. Seeing a doctor on his way out, he asked him what the prognosis was. "Hopeful," Oakley was told. "But more than that, I can't say," the doctor added. "We've never seen a strain of pneumonia like this, so we've no certainty about treating it. If Mr. Karinopolis were younger or stronger—"

"Thank you, Doctor," Oakley said, knowing that the physician had told him more than he should have already.

I couldn't have picked two worst destinations in one afternoon, he thought as he drove his car through even more congested traffic than earlier on his way to meet Mike Maloney. In fact, although he had spent only a short time with Ari, because of the traffic and the crowds at the hospital, he barely arrived on time to meet Maloney at the bar.

Mike seemed to be his usual jovial self, but Oakley detected a hesitation, a seeming unease, in their conversation, even limited as it initially was to social generalities. Perhaps he was still ill at ease over the same thing they had spoken about earlier: the rumors that there were about to be big shake-ups at the police department, and like his colleagues, he was probably running for cover. Oakley, as usual, decided to address the matter directly.

"So, Mike," he said, "anything new about the big scandals in the department that you hinted might break any day?"

"Nope. Nuttin' new. Ever'one is scared shitless that they might be fingered by top brass to save their asses. So ever'one is hidin' out. Pretendin' to be investigatin' this or that crapola all the time, jus' to stay outta the office."

"So how does that affect you?"

"Come on, Oakey," Maloney said with a sarcastic edge to his voice. "Nobody's hands are entirely clean—not the boss's, not the precinct capt'n's, not mine. Everbody's been on the take. With me, nothin' big but a little here, a little there. Enuf to stick if someone wanted to pass the buck to keep their own ass clean."

"I guess this isn't the best time to ask you what you thought of these other cases I suddenly have—stuff that doesn't look like a crime but just smells bad."

"Know what you mean," Mike agreed. "Problem is, there has been so much fuckin' wit' things, no one really knows what's real and what isn't anymore. Like your pansy actor guy. This shit goes on all the time and not just in the pansy world. I could tell you real horror stories about regular people, you know, girl-boy stuff that would curl your hair, like killings that get overlooked by the department after some studio boss calls. And it's nuttin' new. You live in that place where that director was killed in 1922 or '23?"

Oakley nodded.

"Well, as you know, MGM's security people were called to clean up the place before anyone thought it might be smart to call the LAPD. And then, of course, the DA never bothered to look into the murder too closely.

"And it's gotten worse, much worse, since then. Some days, it seems like LA's got the worst police force money can buy. You'da thought whoever is doing the buying could, at least, buy people with an IQ of more than twenty or thirty. And it's even worse over at city hall. You can buy a license for anything you want.

"So am I scared? You bet! I wish I could help, but let's be honest—a strange thing to say when I think about it—the less I know about what's goin' on, the better it is. For you, too. By the way, anyone made a move on you?"

"I think so," Oakley said. "A week or so ago when I was out, the super let someone into my place who was dressed as a gas repairman and claimed I had reported a leak Well, it didn't take much work to discover there was no leak, no call, and who knows who the guy was?"

"Piece of advice, buddy: keep lookin' over your shoulder all the time. If something odd happens, somethin' that don't make any sense and can't be easily explained, take it as enemy action. And you bein' a pansy and all, you're an easy target—a bird on the ground, so to speak."

"Thanks, Mike. I appreciate your advice, and watch your own behind as well."

Needless to say, Oakley had a lot to think about that evening, but try as hard as he might, he couldn't come up with any answers. *I guess there are no easy answers,* he thought as he turned in for what was a restless night, plagued by nightmares in which he was repeatedly being chased off towering cliffs.

CHAPTER 14

Not surprisingly, Oakley felt pretty ragged when he dragged himself to work the next morning. "Benny," he said, "I'd appreciate it if you were a bit less cheery this morning. No hangover—just need to take the pressure off for a while."

"But, boss, you got lunch today with Miss Parsons—plenty of pressure."

Oh God, Oakley thought. *I should have slept in. Lunch meeting with the most powerful journalist in Hollywood when my brain feels like it's turned to cotton.* Just then, both telephone lines rang. *And it's starting to be another one of those days,* he suspected. "Number one, me," he exclaimed. "Number two, you."

"Hey, Oakey, it's your old friend Les. I'm still waitin' for you to return my call of—how long ago?—maybe a year ago?"

"I'm sorry, Les. It's been a bitch some days. What can I do for you?"

"Just have lunch with me or dinner. Want to catch up or at least reassure myself that we live in the same town."

"OK, OK. How about Friday? No," he reneged, remembering his date with Joe Valentine. "How about a late brunch on Sunday?" he suggested, keeping Saturday night open in case Donny wanted to get together.

"That's fine with me. Call you later with where."

"Fine, see you then, Les," Oakley agreed, ending the call and turning to Benny to see who was on his line.

"Sorry, boss, someone here who asked if you were in, and when I said that you were on the other line, he hung up. Sorta strange accent."

Oakley was, despite his slow start to the day, suddenly on full alert. Was this a case of something strange happening without an easy explanation that Mike had cautioned him about? *Not going to take a chance*, Oakley decided and dialed his apartment superintendent, Luis Baragon. After assuring himself that no one had shown up asking to be let into his apartment, Oakley told Baragon that barring an emergency like a fire, a flood, or Los Angeles being Los Angeles, an earthquake, no one, whatever the reason might be, should be allowed to enter his apartment.

With this understood, Oakley spent the rest of the morning tidying up normal business and, happily, finding a check for $250 from Docky Martin. Then it was time to leave for his lunch with the newest Queen of Hollywood, as Louella Parsons was beginning to be called by both newspaper and magazine writers as well as radio commentators.

Traffic was, as usual, a challenge in driving cross-town to the Hollywood Brown Derby. As he pulled into the parking lot across Vine, Oakley noticed with some relief that Parsons's Packard was not parked in its usual spot directly in front of the restaurant, so at least she and Docky hadn't been forced to wait for him.

The maître d' was properly diffident when Oakley introduced himself and mentioned that he was joining Parsons and her husband and quickly led him not to one of the restaurant's red leather–lined rectangular booths but to a large round booth set against the rear wall of the room. "This is her place every day," he said pleasantly as Oakley seated himself. "Would you like something to drink?"

Oakley deferred, saying that he would wait until Parsons arrived, which as it turned out, was within minutes. "Helluuu," Louella Parsons sang out in a loud voice, causing every head in the place to turn as Oakley moved out of the booth and stood to welcome the couple. "You must be Oakley. So nice to meet you. Say hello, Docky."

"I am, and hello yourself, both of you," Oakley said, shaking hands with the pair and thinking how unlike their reputations they appeared. Louella Parsons was the least glamorous person imaginable, despite wearing what was clearly a couturier-designed dress; she looked more like a somewhat dumpy, middle-aged matron from the Middle West with an unflattering hairdo than a Hollywood powerhouse. Docky, who unaccountably because he was a urologist, had recently been appointed medical director of 20th Century Fox, looked older than his forty-seven years, his face deeply tanned and lined.

"Let me squeeze in first," Parsons said, "and you boys sit on either side of me and I'll have my back to the wall. Just like it was in the Old West—makes it hard for anyone to shoot me from the back or sides." She laughed her throaty chortle. "They can only get at me from the front, and then I'll see 'em comin' and can duck."

The maître d' himself took their drink orders. "Martinis for all of us," Docky requested after asking Oakley. "Make 'em doubles."

"Who's going to shoot at you?" Oakley asked with a smile. "The Queen of Hollywood?"

"You'd be surprised, my boy," Parsons said. "Big power breeds big enemies, and there are a coupla people in this room right now who wouldn't mind it if my next stop was at St. Peter's gate. And don't forget, I was writin' scenarios and scripts as well as a column about movies before a lot of these people were born. And it doesn't help my popularity that thanks to my Campbell's soup sponsors, I also make more money every week from my Hollywood Hotel radio show alone than most of them make in a year."

The drinks arrived, and all was silent for a few moments. "Miss Parsons, the usual?" the maître d' asked.

"Yep, Cobb salad. Same for Docky boy. Gotta watch our waists. Oakey, may I call you Oakey? Know what you want or do you need a menu?"

"Cobb salad's fine for me, too."

"So whatcha want ta ask me about?" Parsons inquired.

Oakley decided that he might as well tell her everything. So, after bringing her up to date on the cases she knew about—Eva Sanderson and Billy Williams—he then outlined the experiences of Michael Trevalian, John Wayne, the disappearance of Rachael Baumgarten's valuable violin, and Ari Karinopolis's pneumonia. "I know all of these cases may have perfectly understandable explanations, but call me a cynic, I smell a rat somewhere in all this."

"Darrrling," a thin blonde interrupted, leaning over the table. "Soooo nice to see you here."

"Ditto, Elda," Louella responded. "Docky, you know Elda. Oakley, meet Elda Hopper. Elda—I mean Hedda—meet Oakley Webster, the best private investigator in town."

"Hedda's an actress who was married years ago to the late actor and producer DeWolf Hopper. He was famous for reciting the poem 'Casey at the Bat' a zillion times at baseball games and parties and even on the radio," Parsons added as Hopper stood by looking unhappy that her history was being shorthanded to a stranger. "I've heard that he was always mixing Elda's name up with those of his four previous wives, so she paid a numerologist ten bucks to pick a name for her. It was Hedda. That true, Hedda?"

"Yes," Hopper said, barely containing her anger. "I did have help picking out a new name. And Wolfie was famous for more than the Casey poem; he also starred in dozens and dozens of Broadway plays. Are you investigating something for Louella, Mr. Webster? Helping her get some new dirt?"

"Just sharing lunch," he replied, adding without thinking, "I'm sure if Miss Parsons wants to look into something, she certainly doesn't need to call on a private investigator. All she needs to do is pick up the telephone."

"Reeeeally?" Hopper responded, clearly irritated by the sass of Oakley's retort. "Gotta go. Having lunch with the powers that be."

"Indeed. She's right about having lunch with the powers that be," Parsons said as her eyes followed Hopper's path to a table near the center of the restaurant where the instantly recognizable Louis B. Mayer was seated with the equally familiar Harry Chandler, publisher of the *Los Angeles Times*. "Proves what I suspected."

"I beg your pardon?" Oakley asked.

"Proves that bastard Mayer is going to try and sabotage Lolly," Docky interjected, while waving at their waiter for a refill.

"I've heard that because Mayer and some of the other studio heads are very unhappy with the way I sometimes go after some of their precious contract stars," Parsons explained, "they've decided to create a rival film columnist.

And since Mrs. Hopper's movie career is definitely on a downslide—she never had much of a career anyway—she's available. And because they seem to believe that she can put two words together that seem to make sense, at least to the illiterates who run the studios, she is apparently the chosen one. Considering who is lunching with whom, clearly her column is going to be carried in the *Times* and syndicated by them, too."

"Oh, that's too bad," Oakley commiserated."

"Naaaah," Parsons said as their lunches arrived. "I'll kill her. Having to figure out which of us to give stories to will drive the publicists crazy. Elda—I mean Hedda—has been giving me tips for years in exchange for mentions in my column. But when we double-checked them, it turned out a lot weren't true. So, whoever carries her column, she will always be a second-rater, even when she attracts attention with her crazy hats that she decided to wear as a sort of trademark after her name was chosen for her."

"Hello, Louella," a short, striking-looking woman with huge eyes said as she walked past the table.

"Hello, Bette," Louella replied, who then introduced Oakley to the actress. "Meet Bette Davis. What's the latest on the Oscar race this year?"

"How would I know?" Davis replied. "Those people hate me for naming the statuette Oscar after my husband because its rear end looks like his."

"I know, dear," Louella said, "but I hear others are also competing for the Oscar name credit. But speaking of Oscar competition," Louella added, "they gave it to you last year for your performance in *Dangerous*."

"That was just a consolation prize for the reviews I got for playing Mildred in *Of Human Bondage* in 1934," Davis snapped. "*Life* said I gave what was probably the best performance ever recorded on the screen by a U.S. actress. Norma even led the complaints that I should have been nominated. But that wasn't good enough for the Academy. Screw 'em."

"So what are you up to now?" Louella asked, fishing her notebook and pen out of her purse.

"Why are you asking me? You damn well know what I'm about; that's what you do for a living! I just finished *Marked Woman* for Warner, a gangster film based on a Lucky Luciano story in which, of course, I'm cast again as a tramp. But I guess I can tell you that I'm up for the lead in Warner's *Jezebel*, since filming starts in a couple months."

"Good for you!" Parsons commented, scribbling away, her salad ignored as Docky waved for a third Martini. "Costars? Director?"

"Henry Fonda is my costar. And George Brent and Fay Bainter are in the cast. Willy Wyler is directing. It's another sentimental story about a headstrong Southern girl in the Civil War era, but at least it's an important woman's part, which will please you as much as it pleases me. Anyway, I'm starving. Louella, it was nice to see you and Docky and meet you, Mr.—uh—Webster."

Despite the somewhat fractious encounter, Oakley suspected there was mutual respect underlying the relationship. And he was right: years later, Davis would say of the by-then-often-maligned Parsons: "I had some very rough times with Louella. [But] she was probably one of the greatest newspaper women who would ever be: a pro newspaper woman. Nothing would stop her from getting a story."

"Anybody want some dessert?" Louella asked as Davis walked away. "They invented their grapefruit cake for me."

"I'll have some," Oakley said. No one asked Docky, who was quietly snoring away on his side of the booth. "Who was Norma? And what is the Oscar story?"

"Norma is Norma Shearer who, as you know, is the widow of Irving Thalberg. She has a lot of pull in this town. In fact, the furor over Bette's non-nomination forced the Academy to change the way they pick nominees. Now the entire membership of the Motion Picture Academy votes on the nominations instead of a small committee.

"And the Oscar business? It's true that Bette claims she named the statuette Oscar because she says its posterior looks like her husband's. His middle name is Oscar; Harmon Oscar Nelson Jr.; nickname Ham. He's a musician who was her high school sweetheart. I'm afraid, though, that her Oscar story is about the only interesting thing about him, and I've heard that the marriage is a bit shaky and that she's had a couple abortions. And there are others claiming that they named the statuette."

"I thought what she said about *Jezebel* being a woman's picture was interesting," Oakley said as Parsons returned her notebook to her purse. "First time I've heard something like that."

"I'm not surprised," Parsons said. "Hollywood is run by men, old-world types. To most of them, a woman's place is in the home or in dress shops or, in Hollywood, in jobs sometimes where they can't be seen, like writing scripts in the back room. Or, of course, as some Kansan horse-and-buggy doctor said, 'barefoot and pregnant.' Unless, of course, their mugs sell tickets. Then they put them up on the screen. But women directors? Forget it. Dorothy Arzner, and a couple others. That's it.

"I've fought this prejudice all my career," she continued. "From the days when I was writing a newspaper column back in Dixon, Illinois, I've championed the rights of women in journalism and in the movie business. Sometimes, at least in my early scenarios, it was by writing a story about a 'wronged girl' who gets even. But in journalism, if you're a dame, you're usually thought of as just another 'sob' sister. I hated that.

"So I made headlines on one of the first jobs I ever did for Mr. Hearst when I elbowed my way into the press box for the Dempsey-Turner boxing match in Philadelphia in 1926," Parsons added. "The reporters there had never seen a woman in such a place before, and a lot of them thought it was the end of the world. And sometimes just for the hell of it, I'll take the woman's side in a Hollywood story even when she's clearly in the wrong.

"Back in 1935, a writer named Joel Faith, who works for a Commie rag called *New Theatre*, once wrote that I was 'a poor reporter and a wretched writer.' I checked and he's got only a few thousand readers. I know I'm not Mrs. Shakespeare, but I've got twenty million readers every goddamn day plus my radio audience. All those people must like something I'm doing.

"But for some people like that *New Theatre* guy, I can do no right and never will. Just doing what I do for a living is going to make enemies who then call me every name in the God damned book. When you dig into it, it usually turns out that they're just jealous.

"In any event, my nature inclines me to suspect at least something fishy about Eva's measles attack. But remind me of all of your suspicions again."

Oakley did so, and with each repetition, he was more convinced than ever that there was an unseen agenda lying just beyond his fingertips.

"I'll tell you what I can do," Parsons said, diving into an extra large slice of grapefruit cake. "So many people read my column every day that when I say something, lots of people react. I'm no fool as some people think, and I know that I can cause big things to happen when I mention something in my column. I also know I can do great harm and can make people very angry. I'm thinking of writing something about your suspicions in my column. But I warn you, if what you suspect is true, by writing about it, even as a blind item, I could be putting you in a great deal of danger."

"Blind item?" Oakley asked.

"An item that has no attribution and presumably can't be traced. But it's always possible that someone on the receiving end could, by using his or her head, figure out who is involved, which means that if what you suspect is true, someone might go after you. Just so you know."

"I understand," Oakley said. "But more important, I'm deeply flattered that you'd do that for me. Rather, you'd do that for all these people who may have been harmed."

"I agree with you that there seem to be too many coincidences for comfort," Parsons continued. "But there's something else. People have called me stupid. People have called me greedy, but hell, I like getting gifts as much as the next person. And some have even claimed I make up news, but that's not true and usually happens only when I write something that embarrasses them. That also goes with having power. Long ago, about the time Mr. Hearst offered me a national column, I had to think about what I would do with it.

"I decided that, first and foremost, I would always endeavor to protect the film industry. All too often, Hollywood is its own worst enemy. Because the film industry is made up of people who will, more often than not, lie and stab friends in the back to protect their reputations or to get a leg up on a rival, there is less loyalty here than with a cat in heat.

"Clearly the column makes me the social boss of Hollywood, but the place needed a moral leader, too. And, in all modesty, I am determined to also be that whenever it's called for. I also had to be tough about my source material, so I let it be known that if people wanted their news to be included in my column, I had to get it first. Much has been made about my breaking the story of the Fairbanks-Pickford divorce. But not many people know that I sat on that news for several weeks until I was certain that publishing it wouldn't damage the film industry itself since, to millions of people around the world, Doug and Mary *were* the film industry.

"So that's why I'm going to help you out. If what you're telling me is being deliberately done, I want to get the bastards who are doing it. But, again, Oakley, be damn careful. Hollywood people can, and will, play the game much nastier than they ever do in the movies.

"We gotta go. Wake up, Docky boy," she ordered, poking her dozing husband in the ribs. "Oakey, I'll call you in the next day or two and read you the item I think would do the job. It won't appear in the column for a few days because I write in advance, but you'll know when to duck."

With that, the columnist and her husband walked, Docky somewhat unsteadily, to the restaurant's entrance.

Oakley remained for a time, rooted to his seat trying to sort out the columnist's comments from those that sounded factual and those that were merely self-serving. Much of what she said about defending Hollywood's morality was clearly in the latter category, Oakley believed, especially after the early 1930s when she changed her gossip style from writing only adulatory items about film stars to occasionally tossing out judgmental barbs, especially when divorce or a perceived disrespect of her beloved film industry was involved. Greta Garbo, who famously refused to go along with Hollywood's publicity game, was the subject of a notorious feud with Parsons. So was Mae West who, reportedly, once insulted Mr. Hearst's beloved Marion Davies. Parsons, who, considering what she did for a living, might have been more sophisticated, was particularly offended by West's sex-oriented "shtick."

Nevertheless, because Parsons seemed to believe that she was the film capital's moral arbiter sincerely enough to take Oakley's suspicions seriously and plan on writing about them, Oakley decided to take her at her word. And convincingly, she also seemed as sincere in her concern for his well-being. Of course, Oakley, no longer the naïve kid from Missouri as he was when he first arrived in Hollywood, realized that if his suspicions turned out to be true, Parsons's reputation as being the reigning queen of film journalism (as well as her circulation numbers) would benefit tremendously by scooping a huge Hollywood scandal. *Especially*, Oakley thought wryly, *if I ended up being killed as a result.*

"Wonders never cease," he muttered to himself as he left, concerned about whether to leave a tip or not, then realizing that as Parsons and Docky were daily visitors to the restaurant and that no check had been presented, other financial arrangements were clearly in force. Nevertheless, he tucked two dollars under the edge of his plate.

Before leaving the restaurant, he called his office to check on messages.

"Only a call from Michelle Ryder," Benny said. "Want the number?"

The actress answered on the first ring. "Oh, Oakley, I'm so glad you called. I'm so upset. I need to talk with you."

"Fine, but I'm at a pay phone at the Brown Derby. Could I call you back in a half hour from home?"

"OK, OK. Call me as soon as you can."

CHAPTER 15

Despite it being rush hour by the time he finally left the restaurant, Oakley made it back to his apartment in twenty minutes and immediately called Michelle Ryder back.

"Thank you so much, Oakley," she said, sounding somewhat relieved. "You remember that a few days back, we talked about Eva's measles attack that seemed to come out of nowhere and your suspicions?" she asked. "Well, something similar has happened to me."

"Oh, God, that's terrible!"

"I agree," the actress continued. "Like Eva, my housekeeper, Janine Marchand, has come down with something out of the blue. First, we thought it was the flu, but when it got worse, we took her to the emergency room at Cedars, and they say it's pneumonia. And as far as they know, the only case in town."

"I'm so sorry, Michelle. But remember, it's not the only case in town," Oakley explained. "Ari, whose wife you sent to me, has also come down with pneumonia and is in County General."

"Damn it," Michelle exclaimed. "You're right. I'm not remembering anything today. Call me crazy, but I think she was deliberately infected, like you think Eva was deliberately infected with measles. But I'm also certain that it was me someone was after, but they got Janine by mistake. And I think I know how it happened."

"What are you saying?" Oakley asked.

"A week or so ago, Janine and I were working in my garden when the gardener arrived," Michelle explained. "But it wasn't my regular gardener, and it wasn't his usual day to work. This guy said that he was substituting for my regular gardener who had gone out of town and that it was the only day he could come. It sounded reasonable, so neither of us thought anything of it—not then anyway.

"He did the obvious work, cutting the grass and pulling weeds, and then said that he had seen some bugs on the roses and needed to spray them. He went to his truck and got one of those handheld pump sprays and started squirting the roses. Then, when Janine and I went over to see how he was doing, he turned and sprayed Janine in her face; he would have sprayed me, too, but I had stooped down to grab Misty, my little dog, who was digging in the garden.

"Needless to say, he apologized and said that it was an accident and that the stuff was just a diluted bug spray and it wouldn't bother her. And then he left. But then my regular gardener showed up the next day, his regular day. When I told him what happened, he said that he had never gone out of town and had never asked anyone to substitute for him. It seemed really odd, but I stupidly let it go. That is, until Janine got sick a couple days ago. When she told me that no one else she knew had become ill, I realized that maybe it was connected to the substitute gardener and his so-called bug spray. And being naturally suspicious, I realized that maybe it was me who was supposed to have been infected and not Janine and that whoever his guy was, he missed me because I was dealing with the dog."

"Michelle," Oakley said, "this is terrible news about Janine, but it could explain how both Eva Sanderson and Ari Karinopolis were infected. And John Wayne, for that matter, but I don't remember if I told you about that case. It sounds crazy, but maybe someone has gotten hold of some measles and pneumonia virus or whatever it is and has figured out how to use it to deliberately infect people."

"But why Janine, why me," she asked, "if that was the intention and, as I said, I think it was? I'm not involved in anything that would make someone want to hurt me, other than being a fairly successful actress, which makes some people jealous."

"Forgive me, Michelle, but you are involved in something that would make some people seriously angry with you if what we think is true. You are more or less the center of the group of people who share suspicions about Billy Williams's arrest, and maybe someone figured that if they removed you from the scene, some of the interest in finding out what really happened to him might go away."

"Do you really think that could be it?" Michelle said nervously. "I'm no more responsible for suspecting it was all a frame-up than you are. Please, Oakley, I don't mean to suggest that whoever it was who you think might have been interested in getting rid of me should have come after you instead of me. I meant nothing like that. But—"

"I understand," Oakley said, "and, being objective, you are probably right in thinking that I'm a more likely target. As a matter of fact, I had lunch with Miss Parsons, and she warned me about the same thing."

"Why would she warn you? Now she's involved?"

"I guess you could say so. From early on, she's been more or less aware of my hunch. When she and I originally talked about the possibility that the Billy Williams arrest was a frame-up to destroy his career, I told her of a couple of other cases I'm involved in where—maybe I'm just paranoid—I'm beginning to suspect criminal plots are involved. So I decided I needed some fresh, objective thinking. Miss Parsons has seen just about everything in her career, so I figured that if I explained my suspicions in detail to her, she could tell me if I was crazy or not.

"So I did, and she agreed that there might be more than mere coincidence involved. She already had her suspicions about Billy's situation and agreed that Eva Sanderson's tragedy was certainly odd. And I guess it's OK for me to tell you this because she didn't tell me not to: she's figured out a way to find out for sure if there is some nasty business being done or if it's all accidental—everything but the Williams arrest, of course, which all of us agree smells as fishy as a salmon left out in the sun for several days."

"And so what is dear Lolly going to do?"

"She's going to run an item about my suspicions in her column. To right a wrong, she said."

"Oh, my God, Oakley! You never should have told me that. Never, never ever tell anyone what a person as powerful as Louella Parsons is planning to write in her column, especially if she is using the column to manipulate events. My God, Oakley, if the story became public knowledge, she would be terribly embarrassed, maybe even fired. Because the one thing she and other columnists must have is credibility, and she could lose all of that if it got out that she was trying to rig a story. It would be a huge scandal."

"I didn't—" Oakley said, literally gasping for air. "I didn't mean to…"

"The story is safe with me," Michelle said. "But don't ever breathe a word about it to anyone. No one, not even a girlfriend or a boyfriend, whatever. Anyone you know would instantly repeat something like this to everyone they knew."

"She said it would be a blind item."

"Of course. No other way unless you wanted to paint a target around your head and parade down Sunset Boulevard begging for someone to shoot you. She's protecting your ass while pulling the curtain on what—at least one of your guesses—may be one of the biggest scandals Hollywood has ever seen. That is, if what you suspect is true. Of course, if it is true, she and Mr. Hearst will get all the credit.

"She may say it's to 'right a wrong,' but never forget that the real reason is to build circulation. That's the business she's in, and so is Mr. Hearst who, to build circulation for his newspapers back in 1898, actually faked news to start the Spanish-American War and then boasted about doing it. But it's different now, with all his newspapers and magazines and her with twenty-some-million readers. If it came out that she was overtly trying to build circulation with an item in her column solely based on someone's hunch and deliberately written to provoke a response, it would be a catastrophe."

"I can't thank you enough for your advice," Oakley said, his gratitude evident in his voice. "But if it is true, then we'll know who poisoned Eva Sanderson, and Ari, and your housekeeper. And who framed Billy. And the motive behind the rest of my cases if they weren't accidents."

"Yes, we'll know, but probably if there's only one person behind all this. If it's more than one, we'll probably never know for certain, which is a chance she's taking. And certainly you," Michelle added.

"As she told you, it shouldn't be too hard for whoever is behind what you think is happening to figure out your involvement from her blind item," she continued, "which makes you a sitting duck. If what happened in my garden wasn't an accident, it was still a relatively low-level attack—nothing to what would be done to you."

"I know," Oakley said. "Miss Parsons warned me in nearly the same words."

"I'm sure. She's seen the underbelly of the industry for years. So, trust no one. Say nothing to anyone. By the way, do you know what she is going to write and when it's going to run in the column?"

"No. She said she'll read it to me in a couple days and tell me when it will appear."

"When it appears, do not react, either to your office employees or people close to you. Don't even comment to someone about it being an interesting item. Act like you never even noticed it."

"I get it. Thanks for the advice and, Michelle—"

"Yes?"

"Thanks for caring."

"You're welcome. Before we end this sermon of mine, I need to ask you something," the actress said. "You have a gun?"

"Yep, in the office."

"That won't do you a bit of good if someone breaks into your place in the middle of the night. Keep it with you at all times, even when you go to a friend's house for dinner; take it in something that looks like it's meant to hold work you need to do at home. Even take it to the beach if you go. Put it in a beach bag. If someone wants to get to you, they'll do it without warning and when you are most relaxed. So be a Boy Scout and be prepared at all times. And, oh yes, don't forget to keep the damn thing loaded."

"Thanks for the advice, Michelle. I will. When I know when the item is running, I'll call you."

"OK, but tell only me. Don't leave a message. Again, trust no one. Well, I guess you have no choice but to trust me—and Lolly, of course. Oh, was Docky with you when she offered to do this?"

"Yes, but he had passed out—three double Martinis."

"Thank God for small favors. Gotta go and check on Janine. Good luck."

Oakley sat back and sighed. *I really am up to my neck in it*, he thought. *Maybe I shoulda stayed at the law firm.*

For Oakley, the next two days proved relatively uneventful, although filled with growing apprehension about his safety. He did as Michelle asked and now carried his pistol with him in a briefcase, which prompted Benny to ask if he had decided to change his profession from private investigator to lawyer. He also stopped by a sporting goods store near his office and picked up some new ammunition for his semiautomatic Beretta. The bullets he previously bought for it had been lying around since he first acquired the gun two years earlier, and knowing nothing about firearms, he had no idea whether they were still good or not.

Getting the pistol in the first place was done out of naïveté when, soon after he arrived in Los Angeles, his new acquaintances had a little fun at his expense: "initiating" him as an Angeleno as they later laughed. After realizing that Oakley was still somewhat wet behind the ears, they told him that because savage Indians still prowled the local countryside, he needed a gun to protect himself from frequent raids. He quickly wised up to the joke. The closest thing to Indians still living in Southern California were actors as white as he was who were occasionally decked out in makeup, deerskins, moccasins, and feathers to do a job in the movies.

Aside from teaching Oakley his first lesson about Hollywood—that despite what people back in the rest of the country believed about Hollywood (largely derived from media puff pieces)—few people living in his newly adopted home were actually what they appeared to be. So the gun became a dust collector—until now.

On Friday, about the time he was to leave for the day and his date with Joe (he had left a message earlier changing their dinner date to Don the Beachcomber restaurant because he was too exhausted to even think about preparing a meal at the apartment as originally planned), the telephone rang. It was Louella Parsons with the information Oakley had been sort of dreading: the blind item she was running.

"Here's what I think will do the job," she said, sounding, Oakley thought, ominously pleased with herself. *"Lots of Hollywood bigwigs are rightly holding their breaths over a handsome, young private investigator's suspicions that some recent, baffling happenings in the film capital may not have been accidental but were deliberately planned and executed attacks on some of our most beloved actors and actresses. One incident he cites as not seeming legit is Eva Sanderson's recent, rare measles attack, which caused the tragic loss of her and hubby, Stan Damon's, child and her withdrawal from Metro's big-budget Matrimaniac film. If proved to be true, the revelations could be the biggest scandal to hit Tinseltown since the sex, drug, and murder happenings of the early 1920s.* So, there you are. It's running on Sunday, my biggest circulation day."

"Well," Oakley said as he finished scribbling down the item. "I don't know what else to say but thank you. If this brings the truth out in the open, it will be one of the greatest triumphs for justice in the city's history. And you are to thank for it," Oakley said with true feeling, while pragmatically suspecting he was sounding exactly the right adulatory tone."

"And, thanks for saying I was 'handsome,'" he added, knowing that it was her coded way of telling those who spoke Hollywoodese that he was homosexual while wondering why she had done so. The only effect it could possibly have would be to endanger his friends whom, of course, he couldn't warn without revealing Parsons's motivation. "And, again, thank you for helping so much," Oakley said, actually crossing his fingers as he spoke.

"You're welcome, handsome," she replied. "And don't forget to be careful. And if you're not careful, be sure to do your will right away and make me your heir." She laughed. "Bye, for now. Docky says hello. And good-bye, too,"

Not particularly amused by Louella Parsons's passing shot, clearly intended to be humorous, Oakley called Michelle Ryder. She was home, and after passing the usual pleasantries, he read her Parsons's column item.

"Well, that couldn't be clearer, and the fat will really be in the fire Sunday," she said. "You get your gun?"

After assuring the actress that not only was he carrying the pistol everywhere he went, but he had also bought fresh ammunition for it, Oakley admitted that he was beginning to worry, especially about the reference to his "appearance," which could endanger his friends.

"It could," she said, "but it probably won't. What would be the point for someone to go after one of your buddies?" Ryder asked. "Most likely they wouldn't know a thing about your cases and suspicions, so why waste time and energy on eliminating them? If you need to worry about anyone, go look in the mirror. Have you thought of maybe getting out of town for a while?"

Oakley admitted that he had and planned to go to Hawaii in the fall but couldn't see any way of escaping his responsibilities to his clients before then.

"Oakley," Michele said, "maybe you should find a way. Don't mean to be unfeeling, but if you were hurt or, God forbid, killed by these people, those clients would have to find a way to get along without you. What I'm suggesting is that you hide out for a while."

"OK," he said, "but what happens when I return? I don't see anyone else pursuing my suspicions, so a vacation would only postpone the inevitable."

"Got it. Then what you must do is go nowhere but the office every day, keep your gun with you at all times, and stay somewhere else at night for a while. I'm suggesting that at the very minimum, you get the hell out of your apartment. Disappear somewhere…and maybe while you're away, look for a new apartment."

"Maybe that's a good idea," Oakley agreed. "And I think I might be able to pull that one off this weekend."

"Good. And let me know what your new phone number is and where you'll be. But tell no one else except Louella. Become a hermit or a monk, whichever is your preference. Keep all other contact to your office. Oh yes," she added, "I'd think twice about staying with a boyfriend or some friend-friend—too obvious, and you could get them in trouble as well."

"How do you know all this?" Oakley asked.

"Honey, have you been following my movies? I've been called the Queen of Noir even though I've made some real stinkers like *Death in Detroit*. Everything bad that could happen to someone has been in my scripts and movies. And I'm a fast learner…and rememberer."

"So," Oakley asked, "got any ideas of someplace that would fit the bill as a hideout? But not so far away it would take me forever to get anywhere like my office?"

"Not really. Hey, you know?" she paused. "Actually, I may know of a place that could work, but you might not approve of certain aspects of the place."

"Oh?"

"There is a certain director I once worked with—a famous one, by the way—who has an inordinate liking for young women. I hope I'm not offending you."

"No."

"Anyway, among the investments he made was one that involved fulfilling those interests and those of other like-minded men, many of them major movie stars like Gable, Flynn, and Spec Tracy. He built this huge apartment building on Sunset where, as it turned out, a lot of stars also wanted to live, and then rented out a whole floor to a woman named Lee Francis, who runs the snazziest brothel in town—probably the most famous one in California."

"You mean a whorehouse?" Oakley interrupted, suddenly realizing the direction Michelle's suggestion was going. "You're suggesting that I hide out in a whorehouse?"

"Well, why not? It's got a great location and the building was once home to a lot of big stars like Marie Dressler before she built her own place and 'Saint' Loretta Young who moved out as fast as you could say 'Amen' after she discovered that Miss Francis's place was, as Polly Adler said about her own brothel in New York in the 1920s, 'a house but not a home.' And whatever your inclination is sex-wise, no one would ever think of looking for you there. I forget the name, but I think it was Hacienda something or other."

"Oh, my God," Oakley said. "You mean that grand pile called The Hacienda Arms, right next to Ciro's nightclub? Grand double stair out front. Couple blocks down Sunset from the Garden of Allah."

"Yep, that's the place," the actress continued, obviously quite taken with her idea. "Convenient for the stars who live at the Garden and appropriate. Lee's working girls mostly came to Hollywood to become movie stars but ended up as prostitutes who are making, I hear, as much as a grand a week, much more than most movie actresses ever make. Customers park in the back and use a rear entrance, so if you were living there, no one would ever see you comin' or goin'."

"You could fix that?"

"Believe I can," Michelle said. "Give me an hour and I'll call you back."

Well, Oakley thought with a smile, *I guess that's what friends are for, at least in Hollywood: finding you a nice, upscale whorehouse to hide out in when you need to disappear for a while.*

In fact, it was less than an hour when Michelle called back with good news. She had spoken to the director who owned the place who spoke with Lee Francis, and Oakley was welcome to stay as a favor for the actress, "So long as he doesn't fool around with any of the merchandise," he cautioned.

"Actually, that was my version of what he said." Michelle laughed. "He said you could fool around with the merchandise all you wanted, but unlike your room, it wouldn't be free. But like Metro, which has a charge account at the place, you can charge it."

"MGM has a charge account there?" Oakley exclaimed.

"Sure does. Perfect for providing big-name visitors a little entertainment when they're in town. Ya gotta do something for the visiting firemen."

"I don't think your director needs to worry about me running up a tab for the merchandise," Oakley said. "But why is this room free for me?"

"Look, honey, haven't you learned in your time in Hollywood that when someone does you a favor, it isn't always a good idea to ask too many questions? Besides running on money, Hollywood is run on favors. Let's just say that I did the director a big one once when he got in trouble when a very big-name actor in a film of his became a very big, expensive problem. I was able to smooth things out and saved him from losing a lot of money. People remember things like that—most of the time anyway.

"They're expecting you to check in tonight. Just ask for Lee Francis, and she'll fix you up. You'll even have your own telephone line in your room. But remember, don't tell anyone—boyfriend, girlfriend, postman, your mother, your dad, the dogcatcher, whoever—where you are or what the phone number is. That's why it's called 'hiding out.' And the more I think about it, instead of what I suggested before, it would make more sense if you stayed away from your office, too. Then you could tell everyone you're out of town on a hush-hush job or something like that. Call in a couple times a day to get your messages.

"The girls are being told you're a screenwriter friend of the boss staying there for a while to work on a script. So lug along a typewriter and some paper when you move in. And, oh yes, your name is Mark Savage—name of a character in one of my old films who got killed off. So if someone calls out 'Mark,' be sure to react. It's you."

"Got it. I've got a dinner thing tonight, so I may be a bit late checking in."

"Are you kiddin'? That's when things just get going at Lee's place. Your only problem will be finding a parking place."

CHAPTER 16

By now, it was getting late, too late for what he really wanted to do, which was to cancel his dinner date with Joe Valentine. At this point, it would be difficult to get out of spending the night at Joe's place afterward, disappointing a potential love interest twice in a row. However, the circumstances were beyond his control, so after calling the restaurant and leaving word for Joe that he was running a bit late, Oakley grabbed his typewriter, stuffed a sheaf of paper in his briefcase next to his gun, and left his office, not knowing when or even if he would see it again. Joe would have to live with his disappointment.

As Oakley anticipated, Joe, who had been cooling his heels for an hour by the time Oakley fought his way through Friday night traffic to the Hollywood restaurant, was furious, his anger somewhat abetted by the consumption of two Zombies, the restaurant's signature (and lethal) cocktail, while he waited. No explanation was good enough, certainly not Oakley's excuse—albeit true—that he had been tied up on a long business call. So, a Zombie of his own in hand, Oakley decided he might as well get all the bad news out of the way at once, and explained—with an uncharacteristic lie—that as he had to be in Palm Springs for an early meeting the following morning, instead of ending the evening at Joe's place, he was going to have to "hit the road" for the desert resort immediately following their dinner.

"So why didn't you just call and cancel the dinner, too?" Joe hissed with unveiled sarcasm. "Then you could have been on the road right away and wouldn't have to bother with me!"

"I would have, but it was already too late." As quickly as he said it, Oakley realized that he had made a terrible mistake, unintentionally adding what Joe would hear as indifference bordering on adding insult to injury.

So he wasn't surprised when Joe stood, slammed down the menu he had been idly perusing, said, "So leave then. I am," and stormed out.

Oakley was exasperated, frustrated, and disappointed. He knew he was being unreasonably angry with Joe for not accepting his story, knowing at the same time he couldn't tell him what was really going on. He liked Joe too much to brush the issue aside with the old proverb about being unable to make an omelet without breaking eggs, but he also knew that, clichéd as it was, it stated the situation precisely. Moreover, he knew his unexplained disappearance was going to hurt, anger, or mystify others as well.

"Better them angry or hurt than mourning my death," Oakley said aloud, deciding that he might as well order dinner for himself and waving at his waiter. "My friend was feeling ill and had to leave," he said. "But I'm staying for dinner. First, though"—he held up the tiny umbrella that came perched in his drink—"I'll have another one of these."

It was close to 11:00 p.m. when, after stopping by his apartment and packing a suitcase with clothes and other daily necessities (including the latest whodunit from Agatha Christie, whose mysteries were not surprisingly becoming habit), Oakley pulled his Ford into the parking lot behind The Hacienda Arms, which was already filled with a collection of the most expensive automobiles in Los Angeles. After waiting a few minutes in his car, a huge tan Duesenberg sports car pulled out, and Oakley quickly parked in the space, thinking as he did so that the driver looked a lot like Clark Gable.

After reminding himself his name was Mark Savage and so identifying himself to the doorman at the rear entrance, he was told to take the elevator marked "Private" in the small adjoining lobby to the fourth floor and tell the receptionist he would find there that Miss Francis was expecting him.

The place looked exactly what popular opinion thought an upscale whorehouse would look like at the time: fake Louis XVI sofas upholstered in gold velvet set in a lobby-like room seemingly wallpapered with crimson brocade; a few paintings of ripe, nude women set in heavy, ornate, gold-leafed frames;

and an ostentatious reception desk that looked like it would have been chosen by Napoleon had he shopped for furniture from a studio prop department.

Seated at the desk was a young woman who possessed a body as voluptuous as any pictured in paintings; her face was overly made-up and set in an expression that resembled a decadent Kewpie doll. Oakley, rather "Mark," identified himself, and only moments after the receptionist made a telephone call, a florid, large woman dressed in a flowing, coral-colored, floor-length, silk dress walked briskly in from the adjoining room. "Mr. Savage," the woman announced, her hand extended in greeting. "I'm Lee Francis. Michelle Ryder told me you might be arriving tonight. You are so welcome."

"Thank you, Miss Francis," Oakley said, searching for something appropriate to say to a madam who would also be his host for the duration. "I love what you are wearing," he punted. "Is that what they call a muumuu in Hawaii? It looks so comfortable and flattering."

"Thank you. I believe so. With all the running around I have to do, I need something that puts comfort first. Like I plan for you! We want you to be happy here for as long as you stay with us. I'm told that you are a writer?"

"Yes. I left my typewriter and things in my car. I'll retrieve them after you show me where I'm going to be stashed."

"'Stashed' isn't quite the right term," she said. "We have the best guest room for you with your own bath. I think you'll be very comfortable. Opal, here"—she snapped her fingers, and a black woman in a black uniform and white apron appeared—"will show you to your room and explain everything. We have several meal services here. Breakfast—which is lightly patronized because the girls usually stay up quite late—lunch, dinner, and a late supper served right about now. The dining room is right down the hall. Opal will show you around and give you the times of meal service, room cleaning, and all that.

"But now I must return to my duties. Nose to the grindstone, never a moment off. But we'll see each other often. I usually am in the dining room for the lunch service, but I prefer to have my dinner in my private quarters. Busy, busy time, getting ready for the evening."

"Again, thank you so much," Oakley said, stifling an urge to bow. *This is just a whorehouse*, he reminded himself before realizing that the refined welcome and cinematically overdone decor were part of the reason the place was considered the best brothel in town. You don't get the patrons the place was famous for without the ambience resembling a heterosexual Midwestern male's fantasy.

Mae West would feel right at home here, Oakley thought before realizing that a number of his homosexual friends would also find the place's over-the-top decor equally appealing. "So much for jumping to conclusions," he said aloud to himself, as Opal beckoned for him to follow her down a chandelier-lit corridor wallpapered in what appeared to be gold-flocked brocade.

"Here's yo' room," Opal said, opening a door with a star framing the number 5 mounted on it. It was furnished as he expected with vaguely French Louis something-or-other imitation antiques, which were probably the best fakes money could buy—maybe from Barker Brothers, one of the city's top furniture stores—and a comfortable double bed to boot. *Well, that's to be expected*, he said to himself, noticing that at least the color scheme was done in fairly subdued tones of tan and burgundy. Rich, as they say, but not gaudy, which considering where he was, could mean that the mirror was over the dresser, not on the ceiling.

"I believe Miz Francis said you wuz a writer?" Opal said. "So here be a desk fo' you. And the bath is ova here," she said, opening a door.

After showing him a directory indicating the meal times and other house policies, she asked him if that was all, adding, "This was Miz Harlow's room"—a comment that literally stopped Oakley in his tracks.

"What do you mean 'This was Miss *Jean* Harlow's room?' Why on earth was she here?"

"Well, I guess I shudn' say, but Miz Harlow," Opal added in a low voice, "she had a likin' for sorta rough-type men. An' I guess she wuz able to meet some hereabouts. Story roun' here wuz that she done paid Miz Francis a hunnert dollas for ever' new man she done meet here. Pleez, pleez, don' say I said sumptin' 'bout her. Maybe it be secrit."

"My lips are sealed, Opal," Oakley said. "Don't worry. And thank you for showing me everything." *What a town!* Oakley thought as the maid left. *Every time you think you know all there is to know about someone, it turns out you don't know anything. And now I'm sleeping in Jean Harlow's bed!*

After retrieving his typewriter and suitcase from the car, Oakley decided that because it was too late to call Donny and Les to cancel their mutual weekend plans, and there was really no point in worrying that they might react as angrily as Joe, he might as well go to bed and snuggle up with Agatha Christie's newly published whodunit, *Cards on the Table.*

Putting off Les and especially Donny the next morning was not so easy. Les understood that occasionally work responsibilities trumped social engagements and was apparently convinced by Oakley's excuse that their dinner date needed to be postponed again as he had to go out of town on a case. Les didn't ask for details and none were given.

Donny, however, was a different story. Oakley knew that his boyfriend, lover, or whatever description fit their present relationship would not be put off by a simple "out of town on business" excuse, nor could he tell him he was hiding out. So he decided to tell him that he had to go to Kansas City for a short trip on family business and to save money, would take the train instead of flying, which added a week to the trip. Donny was of course unhappy, but after Oakley added the story about a favorite uncle dying, and as his heir, he was required to appear before the probate judge, Donny reluctantly accepted his excuse.

The following week also proved, thankfully, to be uneventful despite the publication of Louella Parsons's blind item on Sunday. Just so no one would miss it, Parsons, in fact, had led off the column with it. No question, Oakley realized, that millions now knew that there might be something bad going on behind Hollywood's tinsel. Despite consternation over warnings about his safety, he was also pleased and more than a little proud that someone important, in this case, the film capital's most powerful columnist, took his suspicions seriously.

The highlight of his week, aside from an upbeat conversation with Parsons when he called to thank her, was a call from Michelle Ryder to say that, as Oakley had requested, she had spoken with Metro's publicity boss, Howard Strickling, after Parsons's column appeared, and that he apparently knew nothing of any covert mischief. *So much for clarifying anything*, Oakley thought ruefully.

She also asked how the move went. After Oakley explained how welcoming Lee Francis had been, they ended the conversation, agreeing to talk every couple days. All of that, Oakley realized with awe, had taken place on what was once Jean Harlow's private telephone.

He was also getting acquainted with Lee Francis's working girls. Obviously, they were all beautiful, alluring, and to Oakley's unalloyed fascination, outspoken on subjects ranging from women's rights to male endowment. But for some reason he didn't entirely understand—perhaps they sensed without being told that he was a homosexual and thus, a fellow outcast from traditional social rules—he was immediately accepted as a member of their unorthodox group. "It's like you are all members of a club!" Oakley exclaimed after they all joined in laughing over one girl's crack about a certain famous actor's unorthodox sexual proclivities.

As with Oakley, all the girls, in fact most of the employees of the bordello, seemed to have adopted false identities—an understandable but oddly employed tactic because all or most of them seemed to have chosen names of precious or semiprecious jewels. *Opal, for one*, Oakley thought. "But here we have Emerald, Ruby, Amethyst, Pearl, Amber, and so on—everything but diamond," he commented.

"You're wrong," Emerald, a girl of about twenty-three with flaming red hair corrected him. "We had one who called herself Diamond Lil, you know, Mae West's character in that play a few years back? But she had to change it because she was losing business. We couldn't figure out why because to everybody's thinking, Mae West means sex. Maybe in plays and movies as we found out, but not in real life as it turned out. The guys—our guys who are our regulars—thought that because of the name, she must look like Miss West. That may have been hotsy-totsy in the twenties, but most of our customers these days like girls much—how should I say it?"

"Thinner!" a couple of the girls shouted.

"But always with big boobs." Emerald laughed.

Another event that week was a near encounter that was less amusing and also puzzling. Returning from the dining room one evening, he spotted a familiar face emerging from the elevator and, as he was incognito,

Oakley immediately ducked into what proved to be a broom closet. *Who the hell is that?* he thought, suddenly remembering it was the same young, blond, Scandinavian-looking guy whom he had recognized at Aimee Semple MacPherson's service. Oakley still had no idea where he had seen him before; all he knew was that given the circumstances of his present residence, he had to avoid him. Oakley quietly opened the closet door a crack to see if the coast was clear, but it wasn't. The blond man along with an older, somewhat grizzled man who also sported a crew cut, were talking with Lee Francis. *Looks like they are negotiating,* Oakley thought. *Two for one deal, maybe?*

Just then, Opal appeared and led them off down a different corridor than that where Oakley's room was located. As soon as the coast was clear, he scurried to his own room, resolved to, one way or another, solve the mystery of who this familiar person was. It was beginning to drive him crazy.

The next morning when Opal arrived to make his bed, he asked her who the two men were.

"I don' know dere names," she said, "but I tink dat the older man done call the yungun Lonny—sumptin' lak dat anyways. Strange peoples, tho."

"How so?" he asked as Opal began tucking new sheets in the bed.

"Well, as I hears it, the olda man, he go for a differnt girl each time he visit, so long they be blon' wit' blue eyes. But da yungun? He jus' watches... but in da same room. One doin' his stuff, da udder jus' wachin'. Not nachrul."

"Wow," Oakley said, "sounds really strange."

"An' dey nebber leave me nuttin'. Guess dey tink da room clean itself up."

"Thanks," Oakley said. "You won't ever have to worry about that with me."

"I nebber hafta worry 'bout you, Mista Savage. You be a gemmun'. Not so sure 'bout dose guys, tho'. Sometimes, dey makin' lotsa noise in dere."

"Opal," Oakley asked, "do you know who was with them last night?"

"Sure 'nuff. It wuz Amber."

"Thanks," Oakley said as Opal left, resolving to have a little chat with Amber as soon as possible. That was easily arranged that night at dinner by Emerald, who assured Amber that because Oakley/Mark was a friend of the owner—"Miss Francis's boss," she added—he was safe to confide in.

"What you do behind closed doors is your business," Oakley/Mark reassured Amber. "The only thing that interests me is his name. Well, that and why the other guy was in the room."

"I don't know his last name," she said, "but his first name is Henry. The other guy, who he called Johnny, did call him Mr. something or other, but I don't remember it exactly…maybe Grant or something like that—"

Oakley, taking a shot in the dark, interrupted, "Could Henry's last name have been Graber?"

"Could be. The blond kid, I never figured out why he was there. All he did was watch," she said, confirming Opal's story. "Once, after he was done, Henry asked this Johnny person something like 'You want to have a go at her?' I don't remember the exact words, but he was offering me to him like I was dessert. But Johnny shook his head and said, 'No, thanks.' Miss Francis wouldn't have liked that at all anyway since Henry had paid for only himself. Two-for-one is a different price." She laughed.

So, part of the mystery is solved, Oakley thought. Henry Graber, the man who stole the client from the Karinopolis talent agency—which reminded him that he had been remiss in checking on Ari's pneumonia.

The next morning, the first call he made was to Maria Karinopolis, and the news wasn't good. She was in tears. In between sobs, she said that the hospital had called, and because Ari had taken a turn for the worse during the night, they suggested that she return. "I'll come over, too," Oakley said. "I'll be there as soon as I can, he said, regardless of his safety concerns.

Needless to say, the mood was somber in Ari's room at LA County Hospital. Maria was sobbing, and a couple who were apparently their children were looking on sadly as a doctor was feverishly pumping Ari's chest. "I'm afraid…" he said consolingly.

"No, no, no!" Maria shouted.

"I'm sorry," the doctor said as he continued to attend to her husband. "I believe he's expired."

"You believe? You believe?" Maria shouted through her tears. "You're supposed to know! You're supposed to keep this from happening!"

To Oakley and the others, it was clear that Ari had succumbed to pneumonia, however it was acquired. But Maria wasn't hearing anything or believing anything. Oakley soon realized that it was hopeless remaining; being with her children instead of a relative outlier like Oakley was probably the best thing for Maria right now. So, after embracing her and saying how sorry he was—despite the fact that he realized she wasn't hearing anything he was saying—he left, resolved that he would call and commiserate with her when she was less emotionally fraught.

No harm in stopping by the apartment and picking up some clean clothes on the way back to the whorehouse, Oakley thought with a smile. *It's about time I visit the office if only to go through the mail and see what Benny has been up to.*

Everything was peaceful at his place, eerily so when compared with the activity and constant presence of dozens of people at Lee Francis's place. In fact, the only person he saw was Luis the super, attending to some minor repair work on the front of his building.

"Nice to see you, Mr. Oakley. Been out of town?" he asked.

"Yep," Oakley replied with a smile. "Busy, busy. Everything copacetic?"

"Copa what?" Baragon asked, clearly unfamiliar with the slang term suggesting all was normal and dating from the previous decade. "If you're asking how things been ' round here while you were away, they been quiet, except for your visitor the other day."

"Visitor?"

"Yessir. Some guy. Crew cut. Said he had a date with you. I told him you weren't around, probably out of town for all I knew, and he asked if he could leave a present for you in your apartment. I remembered what you had told me before and said that you had forbidden me to let anyone into your place. He didn't seem very happy about that and left. Didn't even ask if he could leave his name or the present with me to give you when you got back."

"Well, life's full of little mysteries," Oakley said seemingly offhandedly, although considering the warnings from Michelle Ryder and Louella Parsons, the incident made him uneasy. "Thanks anyway," he said, as he went up the stairs to his place.

Everything seems normal, he thought, *but why shouldn't it be? No one has been in here since I left. At least no one has been in here and wanted me to know it as before.* After a cursory look-over, Oakley grabbed some fresh clothing, stuffed it into an empty Ralph's shopping bag, and going into his kitchen to check on what was in his refrigerator, suddenly noticed that the back door of his apartment was unlocked.

"What the hell?" he asked aloud. "Hey, Luis, could you come up here a moment?" Oakley shouted out the window. "Before I left, I made sure the back door was locked, and now it's not. Were you in here working?"

"No, sir. I had no reason to go into your place."

"I guess that's yet another of life's little mysteries," Oakley said, now more worried than ever. Nevertheless, as there was no way of penetrating the mystery, Oakley, who always tried to be pragmatic, shrugged, closed, and relocked the door. "Please keep your eye on the place," he said to Luis as they left the apartment. "I'll be away for, maybe, another couple weeks. If you need me for an emergency, you can call me at this number," he said, scribbling the number for his private telephone at the bordello on a piece of scrap paper despite Michelle Ryder's caution that he give it to no one but her and Louella Parsons.

"You stayin' in town?" his superintendent asked. "I thought you were away somewhere. Girlfriend you doan" want nobody to know about?"

"You could say that." Oakley smiled enigmatically.

He was still worried about what was clearly a break-in into his apartment when he arrived at his office. "Hey, boss, whatcha doin' here? I thought you was outa town for the duration," Benny exclaimed.

"The duration of what, Benny?" Oakley said with uncharacteristic impatience. "Summer?"

"No, boss," he explained. "Jus' didn' know exactly when you were comin' back. Glad to see ya, though. Lotsa telephone messages. An' lotsa mail, too."

Oakley seated himself at his desk and started going through the mail. There was the ever-growing blizzard of advertising junk that had exploded after bulk mail rates were introduced several years before; all of it went directly into the wastebasket. There were a few letters, among them a note from Michael Trevalian thanking him for their dinner meeting and adding that the enclosed $50 check was to cover his initial work. There was also another $250 check from Docky Martin enclosed with a tear sheet of his wife's column with the blind item and a note that read in part: "Louella knew this would get a response but has been overwhelmed with letters and calls about it. She'd appreciate it if you would give her a call when you come out from hiding as Michelle Ryder suggested."

"My God," Oakley said aloud with a smile, "does that woman know everything?"

"Hey, Benny, other than the mail and these messages, anything special happen when I was gone?"

"Nothin', Oakey. Well, there was this guy who came by with a package for you but wouldn't leave it."

"Crew cut? Fortyish?"

"Yep, that's him."

For yet another time that morning, Oakley found himself repeating the hoary sentiment "another of life's little mysteries" while troubled by the realization that something was going on that he wasn't sure about.

Best thing to do would be to start returning calls. First, of course, would be Docky Martin, who as soon as he answered, passed the call to his wife.

"Oakley, I'm so happy to hear your voice. I was beginning to wonder if one of my readers figured out that you were the 'handsome, young private investigator' I described and did away with you. Glad you're still alive!"

This lady doesn't waste time cutting to the chase, Oakley thought with a rueful grimace. "Needless to say, I'm pretty happy about that, too," Oakley said. "Docky mentioned that you had been buried in responses to the story. Is that usual?"

"Well, yes and no," the columnist said. "Depends on the item of course. People love mysteries anyway, but they love them even more when big stars like Eva could be involved in a big Hollywood scandal, as I made pretty clear. I think I've gotten some five hundred letters and calls. And all of them asked me to reveal the real story, which of course is not in the cards—not yet anyway. But, getting real, besides still being alive for which we are all grateful, how're you doin' hiding out in a whorehouse? At least it's a good one I hear. I'll bet you could come across some pretty hot news items for yours truly there."

"Not necessarily, but it is fascinating. I'm getting acquainted with the girls—only in a brotherly way," Oakley quickly injected when Parsons chuckled. "They're pretty interesting. Most came to Hollywood from the Midwest chasing their dreams to be in movies and ended up working for Miss Francis and making a lot more money."

"So I hear, too."

"And here's an item for you. One of the maids there told me that my bed-room was once reserved for Jean Harlow who used to come by a couple times a week and pay Lee Francis a hundred dollars to pick out men *she* wanted—reversing the usual arrangement."

"Yeah," Parsons said slowly, "not bad. But using that could be seen as sorta like spitting on her grave. I have to think a bit more about it. But then again, worse things were said about her and her marriages, like poor Paul Bern killing himself because he—or maybe she—thought his…um…equip-ment was too small. Maybe he knew more than he let on. But dead men tell no tales. Thanks, though."

"Right," Oakley said, inwardly squirming over the columnist's use of the clichéd saying until he realized he had been dismissing the mysterious visits by a gift-bearing man to his home and office with a similar cliché.

"So, more to the point: you getting along OK? Anything new on the great investigation?"

"I'm fine, and thanks for asking. A few bumps in the road, though, one serious. Stopped by my place and found that someone had been in it and left the door unlocked. Nothing gone, though, so I'm wondering what the motive was. But the bad news is that in the Eva Sanderson matter, the husband of the couple who once represented Eva Sanderson and still represents her husband and also the girl who replaced Eva died of pneumonia this morning."

"Did you speak to me about that before? What's so suspicious about it?" Parsons asked.

"Well," Oakley said, "nothing, perhaps, other than the fact that the doc-tor at Los Angeles County Hospital said that there were no other pneumonia cases in the entire city that he knew about. Again, call me a nervous Nellie, but it is certainly odd and the connection to the Eva Sanderson case on every level gives me goose bumps."

"I see what you mean," the columnist replied. "I guess you'll stay on top of this without being reminded by me."

"Of course. And thanks for everything."

Chapter 17

Oakley's next phone call was another "keeping in touch" call to Michelle Ryder who, if he were able to award medals for going beyond the call of duty, would be first in line to receive one. Somehow, he felt that if matters turned bad, really bad, everyone else in his professional life—from Les Grady to Louella Parsons to his contacts at the LAPD— would, after missing him for a bit, get along just fine. However, Michelle Ryder, for reasons he didn't fully understand, was clearly committed to his well-being. *Someday, I'll ask her why*, Oakley vowed to himself, while dialing her telephone number. *That is, if I'm still around after all this is resolved*, he thought wryly.

"Hi, Oakey," she virtually shouted into the telephone. "Not dead yet? Made it with any of the girls?"

"'Fraid not, on either count," Oakley said, laughing. "Not really on the agenda, the girls anyway."

"I know, I know. Just kidding. Seriously," she continued, "any rumbles from the enemy?"

Oakley repeated much of what he had just related to Louella Parsons including the news of Ari Karinopolis's death and the story about the visit of a man with some sort of gift to both his home and his office. To his surprise, after agreeing with his suspicions about Ari's death, Michelle seemed much more concerned than the columnist over the break-in of his apartment.

"If your suspicions are correct," she said, "and I'm beginning to be convinced that they are, these people will stop at nothing to get you out of their way, especially after Lolly's column the other day. I must say, she certainly gave it a big play—lead item and long.

"Of course, that means that now whoever's behind this knows that some people in Hollywood are on to them and their schemes as well as you, or at least some 'handsome private investigator.' And how many 'handsome private investigators' can there be, even in a place as large as Los Angeles? I believe it's as clear as a Musso and Frank's Martini that they probably have zeroed in on you already. Still keepin' your gun handy?"

"Sure 'nuff," Oakley assured her. "So what do you think this guy with a gift is all about?"

"Since it's not your birthday, and I'm assuming it isn't," Michelle said, "and he wouldn't leave it with your super as any legitimate delivery person would do, I'd be very careful with the package if and when it ever comes into your possession. Don't under any circumstances try to open it. Call the police, say you think it is suspicious, and let them deal with it."

"And my excuse for doing that would be?"

"Just tell them that you think it's a bomb. If it is, they'll realize you did the right thing. If it is only some clothes being returned by some guy you might have spent the night with, they'll think you're paranoid. So what? Better safe than sorry."

What is it about these damned clichés? Oakley wondered. *Something seems out of kilter and suddenly everybody, including me, starts spouting clichéd maxims left and right. Maybe clichés just go with trouble like cake and icing.*

"I agree," Oakley said, adding, "I really gotta go now. Can't miss dinner with the girls. I'll call you in the next couple days, and thanks for caring, Michelle."

Oakley sat quietly for a few moments, trying to figure out exactly what his next move would be. It seemed that his responsibilities were increasing, and the death of Ari Karinopolis just added more to them because he realized that more than sympathy was called for. And any solution to the puzzle over the Billy Williams frame-up, which he was being well paid to solve, hadn't gotten any clearer, nor had he come up with any way to rehabilitate Michael Trevalian, which of course was the client's purpose. He thought, *I guess there's not much to be done about Rachael's violin.* And with all the time and attention he had paid to it, Eva Sanderson's bout with measles seemed less suspicious than merely a natural occurrence. *Talk about getting nowhere,* he thought.

"Benny, why don't you take the next few days off?" Oakley suggested, realizing that what he wanted most of all was to remove as much static as he could from his life, especially because he was getting fed so much generally useless information and gossip by Lee Francis's girls. "Not much going on here," he said with his fingers crossed. "And you deserve a bit of paid vacation."

"OK, boss. You mad at me about somethin'?"

"Absolutely not. If I'm mad at anyone, it's myself. I can't seem to get anywhere on these damn cases."

"If I could say so, I think one reason is that you started off on the wrong road by thinking that movie star's measles attack was part of some plot instead of her just getting some kid's disease."

"Benny, we've gone through this time and time again. I believe there's something funny about it, but you don't. Maybe we'll find out one day. Now go home and have some fun."

After Benny left, Oakley continued ruminating for a while. Unlike him, he didn't know what he wanted or needed to do next. He was, for all intents and purposes, at a dead end.

"Maybe a drive and a little company would help," he muttered to himself. *Why not combine both?* he realized, by driving out to Hollywood and dropping in on Joe Valentine. *Need to do some fence mending anyway after the debacle at Don the Beachcomber's. Said and done.*

Joe answered the buzzer at his building's gate on the first ring and, over the crackling intercom at least, sounded surprised with Oakley's impromptu visit and not as unhappy as might be expected after their arguement at the restaurant. Joe promptly buzzed him into the building's lush, Spanish castle-style courtyard. He was again struck by how perfectly the place represented the kind of romantic, exotic setting in which, as millions of movie fans probably fantasized, most Hollywood residents lived.

Joe's door was opened the instant he knocked, but to his surprise, it wasn't Joe who opened it. There, a couple feet from him, was the tall, slim, blond man he thought he had recognized at Aimee Semple MacPherson's Sunday service and at the whorehouse.

"Hi, Oakley," he said. "Welcome."

"Do I know you?" Oakley asked, thoroughly confused.

"I guess you don't remember me," the blond said. "We met once before. Some time ago so you probably forgot."

"Guess so," Oakley replied.

"My name is Johnny Cleveland," he explained, ushering Oakley into Joe's living room with its soaring ceiling. "I once waited on you when I was working at Musso's. I told you how I had moved here from South Dakota to become a movie star. Didn't quite work out that way, but here I am anyway." He laughed as Joe walked into the room from the kitchen. "Johnny's my agent," Joe said, "like I once mentioned. Les Grady hired him for his talent agency after meeting him at Musso's, and then when Johnny left Les's place, I went along with him."

"Oh yes," Oakley replied. "A company named New something or other."

"New World Agency," Joe added, "run by a great guy named Henry Graber."

Oakley froze, instantly connecting the dots with the story of Maria Karinopolis's story of how a one-time employee of her and her husband's talent agency named Henry Graber—she called him Grabber—left and stole some of their top clients. *How odd that Les's employee Johnny Cleveland would end up with him not to speak of accompanying him to Lee Francis's place. Hollywood is really a tiny, tiny town,* he realized.

However, in the present situation, he could hardly let on any of this to either Joe or Johnny. "Weren't you also using another name when we met?" Oakley asked Cleveland to mask his surprise.

"Yep," Johnny replied, "I was using a name I thought would work better in films: Bob Barkley. But, so far, I haven't needed to use it. Maybe one day..."

If you're lucky, Oakley thought. *The dream never dies. At least he didn't end up as a hustler.* And then he realized that he might be jumping too quickly to such a conclusion; why was he with Graber at the whorehouse? Didn't that seem a bit more than an employer-employee relationship? Time for another use of a hoary cliché, he decided: wait and see.

"Wouldn't that be nice," Oakley punted in reply to Johnny's hope to break into movies one day.

"Listen, Joe, I wanted to come by because I feel really badly about the misunderstanding at the restaurant the other night. And I want to apologize for being late, which caused it."

"I guess that'll do," Joe said. "I was really pissed off because I had made plans to see you and maybe overreacted. Those drinks they make are lethal, too. So maybe we should just put it all behind us. Blame it on the booze, as they say.

"By the way, despite the fact I was mad at you," Joe continued, "I went ahead and got you a couple tickets for the Gershwin concert. They'll be at the Bowl box office. September 8—that's a Wednesday. I also invited Les who will be in the same box with you. Johnny will be there somewhere also. Want something to eat?" Joe asked with a gesture meant to include both Oakley and Johnny.

"Sure. I can always eat," Johnny said as Oakley also nodded.

"I'll whip up a salad or something. At least it'll be healthy."

And so the afternoon progressed well. Oakley was still trying to figure out what the exact relationship was between Johnny and Joe. He was of course his agent, which meant a certain amount of closeness, but there seemed to be more to it. Were they lovers? Then what was Johnny's role with Henry Graber? *I'm simply no good at relationship things*, Oakley said to himself, sat down, and enjoyed the salad.

This is a work day, he suddenly realized as they were diving into some of the Neapolitan ice cream Joe loved, *and there's no way for anyone to find me if I'm needed. Benny isn't at the office to take messages any longer, and I'm not at home or the whorehouse to answer the phone.* "Sorry, guys," Oakley said, suddenly somewhat panicked that perhaps actions motivated by Louella Parsons's column item might be swirling about him, the putative target, without people having any way of warning him. "I can't play hooky any longer," he said, rising from the table. "Gotta tend to business. Johnny, if I don't see you before the concert, I'll see you there. And Joe, are you going to be able to join us at any point?"

"Probably after the concert," his somewhat reconciled friend suggested. "I'll look for you in your box."

Oakley quickly beat a retreat to the bordello, found a parking space next to a gorgeous French Delage roadster, famously owned by Charles Boyer. *Damn!* he thought. *Even in the middle of the afternoon!*

Just as he feared, he heard a telephone ringing when he was walking down the hall to his room. *Gotta be mine*, he realized. Lee Francis or Kewpie doll would have grabbed it right away if someone was calling for a home or studio delivery—a side business provided by Francis's business when an actor was too tied up in work to make it to the bordello.

It was. "Hey, Mr. Webster, it's Luis."

"Wow, I didn't expect to hear from you so soon. What's up?"

"Well, right after you left, that guy who tried to deliver a package for you before came by again and this time asked if he could leave it. I said that I usually didn't accept deliveries, but as he had tried once before, I said OK. But I thought I should tell you."

Actually, he tried twice before, Oakley thought. *Must be determined to get it to me.*

"But then he asked for something sorta strange. He asked me if you was outa town, and I said, 'Not as far as I knew,' that you'd been here like always. I figured it was none of his business that you might be shacked up wit' someone. Did I do right?"

"Yes," Oakley agreed. "Exactly the right thing to say." As Oakley figured, the last thing for anyone to know is that he might be so aware of what was going on he was hiding out. Just be hard to find.

"Then he said that it was a gift," Luis added. "And that it was a special, very personal present for you and asked that I leave it on the nightstand next to your bed. So what you want me to do?"

"Just put it there," Oakley instructed. "We'll find out what's so special about it when I open it. I'll come by tomorrow sometime."

The rest of the day was spent indulging in what seemed to be a desperately needed nap and then gossiping and laughing with the girls at dinnertime. Then it was early to bed and another hour or so with Agatha Christie.

Why is the fire alarm ringing? Oakley thought as he was jolted awake sometime in the middle of the night. He quickly realized that it wasn't a fire alarm but his telephone shrilly ringing. After glancing at the bedside alarm clock and quickly wondering if it was Jean Harlow's too, Oakley staggered over to the desk and answered the telephone. "Hello? Hello?" he said.

"Oh, Mr. Webster, I'm so glad you're there." It was his superintendent, Luis, calling again.

"Yes, Luis," he said. "I guess you know it's 2:00 a.m. Has something happened?"

"Sí, sí, Mr. Webster. Somethin' terrible has happened. Somethin' blew up in your apartment a little while ago, and it's all on fire. I called the fire department, and they are on the way. There's a big hole in the wall where your bedroom is."

"Oh my God," Oakley said. "Was anyone hurt?"

"Nobody, but everyone is awake and sitting in the courtyard wondering what to do," Luis said as Oakley heard sirens in the background. "Here's the fire department now. Wherever you are, can you get over here soon?"

"I'm on my way," Oakley said, hanging up the instrument, falling into the clothes he had worn earlier, and running down the back stairs of the bordello instead of waiting for the elevator. Idly noting that the Delage was still there, he backed out of his space and exited the parking lot on a nearly deserted Sunset Boulevard. Luckily, because of the time of night—actually morning—there was little cross-town traffic, and he made it to his place in the fastest time he had ever managed.

The building his apartment was in was lit with emergency floodlights and looked like a disaster-movie set. Fire engines were parked randomly in the street, and seemingly, hundreds of people were standing around, curious to see what happened. Smoke was still pouring from the area between his building and the next, right where his bedroom would be and where the firemen were apparently pumping a heavy stream of water.

He left his car in the middle of the street and ran over to the site where he quickly found Luis and saw, brightly lit, both the gaping hole on the side of his building's second floor and the damage done to the adjoining building where all of the windows facing his apartment had been blown out.

"Was anyone hurt over there?" he asked Luis, pointing to the adjoining building.

"Not seriously," the superintendent replied. "The fire department people helped them and called the ambulances, which are here now. Jus' some cuts from the broken windows. The guy below your place wasn't at home, and nothing was damaged there by the explosion. But his place is a mess now from all the water."

"What do they think happened? Oakley asked. "Maybe that the gift that was delivered was a bomb?"

"I told the police about that, and they agree. Here's the police guy I spoke with," Luis said as a man dressed in civilian clothes approached the pair.

"Police Detective Peter Wilson," the man said, introducing himself and shaking Oakley's hand. "I'm guessing you were the intended victim. Could we have a chat?"

Ironically, the most private place the pair could find was Oakley's living room, which was relatively undamaged because the bedroom door had been blown shut by the blast.

"Let's start with your telling me where you were tonight," Wilson said.

Without going into the reasons why he was at Lee Francis's bordello, something he instinctively knew would create more questions than it answered, Oakley's simple statement that he was visiting a girl at her bordello clearly satisfied the detective's curiosity. Oakley smiled to himself and wondered if there was another clichéd maxim for the kind of white lies he seemed to be falling back on more and more lately.

"Your building superintendent tells me that someone left a package for you this afternoon and asked that it be placed next to your bed. It was clearly a bomb that was on a timer set to go off when you were asleep if you didn't open it earlier and blow yourself to kingdom come then. Any idea of who may have wanted to do you in?"

"Well, Detective Wilson," Oakley said, "I'm a private investigator and, unlike people employed in less adversarial jobs like Luis Baragon here at the building, sometimes people get pretty mad at me. Of course, I'm wondering if this is one of those times, but I have no idea who may have done it. But it's clear that someone seems pretty determined. Luis told me that the same person tried to deliver the package earlier, and also, I was told by my assistant that someone matching the same description tried to deliver it at my office."

"Do you have that description?"

"Because I never saw the person in question," Oakley said, "I think it might be best to ask Luis."

The detective agreed, and after asking a few more routine details including a request for a list of Oakley's clients, he left. No damage in giving him the list of his clients, Oakley reasoned, as the story of the bombing was going to be in all the newspapers the next morning, and he would have to call all of them anyway to explain that he wasn't killed without going into too many details, including that he was hiding out in a whorehouse.

As soon as Detective Wilson was gone, Oakley walked over to his bedroom and opened his door. In the reflected light from the emergency lighting equipment outside, he saw that virtually nothing was left of the room. The huge hole he had earlier observed from outside the building seemed even larger from the inside. Some fragments of wood that would probably make good kindling in the living room fireplace seemed to be all that was left of the bed and the nightstand next to it. Springs from the bed's inner-spring mattress support were flung everywhere—some so forcefully that they were impaled on the ceiling and walls of the room—and everything was covered with what appeared to be a thin coating of "snow," a.k.a. exploded cotton from his mattress. *God knows what's left of the clothes and stuff in the dresser,* he thought, observing the heavily damaged piece of furniture. Aside from a buckled door, the closet and, he hoped, his clothes in it, seemed to be intact.

Oakley went out to his kitchen and despite the time of the morning, found a beer in the refrigerator left over from the Chinese dinner with Donny and opened it.

"Oh God, Donny!" he said aloud. "I've got to call him before he hears about this some other way." Happily, Oakley's telephone was still working.

Needless to say, Donny sounded somewhat sleep-drugged and then unhappy with being awakened in the middle of the night by a telephone call until he realized who was calling him. "Are you OK, Oakey? What's going on? What time is it anyway?"

"It's around four in the morning," Oakley explained, causing Donny to groan. "Someone tried to kill me," he added and then explained what had happened to his place as well as that the Kansas City story was made up and he was really hiding out in a whorehouse. "So, love, I've got no place to live after I leave Lee Francis's place, so I guess you just might have someone occupying that Murphy bed with you until my place is fixed—that is, when I feel safe enough to resurface."

Even if delivered to a fully awake and operating person at high noon, all this unexpected news could be nearly too much information to deal with. Donny was neither awake nor operational. *What's the matter with me?* Oakley asked himself. *Donny had no idea that I was hiding out at the bordello and that the story of having to return to Missouri because of a death in the family was a complete fabrication to cover my disappearance. This meant that Donny had no inkling that the reason for my disappearance was due to a suspicion—shared with several of his film industry friends— that my life was in danger.* And, given the time of the morning, Donny, Oakley realized, wouldn't know of the bombing, which could be considered a blessing because he had been out of the loop all along.

"I guess that might be too much news about what I've actually been doing," Oakley said reassuringly. "I need to tell you what's been going on. I guess it's now time to 'fess up. The reason for all the secrecy was part of a deliberate plan to save my skin. How 'bout I drop by your place around seven?"

"Are you OK?" Donny asked, his voice still so clouded with sleep that he was not hearing Oakley's story. "You want to come by? I thought you were in Missouri."

"I know. I just explained that that was a cover for me to disappear. Do you remember anything I said or were you too sleepy?"

"Somethin' 'bout a bomb."

"Right. Someone tried to kill me by bombing my apartment. I said that I wasn't there, and I also explained that the story I told you about going out of town wasn't true. It was a cover so I could disappear because it looked like there were some people determined to kill me because of what I was tracking down. And judging from the morning's events, clearly it was the right thing to do. But it wasn't right to leave you in the dark. That was only because I had to move quickly and had no time to call you or anybody. So, may I come by and fill you in on what's really been going on? In a couple hours?"

"Sure. I'll rustle up some breakfast for us."

Oakley went downstairs and sought out the policeman left in charge by the departed Detective Wilson. "I'm going to get together some personal things and leave in a while. Could I leave a couple telephone numbers with you to relay to Detective Wilson so he can find me when he needs me? I'm not sure where I'll be until all this is repaired. So that's the best I can do. And, anyway, I don't think there is much for me to do around here now. Would I be correct?"

The police officer agreed and wrote down Oakley's office number, Donny's number, and that of his private line at the bordello. Oakley also made a mental note to tell Donny that he might get a call from the police looking for him as well as telling Benny that his impromptu vacation lasted one night and that he had to get back to work to cover the office phones.

Despite the bombing, he assumed his life was still in danger and he had to remain in hiding.

By the time Oakley arrived at Donny's apartment, he had made coffee and started scrambling eggs. As soon as the pair sat down at his kitchen table, the inevitable questions poured petulantly from Donny's mouth: "What's going on?" and "Why didn't you tell me about it?"

Without rehashing all the details, Oakley explained that Michelle Ryder had convinced him that, thanks to Louella Parsons, his suspicion that someone was attacking Hollywood personalities in ways disguised as everyday happenings was now public knowledge, he had better disappear. At least until his suspicions were proved fanciful or the culprit or culprits caught. Of course, exactly who would be doing the catching was a question that hadn't been answered because the plot—if there was a plot at all—was only a matter of innuendo. That was until last night when a bomb blew a hole the size of Oakley's Ford in the wall of his bedroom.

Ryder had also found a place for him to hide out: Lee Francis's bordello. Apologizing for his neglect, Oakley gave Donny his telephone number at the whorehouse and also told him he had given the police Donny's number as he planned to stay with him as much as possible until everything was resolved—that is, if he was still welcome.

"Of course you are!" Donny exclaimed. "Stay here all the time if you want."

Without worrying his lover that such an arrangement might endanger him as well, Oakley assured him that, for the present, it would be best to continue living at the bordello, but he would stay over as often as he thought it was safe.

Just then, Donny's telephone rang. It was Detective Wilson looking for Oakley whom he needed to stop by the Rampart Division police station that day to, as he said, "fill in the details." Oakley agreed, knowing that there were as many details that needed to be evaded or modified, among them the fact that he was actually living at Lee Francis's bordello instead of, as he had told Wilson earlier, being there as a customer.

His visit seemed to satisfy the detective who, during their conversation, seemed more interested in boasting about how his team was going to track down the bomber from the evidence they might find than what Oakley had been up to the previous night. "I guess that's the end of that," he said softly as he exited the station.

Next stop was his apartment and a conversation with the superintendent and the building's owner, presumably on site by now. It would be important to find out when his apartment would be repaired and he could return, at least nominally if not physically. As it turned out, the news was good. The owner had, with a representative of the building's insurance company, inspected the damage and determined that because it appeared the blast had not damaged any of the structure itself, repair was relatively easy and should be complete in a month or so—certainly by the time Oakley and Donny returned from Hawaii in mid-October from the trip Donny had booked for them. *I guess I'll be as safe in the middle of the Pacific Ocean as at the bordello*, he thought, dismissing his present cause for disappearing as a reason for canceling the trip. *Good timing for a vacation, honeymoon, or whatever it is anyway.*

Less pleasant was the insurance representative's news that although the room's interior would, as with the wall itself, be as new again, replacing the bedroom furnishings the blast had destroyed was not covered by the building's insurance and thus would be Oakley's responsibility. But, as he said aloud, reverting again to another cliché, "Such is life."

While he was gathering items of clothing in the apartment, he was startled by the sudden ring of the telephone before realizing that there was no reason for someone not to call him there; it was still his home. Nevertheless, the person calling, Michelle Ryder, sounded startled when he answered.

"Why the hell are you there?" she yelled into the receiver. "I just heard that there was an explosion at your building and started calling around to find out if you were OK."

"Yep, big explosion. And it was my place that got bombed," Oakley said. "That's why I'm here—seeing what happened and getting clothes and things I need at the bordello. Someone left a bomb yesterday, which blew up in the middle of the night. So I guess you saved my life by setting up the arrangement with Lee Francis."

"Oh my God!" the actress exclaimed. "I guess this proves that your suspicions were correct. Coppers been there?"

"Beat me to the place. Just had a visit with the detectives at Rampart Station. Told them I was at the bordello visiting one of the girls last night, which is why I wasn't killed."

"They buy that? I mean, Oakey, pardon me, but you don't generally come on as the usual customer for a bordello. That's why hiding out there was such a great idea if I do say so myself."

"You may be right," Oakley replied, "but they seemed to buy it. Why not? Their job is to find out who did the bombing, and since it was clearly evident that I wouldn't have planted a bomb in my own bedroom, they're focused elsewhere."

"So you think if they find out who delivered the bomb, that'll be the person behind all the other mischief."

"Maybe. But I don't think they'll find the person, which is why I'm going to hang out at Lee's place for the foreseeable future—that is, if they don't mind."

"Believe me, they won't mind. You're there because the owner of the building agreed for you to be there. Don't worry."

"Michelle, could you do me a favor because I'm trying to get out of here as quickly as possible? Could you call Louella and, since she's certainly heard about the explosion by now, tell her what happened, that I'm OK, and that I hadn't called her because my hands were full with the police, the insurance people, and figuring out what's left and what was destroyed at my place?"

"'Course, hon. I think it's about time we have another little visit to the Tea Room at BW. Bet you're in the mood for a couple double Ms."

"I am, but I'm really upset by this bomb business, and since no one knows who did it, I plan to stick pretty close to Lee Francis's place, my office, and a certain apartment at the Bryson for the next month or so. Let whoever planted the bomb think I was hurt or something. Except for going to the Bowl for the Gershwin concert in ten days or whatever—on the eighth—that'll be it. I think I'll be safe surrounded by twenty thousand people. And then going to Hawaii a week or so later with a friend who set it up. Better than hidin' out in a whorehouse."

And so it went for the next week or so. Oakley, as planned, stayed close to his business and called the whorehouse home. He continued to be delighted with the girls' gossip, unorthodox opinions, and the way they had apparently accepted him as a sort of big brother. Even Ruby, the receptionist, had thawed to the point that Oakley felt comfortable in suggesting that she tone down her makeup a bit. He resigned himself to being unable to do anything to change her shape, but he made several suggestions, mostly involving less provocative clothing, of how she could tame it all. And he was surprised; she actually did so because, as Lee Francis explained, he was a "classy guy."

More often than not, he spent the evenings with Donny at the Bryson but, out of caution, usually returned to the bordello late at night to avoid endangering the person he was more and more accepting as a permanent fixture in his life.

CHAPTER 18

"**Just another perfect** night at the Bowl," Oakley commented to Donny as they delightedly discovered that their seats for the George Gershwin memorial concert were only about one hundred feet from the stage and the iconic arched band shell of the famous concert venue. "Interesting concert," he added as they scanned their programs. "Sort of a grab bag but a good one. Really nice of Joe Valentine to get us these seats."

"Where's he tonight anyway? I thought he'd be here." Donny asked.

"He is. Somewhere in the orchestra with the violins," Oakley explained, "probably in the back."

For the salute to the composer who died on July 11, the Los Angeles Philharmonic Orchestra administration had assembled a showcase of his music and whom they felt would best present it. Among the performers appearing was the Philharmonic's director, Dr. Otto Klemperer, who would open the concert leading an orchestrated version of Gershwin's *Piano Sonata No. 2* (to be played at a funeral pace as a memorial); Fred Astaire singing "They Can't Take That Away from Me," which he had introduced earlier that year in the film *Shall We Dance?*; *An American in Paris*; and the pianist and comedian Oscar Levant showing his stuff in the composer's *Concerto in F*. The two-and-a-half-hour concert was being broadcast live by CBS.

"Oscar Levant," Donny commented as he read through the commemorative program. "I've always thought of him as mostly a comedian. Wasn't he the one who once said about Hollywood: 'Peel away the phony tinsel from this town, and you know what you'll find? Real tinsel!'?"

"Right. But he's as good a pianist as he is a quipster," Oakley added. "Hey, look who's here? Hi, Les," Oakley said coolly. "Meet my friend Donny Wells; Donny, meet Lester Grady, big-time and occasionally unethical talent agent."

"Unethical?" Les said. What are you talking about?"

"Because of Joe Valentine who got us these wonderful seats," Oakley said as Grady joined them in the box. "I only recently learned that he was once your client as well as Rachael Baumgarten … I always thought that having two clients in the same racket wasn't exactly kosher in the PR world, but I gotta say it must have been pretty convenient for you to do a favor for Joe by getting his Rachael's Philharmonic gig when her violin disappeared."

"Oakey, that's not the whole story. Let me…" Les said in an imploring tone.

"No. Let me finish. Whatever the story, it was a pretty suspicious situation. That is, until your assistant Johnny quit and took Joe with him to another agency. Oh yeah, I met Johnny at Joe's place when I stopped by the other day."

"I'm sorry you're so burned up about this, and here and now is probably not the best time for us to argue about it," Les said. "And speaking of the Devil, guess who's coming down the aisle?"

"Wouldn't you know it?" Oakley said sarcastically, realizing that a further confrontation with Les had to wait. "It's bad-boy Johnny himself. And who's that with him?" he added, recognizing Johnny's somewhat beefy, crew-cut companion from Lee Francis's bordello.

"That's his boss, the guy who runs the company he's working with now," Les said unhappily. "Something called the New World Agency. Name is Henry Graber."

Wouldn't you know it? Oakley thought. *The guy who screwed Maria and Ari Karinopolis by stealing some of their clients. The man who Maria Karinopolis called Grabber.* "Aren't we lucky?" Oakley snapped.

Making matters worse, certainly as far as Les was concerned, the seats the pair were looking for were situated in the box directly behind that occupied by Oakley and his friends. Introductions were unavoidable and clearly uncomfortable—at least for Les—but thankfully, also curtailed as the house lights were dimmed, and the program commenced. *Somehow, the darkened setting was no longer romantic,* Oakley thought as Donny draped an arm around his shoulders, *but suddenly and inexplicability menacing.*

Understandably, during the intermission, conversation between them was somewhat forced despite Donny's offer to share some of the picnic dinner he had picked up earlier at Gotham's Delicatessen on Hollywood Boulevard. Johnny seemed pleased by the gesture, but Graber took one look at the sandwich he was offered and sneered. "What is this stuff?" he said, peeling off the top slice of bread. "Watercress? Men don't eat watercress. That's food for rabbits and"—he looked squarely at Donny and Oakley before throwing it on the ground—"fairies."

Not much to be done about his manners, Oakley thought as they turned their attention back to the stage where the final part of the concert was commencing. It would include songs from *Porgy and Bess* by members of the original, 1935 Broadway cast augmented by the soprano Lily Pons who, the previous year, set the Bowl's all-time paid attendance record (26,410), singing *Porgy*'s hit song "Summertime." The concert would conclude with Gershwin's tremendously popular *Rhapsody in Blue* performed by the popular pianist José Iturbi.

Halfway through the final number, Oakley turned to Donny to make a comment and noticed that he was shivering. "What's up?" he asked.

"I dunno, just cold. Shoulda brought along a blanket like everyone else. I always forget that it can get chilly at night in LA."

"I have a blanket in my car," Les interjected. "At least there should be one. There was one when I last looked. I hardly ever need to put anything back there."

"Thanks," Oakley said. "I'll get it so you don't need to miss any of the music. I know this piece like the back of my hand, and between you and me, Iturbi's playing isn't so hot tonight anyway. Where's your car?"

"Parked behind the stage in the section marked for performers and press," Les said, handing Oakley his keys. "You know it—the brown Nash."

It took Oakley a few minutes to find his friend's car in the dimly lit parking lot, jammed in with the vehicles of the many performers appearing that night and the large crowd of press covering the event along with the CBS remote broadcast vans. Eventually he found Les's Nash, completely blocked in between several latecomers' cars, among which he couldn't help noticing was a spectacular Packard sedan. After taking a moment or two to figure out which key was intended for the Nash's trunk, he opened it and grabbed the blanket. Then, even in the dim light, he saw something else that stopped him in shock. Underneath the blanket was something that was the last thing he imagined to see in Les Grady's car: a violin case.

Oakley dropped the blanket back into the trunk and lifted the violin case out. "What the hell?" he asked himself aloud and then carried the case over to a bench below one of the parking lot lights to better examine what he had found. Inside was one of the most beautiful musical instruments he had ever seen. Even in the limited light, it seemed to glow with an inner, golden fire.

When Oakley had visited Joe, he had showed Oakley where to find the name of a violin's maker, that is, if it were important enough to be labeled in the first place. So without removing the instrument from its case, Oakley held it up to the light and peered through one of the sound holes on the top of the instrument to see if there was a label. There was. Even though he couldn't read all of the notation, he could discern at least the name of the maker: *Stefano Scarampella di Brescia*. It was Rachael's missing violin.

Oakley closed the case, returned to Les's car and retrieved the blanket with which he wrapped the violin, and retraced his steps to his seat.

"Les, I think we have something to talk about," he said as he handed the blanket to Donny. "I found something in your trunk, which was the last thing I ever expected to see in it."

"And what was that?" Les, still defensive from Oakley's earlier confrontation, asked, suddenly noticing the violin case.

"This," Oakley said. "I opened the case, looked at the label inside the violin, and there is no doubt that this is Rachael Baumgarten's missing violin. So, I'm wondering what's the story? Was all that conversation at the Brown Derby some sort of song and dance to cover up the fact that you had stolen your client's violin? And why the hell would you do something like that? Was this part of some sort of deal with Joe Valentine to get him the gig?"

To describe Les's reaction as stricken was to put it mildly. To Oakley and Donny, he looked like he was going to pass out from shock. "I don't—" he muttered. "I don't have any idea of how that got in my car. I swear to God, Oakley. You know me. I would never have done anything like this."

Recovering somewhat from his initial shock, he added as the music ended, "Why would I have done it? I had nothing to gain and lots to lose from Rachael's loss of the violin, and there was certainly no deal with Joe to get him the Philharmonic job. Tell him, Johnny," he said, turning to his former employee in the adjoining box. "You were working with me then. I was as shocked with the disappearance of her instrument as Rachael was. Tell them, Johnny."

"Well..." Johnny started to say. "I—"

"Actually, Mr. Cleveland was actually working for me then," Henry Graber interrupted, standing as the rest of the Bowl's audience stood in applause, "only you didn't know it. Gentlemen, I think this conversation needs to continue in a more private setting. So now, if you all would make your way to the parking lot."

"Screw you, buddy. We're not going anywhere except to the police station over on Ivar," Oakley said.

"Sorry. I think you are going to the parking lot," Graber replied, suddenly brandishing an evil-looking Luger P.08 semiautomatic pistol and pointing it directly at Oakley and his friends. "Now let us move along, please."

Oakley, saying nothing, turned and led Donny along the path to the parking lot. He was furious with himself for not following Michelle Ryder's explicit directions to carry his recently acquired handgun with him at all times. But, he figured, how the hell was he going to be able to carry it without it being seen when dressed informally for a summer evening concert in September? So he left it in the glove compartment of his car, figuring it would be handy enough if in the unlikely event he might need it, like right now.

"That's far enough," Graber said as the group reached the parking lot adjacent to Les's car.

"So what are you going to do next?" Oakley asked him. "It seems to me that despite the heavy armament, you are somewhat outnumbered."

"That can be easily remedied, Mr. Webster, as you might imagine. As a matter of fact, you are likely to be the first part of that remedy," he added, pointing the Luger at Oakley and releasing the safety. "We have had enough of your meddling in our affairs. We have tried to warn you to, as you Americans say, 'lay off,' but nevertheless, you have continued to get in our way."

"Pardon me for asking," Oakley interjects while moving toward his car, "but what exactly were those affairs?"

"Please stop, Mr. Webster. If you want an answer to your question, you'll have it. But do not tempt me to remove you from our gathering before that."

"I figured, Henry—"

"Heinrich," Graber said.

"OK, Heinrich, as you clearly intend to, as you say, 'remedy' me," Oakley said, "is it not a tradition in your country—I'm assuming that would be Germany—for someone about to be executed to be offered a cigarette? Mine are in the glove compartment of my car, and I'd like to retrieve them."

"You are correct, and you may have one of mine."

"I would prefer one of my own brand," Oakley said. "Is that too much for a condemned man to wish?"

"*Nein*," Graber said. "But move slowly. If you try anything foolish, believe me, final cigarette or not, it will be your last move."

Oakley walked slowly but purposefully to his car, opened the passenger-side door, and after leaning into his car to shield his movements with his body, opened the glove compartment. It was a matter of moments to retrieve both the pack of Chesterfields, which he stored there in case he ran out, and his Beretta, which he slid into his right trouser pocket.

"OK?" he asked, turning toward Graber and holding up both hands, one clearly clutching the pack of cigarettes.

"Ja," Graber said. "Please walk back slowly."

Oakley did as directed. "May I have that cigarette now?" he asked. "Does anyone have a light?"

"I have one," Johnny said, springing forward.

"Stop, Cleveland. Are you crazy?" Graber snarled. "Let one of his compatriots provide the match."

"Pardon me," Johnny said, clearly irritated with the rebuke, "but despite what I have done for you, I believe I am still one of his compatriots."

"That's enough," Graber commanded. "Be silent."

"Another wish of a dying man," Oakley interjected, drawing deeply on the cigarette after Donny had lit it for him. "What were those things you have done for Mr. Graber, Johnny?"

"Well," Johnny began, "for one thing, it was I who stole the violin and hid it in Les's car."

"So that explains that," Les commented. "But why?"

"That is enough, Mr. Cleveland. You will please be silent," Graber commanded.

"No, I won't," Johnny said. "You asked me to do some things that made me sick to my stomach, and now you are planning to shoot one of the first people in Hollywood who understood my dream."

"Mr. Webster?"

"Yes. When I was a waiter at Musso and Frank's, I told him of my dream, and unlike everyone else in Hollywood except for you, Les, he didn't make fun of me. And now Joe…"

My people skills must be pretty good, Oakley thought, somewhat humbled. *Whatever you may have thought I said, I wasn't encouraging you; I was dismissing you as just another Hollywood failure.*

By then, the applause following the concert had run its course, and the performers and press were beginning to stream into the parking lot. "Please move, all of you," Graber ordered, indicating that Oakley, Les, and Donny should relocate a few yards away—between the edge of the lot and one of the many hills surrounding the Bowl—for more privacy. Just as they were about to do so, a voice rang out from the passing crowd, and a man carrying an instrument came running toward the group.

"Johnny? Is that you, Johnny?"

"Joe, Joe, thank God you are here," Johnny shouted as Valentine ran over.

"What the hell?" Joe said, taking in the situation. "Henry, what are you doing with that gun?"

"Mr. Valentine, it's indeed unfortunate that you have joined our little party. But now that you have, please join Mr. Webster and his friends. I believe that you know them."

"What's going on?"

"What was going on before you interrupted us is that Mr. Webster has finally reached the end of his meddling in the affairs of the German Reich and is about to experience the consequences. I suggest that if you do not wish to follow him, you remain quiet.

"Now, Mr. Webster. Before we were so rudely interrupted, you asked my employee, Mr. Cleveland, what he had done for me. So let me tell you. He did what I asked him to do or didn't do myself. As he said, following my orders, it was he who stole Miss Baumgarten's violin and hid it in Mr. Grady's automobile. He did a few other chores on behalf of my government also."

"And what were they?" Oakley asked.

"It was he who conveyed the measles virus to Republic Pictures to infect a particular actor but unfortunately bungled the job and regrettably infected Mr. Wayne. That was a mistake, but one he didn't make when Mr. Karinopolis, my former employer, was infected with our pneumonia virus."

"That was your doing?"

"*Ja*. It was fairly easy to do. Mr. Cleveland simply waylaid the regular delivery man from the delicatessen from which Mr. Karinopolis ordered his lunch, smeared some of the pneumonia virus on his sandwich, which was already cold enough to preserve the viability of the agent for a short while, and that was that. By the time the real delivery person was found, events had progressed so far that no one really paid much attention."

"Where did you get the virus or bacteria or whatever it was that you used?" Oakley asked. "Isn't it hard to obtain and harder to preserve? And how does it work?"

"Fortunately, Germany is leading the world in medical research," Graber said, "and many disease strains have been isolated and preserved by freezing at laboratories in Munich. So the only problem was keeping them frozen while transporting them to the United States, which was accomplished in the kitchens of the *Bremen*. The disease strains were subsequently carried from New York to Los Angeles by your very efficient Transcontinental & Western Air, and here in Los Angeles, they are kept in a freezer at a friendly restaurant. When they hit warm air, they quickly start to sublimate into an infectious mist which can be breathed in by the victim. It isn't a sure bet, as you say, but it has the advantage of being virtually untraceable.

"But to continue answering your question, Mr. Cleveland's most successful work was convincing a young homosexual sailor, a guest at a festive gathering at the consulate, to lure the homosexual actor Williams into a trap, which we were then able to manipulate in such a way that his career was ended ignominiously."

"So that was your doing, then?"

"*Jawohl*, entirely," Graber continued. "But when we then tried to eliminate the sailor, we were too slow—rather, Mr. Cleveland was too slow—about it. By then, the sailor had, as you also say, 'shipped out.' That was a mistake. Otherwise no one would have ever been able to prove that what happened to Mr. Williams was not just the natural outcome to a regrettable assignation."

"My God," Oakley said. "May I smoke another cigarette? I have a couple additional questions if you don't mind."

"*Nein*, go ahead. I'm rather enjoying this."

"So, you then also found a way to infect Eva Sanderson."

"*Ja*," Graber continued. "It wasn't as easy as it was with the Karinopolis matter or, for that matter, the effort at Republic Pictures, as poorly as that turned out. I just impersonated a gas company repair man as I later did at your apartment and, while I was in Miss Sanderson's kitchen, applied the measles virus to the sandwich that the maid was preparing for her lunch. Thankfully, as with the Karinopolis sandwich, it was cold also, and the strain remained active. All they had to do was breathe in the virus or bacteria it gave off as it warmed. "

"Then, was it you who infected Michelle Ryder's housekeeper, posed as a gardener?"

"*Ja*, a regrettable incident. I understand that the woman recovered, and of course, I failed to eliminate Miss Ryder."

"Then, I'm assuming that it was you or Mr. Cleveland who planted the bomb at my apartment?" Oakley asked.

"It was I. As I just said, I had earlier visited your place as a gas company employee and planned to modify your stove so when you turned it on, it would explode. But your superintendent was too attentive. And then, when I came to deliver the bomb, twice actually, you were not there, so I finally left it after previously wiring it with a timer to trigger an explosion in case you failed to open it immediately. Where were you anyway?"

"Actually, I—we, myself and a number of my friends—suspected that I was becoming a target and suggested that I go underground, arranging for it to be in the least likely place imaginable, which allowed me to see you checking in for your assignation with Amber at Lee Francis's place of business. Why was Johnny with you?"

"After he began working with me, I discovered that he had unfortunate homosexual tendencies. So I decided that he should be introduced to women. I brought him along several times, but he always made excuses for not enjoying the merchandise available at Miss Francis's place," Graber explained, shaking his head either in apparent disgust at being caught at the bordello or because of his failure to convert Johnny. "He represents a misjudgment on my part, which will be remedied."

"So who was it who wrote the letter to Universal about the Jewish members of the cast and crew of *The Road Back*?" Oakley asked. "The one that caused a young friend of mine, Michael Trevalian, to end up on the cutting room floor?"

"That would have been me," came a voice from the shadows. A tall man in his midforties emerged from the large Packard that had earlier impressed Oakley. As he walked into the light, one couldn't fail but notice the monocle he wore in one eye, what was clearly an old dueling scar on the cheek of his thin, aristocratic face, and that he was also armed with a Luger. His obviously expensive and probably handmade gray suit cut in a somewhat military fit bore a small decoration in the left lapel. Oakley, without clearly recalling how he was familiar with the decoration, guessed it was the black-and-white ribbon of the Iron Cross, probably won, he surmised from the man's apparent age, during service in World War I.

"I would appreciate it if all of you were to gather over here," the man indicated a shadowy corner of the lot, waving his pistol in the direction he wanted them to go.

"Let me handle this, Dr. Gyssling," Graber insisted. "I have been trying to remove this problem for some time, and I would like to finish what I have been doing."

"Heinrich, what you have been doing, you have been doing at my order. And how you have been accomplishing it has become a problem, certainly now you have been talking too much," the man, who Oakley now realized was the Nazi consul general himself, said. "So leave this to me."

As the group was slowly moving as ordered and Graber and Gyssling were arguing about who was in charge of the situation, Oakley saw his chance and pulled his own pistol.

"That will be enough of this, folks," he interrupted. "Mr. Graber, Herr Gyssling, please put down your guns. Johnny, run over to the seating area and find a security man. Tell him we need the police here as quickly as possible."

"Stay right where you are, Mr. Cleveland," Graber ordered. "Have you forgotten who you work for?"

Johnny turned. "That was then, Mr. Graber. This is now. You're nothing but a God damn traitor, and I've had enough of this," he said as he began to walk away.

"Halt! I said for you to halt!" Graber shouted. In reply, Johnny turned and gave him the Nazi salute with only the middle finger extended.

Shaking with rage, Graber pointed his Luger at Johnny and fired, hitting him in his shoulder.

"Johnny, Johnny," Joe shouted, running over to comfort his friend who was writhing in pain on the ground.

"Now is the time to finish this," Graber growled, aiming his pistol at Johnny's head.

"Stop right there, Heinrich," Oakley said. Graber turned just as Oakley fired his pistol, hitting Graber in the leg.

"I think this has gone far enough," Gyssling said. "Now, please hold your fire, Mr. Webster. There is no reason for this confrontation to continue. All that would happen is that more would be injured.

"All of you—certainly Mr. Webster—know what has been accomplished. Since all of the incidents that concern you are believable as having been caused solely by accidents, lack of immunity to disease, or indiscretions as in the case of Mr. Williams, to publicly claim that any of them were deliberately motivated would be wasting your breath.

"As Mr. Webster has probably discovered by now, American media has no interest in exposing any of the activities that would negatively affect the film industry's international receipts from Germany and other countries that may soon decide to join the Reich. So you may accuse us of whatever you want, but few will pay any attention."

"So," Oakley asked as he laid his pistol on the fender of a nearby car, "granted that what you are saying is the case, and that we might as well forget what we know, please tell us—I certainly want to know—why you have done what you have done. We suspect that Michael Trevalian was cut from *The Road Back* because he had some Jewish blood. I cannot imagine how much effort was necessary to discover that, but that was your problem.

"And it has been explained that infecting John Wayne was an unfortunate accident. Was Ari Karinopolis killed because he was a Jew? And did Johnny, who by now has, I believe, wised up, ordered to steal Rachael Baumgarten's violin solely because she was Jewish? Was anti-Semitism the sole reason all this was done?" Oakley asked. "If it was, which seems pretty obvious, there are a lot more Jews in Hollywood for you to target in a lifetime, and some of them run the very studios you need to fill Germany's love for American movies. So isn't that a pretty daunting challenge? And if anti-Semitism is the reason, then why did you frame Billy Williams? And were you responsible for Eva Sanderson's tragedy?"

"To answer your Jewish question first, Mr. Webster, you are correct in concluding that it was because of their tainted blood that we decided to eliminate or remove from importance the people in question. In fact, unknown to you, there are many other cases where we have removed film stars who are Jewish or forced changes in films that make heroes of Jews. It may take my lifetime and the lifetimes of many other Germans, but we consider the new Reich as enduring for a thousand years, so we are not worried that, eventually, we will succeed.

"Through our efforts and those of similarly minded American citizens, the Jewish element eventually will be removed from the Hollywood studios.

But for now, the love of money by the Jewish studio heads trumps, as they say in your game of bridge, any objections to taking our advice on certain film productions.

"So, when we discovered that Miss Sanderson was partially Jewish, because of her very high profile in a major film, it became urgent that we dispose of her—"

"What?" Oakley shouted. "Eva Sanderson is Jewish? You're crazy!"

"Not crazy, Mr. Webster. Meticulous. Because of her prominence, we began checking on her ancestors, and it wasn't long that it was discovered that one side of her family descended from Jews who once were moneylenders in Stockholm."

"That's outrageous," Oakley said. "But no way did Billy Williams have a drop of Jewish blood."

"As I have said, the new Germany is committed to purifying the human race," Gyssling continued, "and besides removing Jews in positions of power and influence and suppressing anything that makes heroes of Jews, that also includes the elimination of the decadent stain of homosexuality.

"Let me remind you, when, in 1934, it was discovered that a group of homosexuals led by Ernst Röhm, head of the Sturmabteilung, the SA, planned a coup against the state, the Führer acted bravely and heroically to save Germany. He personally arrested Röhm and saw to it that the rest of the deviants were eliminated in the Röhm-Putsch. I believe your media refer to it as 'The Night of the Long Knives.'

"For the same reason that we cannot allow movies that make heroes out of Jews like the Dreyfus dog," the Nazi added, "we must do everything we can to eliminate people who flaunt a deviant lifestyle from positions of power and importance—idolized, as your publicity people say, by millions of movie patrons. And for years, Mr. Williams, one of your most popular male film stars, has done just that, which is why it was necessary for him to be removed. And there will be others.

"So now I have only one more thing to do before we go our separate ways. Hopefully before the police, who have undoubtedly been called, arrive."

"And that would be?" Donny said. "Hasn't enough happened tonight?"

"Young man," Gyssling said, "you are correct. Much has been explained. But there is still something else to be resolved—what I believe is called in your slang a 'loose cannon.'"

With that said, the Nazi walked over to Henry Graber, obviously in pain on the ground. "Heinrich, you have spoken too much about matters that were not to be spoken about," Gyssling said. "You are a threat to the Reich."

"No, nein," Graber moaned. "Bitte!"

With that, Gyssling stood over Graber, who was trying to crawl away, and shouted, "For the Reich! Heil Hitler!" and then shot him in the head. "Let the police find him," he said. "Trying to figure out what happened to him will be a good exercise for them. I cannot imagine that any of you would have the bad judgment to speak of this in the future, but if you do, you would only implicate yourselves. I, of course, enjoy diplomatic immunity.

"So, let me wish all of you a good night but not *auf wiedersehen*. There is no need for us to meet again." With that, he returned to his Packard and was driven away.

Obviously, none of those remaining were as comfortable with leaving Henry Graber's body lying in the dirt of the parking lot. However, to move it or run for help could, as the Nazi suggested, involve all of them in an investigation of the crime. Knowing fully that what he was doing was, in contemporary slang, a "cop-out," Oakley called the police from a nearby pay phone and reported that as he was leaving the concert, he had discovered a body in a poorly lit corner of the parking lot. Anticipating that the next question would be a request for his name, Oakley hung up. After making sure that his bullet had exited Graber's leg and was, for all intents and purposes, apparently lost somewhere in the foliage surrounding the area, he said, echoing the German's comments, "Let them figure out what happened."

Oakley bent, retrieved, and pocketed his pistol's spent cartridge case and joined his pals. He decided to leave the cartridge case from Gyssling's Luger where it lay, gleaming in the parking lot lights. "Would serve the bastard right to have it traced to him," he said with a rueful smile.

Because of Johnny's condition, a painful but not life-threatening wound, Oakley suggested that Joe take him to the emergency room at Los Angeles

County Hospital rather than the closer Hollywood Presbyterian because, given the usual late-night crowd in the huge hospital, the ER doctors would be more likely to quickly deal with the injury than inquire too deeply into how he had been shot.

As it turned out, a not–entirely plausible story that Johnny had been wounded in a random shooting near the Hollywood Bowl was accepted, and as the bullet had cleanly exited the wound, it was cleaned and dressed and Johnny was released in Joe Valentine's care with the request to return in the next day or two to have the wound checked. How Johnny handled the fact that he committed several heinous crimes that would never be traced to him was a matter for him and his conscience; aided by the clearly infatuated Joe Valentine, he might be able to work it out.

For their part, Oakley and Donny decided that perhaps Donny's apartment was the best place to head for as the repairs to Oakley's apartment caused by Graber's bombing had only begun. And after the physical and emotional drama of the evening, certainly being with his lover would be far more pleasant than the evanescent presence of Jean Harlow in the otherwise-impersonal setting of his bedroom at the bordello.

"Hey, Les, what are your plans?" Oakley shouted as Grady was about to leave. "Maybe, now that some issues have been settled, we should work on our one-time friendship. Why don't we all get a drink? Musso's? Should still be open for the latecomers."

⅄

"Hey, Oakley," Michelle's voice exploded on his telephone at the bordello the next morning. What is this I heard about a little shootout at the Bowl last night? You OK?"

"I'm fine," he said, amazed at how fast news could spread in Hollywood. "How the hell…"

"Les Grady called me," she explained. "I guess he was trying to score brownie points with me, and told me the whole thing. Goddamn Nazis. Got one of them I guess, so that's a start. I called Lolly and filled her in on the whole story, so you may be getting a call from her. She, of course, is absolutely furious that after all the effort, because it involved a partnership between the Hollywood studios and the Nazis which would go against her and Mr. Hearst's resolve to write nothing that would damage the film industry, she can't write a word about it. I suspect that her anger has a touch of relief about it, though," Michelle said. "Although her family attended the Episcopal Church back in Illinois when she was a kid – and now of course, she is loudly Catholic, her father, Joshua Oettinger, and maybe her mother, too, were Jewish.

"But…"

"And because of the Nazi plan you discovered, she is determined that little fact will stay buried. At least from her millions of readers and listeners.

"Anyway, I called for two reasons," Michelle added. "First to make sure that you're OK, and second, I think that it's appropriate for a little get-together for everyone who knows the real story. So could you and your friend, Donny—that's his name?—come by my place around six tomorrow night, and we'll have a little celebration."

"To celebrate the fact I'm not dead?" Oakley asked with a laugh; his first in a while, he realized.

"Well, if you put it that way, I guess so!" she laughed, giving Oakley her address in Beverly Hills. "Tell me how to reach the people involved in the other cases so I can invite them too."

Michelle's get-together may have been impromptu, but it ended up as a gathering that had it been publicly known—especially the reason for it— would easily have been headlined by any newspaper.

Not only was it a rare party given by one of Hollywood's top stars, but the guests included Billy Williams, once America's leading man and soon to be Los Angeles's top interior designer, and his lover, Martin Howard; America's most powerful newspaperwoman, Louella Parsons, and her Docky; and the still-bereaved star, Eva Sanderson, and her husband, Stan Damon. They also brought along their agent, Maria Karinopolis, who despite being dressed in mourning, seemed happy to be out and about for the first time since the death of her husband.

Joan Crawford and her husband, Franchot Tone, arrived at the same time as Oakley and Donny, and after gushing that she was happy to finally meet him, with her husband, launched into a quick a capella version of "For He's a Jolly Good Fellow."

"I didn't know you could sing as well as act," Oakley said after thanking Crawford.

"Hell, Cranberry always wanted to be a classical singer instead of an actor," Billy Williams interjected. "She even recorded a duet with Rosa Ponselle," he added, referring to the opera soprano who, in her time, was generally considered to be the greatest singer in the world.

"Look," Crawford said with an uncharacteristic blush, "a singing career was only a wild dream of mine at one time. Eventually, I had to make a choice, and anyway, a poor girl like me was lucky to even have a choice. I chose movies. But Franchot and I have a voice coach, and well, you never know..."

Eva Sanderson came up to Oakley and embraced him. "There is no way I can thank you enough for your work," she said through tears. "Michelle has told me how you actually risked your life to solve this and without a cent of remuneration."

"It was the least I could do, Miss Sanderson, after what you and your husband went through."

"Call me Eva, please. We are still devastated at the loss of our child. But by finding out that what happened had nothing to do with us other than that I was a person with some Jewish blood in a position of high visibility... well, as Stan and I were blaming each other for what happened until you discovered the truth, what you may have done was to save our marriage. We're eternally grateful for that, and I'm actually thinking that I might even return to films one day. And maybe try for another child. Thank you so much."

Surrounded by all this Hollywood glamour, Benny, Michael Trevalian and Laurel Fox, Rachael Baumgarten and Les Grady, and Johnny Cleveland and Joe Valentine may have felt somewhat bedazzled out of their social comfort zone, but they clearly enjoyed themselves.

Oakley was, understandably, overwhelmed by this outpouring of such high-powered affection until Louella Parsons poked him in the ribs and brought him down to earth.

"Stop looking so glum, kid. So you solved a biggie? But how do you think I feel with a huge story and not being able to say a God damn word about it? You, I, and a couple others in this room helped stop some really bad stuff—at least for the time being—made a few people really happy, and you picked up a few new friends along the way. So enjoy being everyone's hero. Have another glass of bubbly, Oakey. Have fun."

Which he did.

EPILOGUE

O akley and Donny, lounging on the Promenade Deck of the SS *Malolo*, were enjoying a couple of the then-iconic Hawaiian cocktails, the Sea Breeze, a heady combination of gin, apricot brandy, grenadine, and lemon juice, as Honolulu's familiar Aloha Tower heaved into view.

"You were certainly right," Oakley remarked to his lover. "The trip was perfect. Just what I once dreamed about before I rear-ended Joe Valentine's car."

"And it's only beginning," Donny said. "The Ala Moana hotel is wonderful and then the *Lurline* back to LA after a week in paradise. What's this about hitting Joe's car? Was it before he met Johnny?"

"I think it was about the same time. I was driving along in stop-and-start traffic on Franklin Avenue, and he stopped to turn into his garage and I hit him. That's how we met. He plays a mean fiddle."

"Nothin' to match your talent for sleuthing, though. Look what you solved!"

"I didn't really solve much of anything," Oakley said. "I just smelled a rat when I first read about Eva Sanderson's case of the measles and everything sorta happened from there. As it turned out, it was all caused by hate—hate for Jews, hate for people like us."

"Well, it's over, now," Donny said.

"Not really. Nothing's really changed if you think about it," Oakley said sadly. "Gyssling masterminded the whole thing, but because of his diplomatic immunity, nobody can do much of anything about it, and unlike Henry Graber, he wasn't directly linked to any of the crimes anyway. I wouldn't be surprised if, now that he knows some in Hollywood are on to him, he may seek another posting. And Graber's dead. Maybe the government will pay closer attention to what the Germans are up to, but who knows?

"Certainly, it all may stiffen the spines of the studio heads a bit, but Hollywood being Hollywood, money is still money, and that's still the bottom line. It would probably take a war to break that bond."

"But now, the Germans know that people like Louella Parsons is keeping an eye on them. Won't that keep them in line?" Donny asked.

"Think about it, Donny," Oakley continued. "So Louella Parsons may know more than she did before, but what good is that? Do you think Mr. Hearst will let her say any more than she did before, which was nothing? She basically snuck the blind item about my suspicions into the column. And of course, she never told him the result because she couldn't.

"Remember, the real story about the mischief, the story I suspected, was only confirmed to us at the Hollywood Bowl. I told Michelle, Louella, and our friends, but the satisfaction of a big scoop was not in the cards for Louella. It drove her nuts having such a huge story that she couldn't use. Maybe she can get some mileage out of this by revealing some of the other tricks the Nazis are up to in America."

"Like what?" Donny asked.

"There are a few nasty things being drummed up by the German Bunds," Oakley explained, "which are basically white supremacist groups across the country, and something called the Silver Shirts, who contend that democracy is nothing more than a Jewish plot to take over the world. Stuff like that.

"And here in Hawaii, it's nice and peaceful, but on the other side of the same water we're floating on, there's a war actually going on between Japan and China, and that nearly half of the population of Hawaii is Japanese. So are we next on the list when they want something we have and they don't? Like Hawaii?

"I hate to be pessimistic in the middle of all this gorgeousness, but I gotta believe that something is going to explode one day."

"Jesus!" Donny exclaimed. "Stop it, Oakley. I can live with your being a cynic, but don't start being some sort of Cassandra. Relax, damn it! Think about having some fun. Isn't that what we're here for? Why don't you learn to surf-board when I'm stuck with my tourist group; you once said you thought you'd like that. Do something like that instead of always looking for a plot behind every door, like you did with the Sanderson story and all that happened afterward."

Oakley smiled. "That's exactly what I intend to do. But now that you mention the Sanderson case 'and all that happened afterward...'

"Wasn't I right?"

The adventures of Oakley Webster in Tinsletown will continue in 2017 with *1939 – Hollywood: Triumph, Tragedy, and the Mafia.*

40457084R00129

Made in the USA
San Bernardino, CA
21 October 2016